Totally Bound Publishing books by Sierra Cartwright

Mastered
With This Collar
On His Terms
Over the Line
In His Cuffs
For the Sub
In the Den

The Donovan Dynasty
Bind
Brand
Boss

Mastered

IN THE DEN
THE 10TH ANNIVERSARY EDITION

SIERRA CARTWRIGHT

In the Den
ISBN # 978-1-80250-736-2
©Copyright Sierra Cartwright 2024
Cover Art by Kelly Martin ©Copyright June 2024
Interior text design by Claire Siemaszkiewicz
Totally Bound Publishing

IN THE DEN

Dedication

For Jason and Catrina, with thanks for the
insights.
Scarlett, you are a source of constant inspiration.

Chapter One

Master Damien Lowell always got what he wanted.

Granted, sometimes the challenge was greater than he anticipated. But that didn't matter. The more difficult the task, the more he relished it.

Working hard for something otherwise unobtainable flexed his mental muscles, sharpened his senses, and fed his creative energy.

Right now he was standing with his arms folded across his chest, his focus on the gorgeous dark-haired Domme on the other side of the room.

Tonight she'd used kohl liner and false eyelashes to add drama and depth to her startling green eyes.

Her thick hair hung over her shoulders and cascaded down her back in a shining mahogany wave.

She wore thigh-high black boots with heels so tall he was amazed she could walk in them.

Her alluring fishnet stockings were attached to a garter belt, and her tiny black skirt barely covered her buttocks.

She'd topped the breathtaking outfit with a leather corset that he itched to unlace.

As if sensing his lazy perusal, she glanced over and raised her glass in salute.

The meeting of their gazes punched him in the solar plexus.

Fuck.

He inclined his head, acknowledging her.

In return, she offered a soft, seductive smile.

Are you noticing the way I'm behaving like a besotted idiot, Mistress Catrina?

As she sipped, she continued to regard him.

This was a bit of an unusual circumstance for him at the Den.

He'd bought the massive mountain estate years before, and he'd turned it into a private and exclusive BDSM club.

Of course female Dominants were welcomed and granted the respect due their position, yet less than a dozen had applied for membership.

Most of the women he associated with here were subs. They didn't meet and hold his gaze like Mistress Catrina was doing.

Disappointment arced through him when she severed the contact and returned her attention to her submissive.

After snagging a canapé, she offered it to the bare-chested man kneeling before her. Since he sported spiky blond hair, the pair presented a striking contrast.

The man, on a leash and wearing nothing other than tight, gold-colored shorts, looked up at her adoringly.

Smiling, she brushed a gentle hand across his forehead.

Then, capturing his chin between her fingertips, she drew him in closer before popping the treat into his mouth.

All the while, Damien pictured the Domme on her knees, affixed to *his* leash, fully understanding what it meant to submit.

He'd known Catrina Davidson for several years.

From everything he'd observed—and he missed nothing that happened at the Den—she was an excellent Mistress.

Recently she'd attended a private event he'd hosted.

That evening, he'd witnessed a deeper, more contemplative side of her. At one point, she'd stood in front of a window, gazing into the distance.

When he'd joined her, she'd turned to face him.

For a moment, before she'd schooled it away, he'd seen a groove furrowed between her sculpted eyebrows.

When he'd asked how she was enjoying the evening, she'd responded with her customary politeness and thanked him for his hospitality.

Almost immediately, she'd excused herself.

Soon after, she'd left the premises entirely.

Damien didn't often allow his thoughts to be consumed by women, especially dominant ones.

But since that night, he hadn't been able to get thoughts of Mistress Catrina out of his mind.

And now, his interest was renewed.

Renewed?

Hell.

Captivated was more like it.

"How's it going, Boss?"

Dragged from his musings, Damien turned his attention to the Den's second-in-command, Gregorio.

Hiring the man had been one of the smartest business decisions Damien had ever made.

Gregorio lived onsite in a caretaker cottage and ensured the safety of their guests, as well as overseeing the estate when it was open for a production company's use.

Additionally, he managed the calendar, the employees, the accounting, and maintenance. Since he could top or bottom, he was even more valuable to the house.

Gregorio folded his arms across his chest.

Tonight he had on a black T-shirt beneath a leather vest. With his silver earring and motorcycle boots, he looked suitably intimidating. "Your demonstration starts in fifteen minutes, Boss." Gregorio hooked a thumb and pointed over his shoulder. "Good turnout."

They'd had plenty of reservations for the open house extravaganza.

Pleased, but knowing they needed to be more vigilant than ever due to the number of brand-new visitors, Damien nodded. "There are a lot of new faces."

"And buttocks," Gregorio added with a grin.

Despite a widespread snowstorm across the Colorado mountains, guests had arrived from all over the region, including parts of Wyoming, Kansas, even Montana.

Gregorio had planned ahead, reserving a block of hotel rooms in the nearby ski town of Winter Park. They'd hired a bus company with skilled drivers to safely shuttle people back and forth.

"Susan is in the ladies' locker room to prepare."

Since Brandy—one of the house submissives who used to participate in demonstrations—was no longer working at the Den, Susan had volunteered to fill in.

They'd practiced once, when she arrived for the evening, but this was the first time they'd put on a demo together for the rest of the members.

"She'll meet you in the entranceway. Your items are laid out on the mantel as requested."

Damien nodded. "Great job, as always."

"All in a day's work, Boss." Gregorio gave a sharp nod. "I'll be assisting you onstage." With that, he excused himself.

Mistress Catrina was no longer in sight, and Damien wondered if she'd taken her submissive downstairs to one of the private rooms.

Demonstrations typically drew most of the neophytes and people curious about joining the Den. So that meant that during presentations, long-time members often took advantage of uncrowded conditions in the dungeon to connect and scene—of course with House Monitors ensuring rules were followed.

After surveying the happenings at the front desk, he went upstairs to his private third-floor suite and flicked on the fireplace to banish the winter chill.

The blinds were open so he could see the snow that had already drifted into huge piles.

A worker was attempting to keep the patio clear of the persistent flakes.

Several hardy souls in various states of undress stood around the firepit with its tall, dancing flames. Nearby, numerous gas heaters offered a respite from the cold.

Another stunning Colorado night, cold and windy, perfect for sleep—or other things—in his custom-built bed.

After changing into black leather pants and a short-sleeved T-shirt, he clipped a whip to his side and went back down the stairs.

In a corner, Mistress Catrina appeared to wait for the show to begin.

Which meant she hadn't vanished to the basement after all.

Schooling his face in order not to reveal how ridiculously pleased he was, he strode over to her. "Milady," he said by way of greeting.

"Damien," she returned, glancing at him through her gorgeous long, enhanced lashes.

He wondered what she looked like natural, naked, on her knees, her lips trembling as she waited for him.

Ruthlessly, he shoved the thought away, refusing to allow his imagination free rein.

He'd enjoyed success in business because he was pragmatic, not fanciful. "Enjoying the evening?"

"Of course."

"I'll take that as a polite lie."

She scowled. "Your events are always fabulous."

"So why aren't you having a good time?"

"You're the one who said I'm not," she countered.

Her scent was as exotic as she was...musk and vanilla, layered with a pervasive sexual need.

Could he possibly be the only one who noticed the pheromones she was radiating?

"Where's your boy?"

"Outside having a smoke. Bad habit." She shuddered. "But who am I to judge?"

"Who, indeed?"

"If he were mine, I'd attempt to do something about that."

Her revelation took him aback. "That collar isn't yours?"

"No. I've never formally collared anyone. Bradley, however, belongs to Master Lawrence. He's on a business trip and was afraid his boy was lonely. Which he was, so he asked me to help out. We're hoping he makes it up here tonight." She shrugged, her creamy shoulders rising and falling before settling into a tantalizing, gentle slope. "But with the weather…"

A sudden urge to wrap his fingers around her upper arms and drag her to her toes slammed into him.

What the hell is wrong with me?

Acting on his sudden, primal instincts would violate personal as well as house rules.

He owed her the same respect accorded to all Dominants.

In all his years of being a Dom, he'd never had the urge to drive a Domme to her knees.

Until now.

Until *her.*

"Are you planning to attend my demo?"

"No," she responded quickly.

When he'd first met her, he'd ascertained she was blunt. Over time, he'd learned to appreciate her honesty. "Perhaps you should."

She tilted her head. "You think you can teach me something?"

"A lot of things," he confirmed.

"That's more than a bit arrogant, Damien."

He longed to hear the word 'Sir' on her lips. "Is it?" he challenged. "We can all benefit from continuing education."

"Including you?" she fired back.

At her direct hit, he inclined his head.

"Setting the scene and an intro to flogging is meant for newcomers, is it not?"

Since she was one hundred percent correct, Damien didn't respond.

"Have you heard complaints from my subs?" The words were tight, as if her breath were constricted.

"Not at all," he reassured her.

"Seen egregious lapses in good judgment from me?"

He scowled. "Of course not."

"Then why the invitation?" She studied him. "And insistence? Do you have a personal reason for asking, perhaps?"

Too fucking close to the truth.

He wanted her with an intensity that twisted his insides. "Seeing others in action can enhance a Dominant's skill."

"And of course, you make it a point to continue your own education every week?"

Touché. Rather than responding directly, he kept his tone neutral. "I have many opportunities to observe others."

"So does every Dom who attends your events or play parties." With keen interest in her eyes, she observed his reactions. "Or even views videos."

"Have you ever tried submission?"

She blinked with shock, his question evidently catching her off guard.

He pressed his point forward. "Some of the most skilled Dominants have embraced or at least tried submission."

"Including you?"

"Actually, yes. I want to be the best at what I do."

Her mouth parted for a moment before she pursed her lips. "More arrogance, Damien. Doesn't pride come before a fall?"

Tipping his head to one side, he acknowledged her barb. "If you're ever interested, Catrina, I'd be delighted to master you."

"If you ever crave a beating, Damien, I'd be happy to put the smack down on your ass," she returned. "But you'll have to ask in a very pretty way, like a good boy."

He resisted the nearly overwhelming impulse to toss her over his shoulder and paddle her sweet ass until she begged for an orgasm.

Bradley, her sub, entered through the kitchen door, and when Catrina noticed him, she smiled indulgently.

What would it be like to see that same expression directed at him?

The man shook snow off his gold boots before walking toward them.

Eyes only for her, he knelt then placed his forehead on the floor in front of Catrina.

"Good boy." Crouching beside him, she rubbed his head.

Damien took Catrina's arm to help her up.

Her skin was warm, inviting.

Tempting.

Electricity jolted through him.

If she experienced the same sensation, she hid it well.

Against her ear, so no one else could eavesdrop, he said, "With your hair framing your face, you'd look stunning in that position."

She drew her dramatic eyebrows together as she scowled.

Without a word, she extracted herself from his grip.

Just then, Master Lawrence arrived, nodding at Damien and kissing Catrina on the cheek.

"You're here, Master!" Bradley exclaimed.

Damien could and maybe should excuse himself, but he didn't.

At Lawrence's urging, the boy thanked Catrina.

"Always a pleasure," she reassured them both.

After standing, the young blond man followed his master down the stairs at an enthusiastic trot.

Susan walked into the room and sought his gaze.

After giving her a nod of acknowledgment, he addressed Catrina. "Should you change your mind, my offer always stands."

"When hell freezes over."

He couldn't help his grin. "With the snow and cold, anything is possible." With that, he excused himself.

His trap had been laid.

And soon, Mistress Catrina would be his.

All mine.

And I'll never share you…

Chapter Two

What the hell just happened?

When Damien walked away, Catrina exhaled.

Damn you.

Who the hell do you think you are?

His outrageous proposition had stunned her, leaving her shaken, and she glanced around to be certain no one had overheard him.

As if I'd ever get on my knees for a man ever again.

Even you.

So why were flutter-kicks racing through her stomach?

Catrina prided herself on being a take-charge person.

From her time as class president in high school to editor of the college paper, and now, as the founder of her own company where she focused on the financial success of women, she'd always been outspoken and driven.

After the end of her engagement five years before, she'd gathered up the shattered pieces of her heart.

When she'd been ready to date again, a friend had introduced her to Todd, a nice, seemingly agreeable man.

In the bedroom, though, he'd bored her.

She'd realized she couldn't live with unimaginative, he-finishes-first sex every night for the rest of her life.

One evening, after she'd stroked his ego, reassuring him he was an excellent lover, she suggested they try new things in the bedroom.

With a little skepticism, he'd agreed.

When she brought in a toy, he'd grabbed it from her and tossed it aside.

Then they' had sex, and she'd been left unsatisfied. Again.

Later that night, he'd walked in on her masturbating in the shower.

He'd lost his cool, turning off the hot water while yelling that she was an insatiable freak.

His words and never-before-seen temper had left her reeling.

And worse, uncertain.

Then he'd forced her to her knees and brutally clamped her wrists, demanding she lick his balls.

By the time he'd let her go, bruises had been forming on her skin.

Shaking, stunned by this side of him, she'd demanded he leave, and she'd vowed she'd never be forced into a situation like that ever again.

The next day, when she'd arrived home from work, his few belongings had been gone from her apartment and his key had been sitting in the middle of the dining room table.

A few months later, she'd met a handsome gentleman at a party. After hearing about her previous, disastrous relationship, he'd said he'd be honored to worship at her feet.

He hadn't been joking.

Ever since, she'd been involved with submissive men who catered to her every sexual need. In return, she catered to their desires.

What could be better?

At times, though, a horrible, niggling voice whispered that she was missing intimacy.

Anytime the awful thought caught up to her, she'd turn up the volume on her television or distract herself on her elliptical machine, music blaring from earbuds.

She'd remind herself she had plenty of friends for problem solving and conversation.

Her days were full in every way, and she didn't need anyone to hold her or to share a life with.

Even someone like Damien Lowell.

As if reading her thoughts across the distance, he glanced over his shoulder.

With a tiny shiver, she turned away.

When she looked back, he was gone.

Thankfully.

No way did she need someone like the arrogant Dom bossing her around, taking his satisfaction, leaving her frustrated.

Definitely not.

Minutes later, Gregorio moved through the rooms, announcing the imminent start of Master Damien's demonstration.

Now that Master Lawrence had claimed Bradley, Catrina was at loose ends.

Maybe she could avail herself of the services of a house sub.

Or perhaps Gregorio with his pirate-like looks, silver earring, and sexy body might be talked into playing with her.

She swept her gaze over the room and found him. But since he was deep in a conversation with a couple she'd never seen before, she'd need to wait until later.

More out of boredom than curiosity, and not because Damien had issued a challenge, Catrina snagged a sparkling water mixed with cranberry juice and wandered into the living room.

The usual furniture had been removed, and several rows of fold-up chairs had been arranged in a semicircle near the fireplace.

She stood toward the back where she wouldn't be noticed.

From here, she had a clear view of Damien and the pretty sub on her knees, facing him, her head bowed. Catrina appreciated the woman's lush, feminine form. She wore her hair in a blonde bob that shaded her face.

Since both were turned sideways to the room, their expressions and all Damien's gestures were obvious.

Moments later, Gregorio entered and stood near Damien.

Without being told, the gathered crowd hushed as Damien touched the woman's head.

In response, she trembled.

Catrina could only guess how much courage was needed to participate in a demo, especially with the house owner. The sub's nervousness radiated through the room.

Damine's biceps flexed as he made tiny, massaging motions. To soothe or reassure the sub? Either way, his silent communication was impressive.

"I'd like you to stand," he said, his strong, baritone voice echoing through the space. "And tell us your name."

"Susan, Sir." She kept her eyes on the wooden floorboards, even as he offered a hand to help her up.

Warmth shimmied up Catrina's spine as she remembered the sensation of his firm grip on her arm.

She didn't normally accept help, and it surprised her how much she'd liked it.

Softly, he went on. "I appreciate your show of respect."

Interesting.

Damien had not used that tone with her. Instead, he'd spoken to her as an equal, rather than a man intent on seducing a woman.

"Look up at me, Susan," he continued.

She did, her eyes wide and unblinking.

"I want you to be completely comfortable with everything we do here tonight."

"Yes, Sir."

In that same, reassuring voice he went on, "Is there anything you're uncomfortable with?"

"I'd like to leave on my panties, Sir," Susan whispered with her head turned.

He took her chin and recaptured her gaze. "Of course you may leave on your panties. Anything else I can do to reassure you?"

She shook her head but started to fold her arms.

"It appears there may be something you're reluctant to tell me?" His question was astute.

"Ah... I have very sensitive nipples, Sir."

"Then I'll treat them with all due respect."

"Thank you, Sir." She gave a tentative smile.

"And do you have a safe word, Susan?"

"Stop."

"So, to be clear, stop means *stop*."

"Yes, Sir."

"And a slow word?"

"Yellow, Sir."

"Got it. We'll take a break if you use the word yellow."

"Thank you, Sir."

"You're also aware that 'halt' is the house safe word?"

"Yes, Sir."

In that instant, Catrina understood why Damien taught demos at the open house events. It was one thing to inform Doms that they needed to make their sub feel comfortable, but Damien was a genius.

He was repeating what Susan said, but not in parrot-fashion. With the way he spoke and used physical touch, he built trust and simultaneously soothed Susan.

His approach was as subtle as it was elegant.

Maybe he had been correct in thinking she could learn something from him, as much as that thought rankled.

Transfixed, she took a drink while he undressed his sub.

Damien could have ordered Susan to strip. Instead, he squeezed her shoulders and ran his fingers over the skin he bared. "Now I'd like to remove your bra."

Catrina gulped. The seduction in his tone made her wish the words were directed at her.

"Yes, Sir," Susan said.

He moved around the back of her to unfasten her bra.

Her shoulders were rolled backward so that the bra remained in place.

"Thank you for your trust," he continued when he stood in front of her once more.

Slowly, he drew the straps down her arms. "Remember you can stop or slow down at any time."

"Yes, Sir."

When he'd removed the lacy black brassiere and handed it to Gregorio, Damien brushed her hair back and said, "You're beautiful, Susan."

As if a switch had been turned on, she smiled, and her cheeks flushed with color, making her look radiant. Hesitancy had been replaced with confidence.

Under his guidance, she'd blossomed.

Catrina couldn't look away even if she wanted to as he cupped Susan's breasts and eased his thumbs across her nipples.

Her eyes closed.

As he continued, she moaned and moved toward him, curling her fingers around his wrists.

Catrina clutched her glass tighter as shock tightened her throat.

Damien's concentration seemed riveted on Susan. It appeared as if neither were aware of the dozens of people watching them.

For the first time, Catrina observed submission and dominance from an entirely unfamiliar perspective. For them, nothing seemed to exist outside of one another, and Damien's attention didn't wander from the woman under his command.

Catrina took care of her men, meeting their needs in a transactional type of way. In return, she had at least one magnificent climax. The lack of connection had been fine. Until now.

"Tell me what you want, Susan."

"An orgasm, Sir."

He smiled. "Oh, you'll most certainly earn that."

"Thank you, Sir." Her knees buckled.

"Can you wait?" he asked.

"If it's your desire, Sir."

"You're a very pleasing submissive. Tell me what we're demonstrating this evening."

"A flogging, Sir."

"I'd like to make love to you with the leather strands." Damien's words oozed hypnotic appeal.

As if she were the one standing on the stage in front of him, Catrina's insides melted.

"Yes, Sir."

Catrina had never looked at a man the way Susan was looking at Damien, eyes wide with trust and reverence.

Damien led Susan to the hearth and placed her hands on the mantel. "Legs farther apart for me," he said, his words like a caress.

Susan moved into position.

"I can secure you in place, if you'd like."

"I'll remain as I am, Sir, if that's okay with you?"

"Certainly," he replied.

"Thank you, Sir." Though she'd been trembling earlier, Susan was now still.

Damien had said he wanted to make love to Susan with his flogger, and that's exactly what he seemed to do. He started with tender leather kisses, licking at the woman's shoulders and back. He let the strands fall in gentle waves.

Catrina had never wielded a handle with such skill. She told herself it was because a man's skin was much tougher than a woman's, but now she questioned whether she'd assumed too much.

As the scene unfolded, holding her spellbound, he brought Susan's body to life. He increased the intensity of his blows on her panty-covered buttocks. Her cries were whimpers of desire, not of distress. She appeared to surrender not only to Damien but to the flogger.

Goose bumps rose on Catrina's arms, and her skin tingled with anticipation.

Suddenly, she didn't want to watch Damien please another woman.

Confused by the irrational thoughts, she gulped the last of her drink then slammed the empty glass down and headed toward the foyer.

"I'd like to be on the next shuttle to Winter Park," she told the submissive at the door.

"It will be about twenty minutes, Milady. Jeff's just on his way back now."

Catrina nodded, said thanks then strode purposefully to the women's locker room.

The place was empty, and she exhaled in relief.

For several moments, she struggled to rein in her wayward emotions, smoothing her hair, straightening her skirt, and splashing mountain-cold water onto her face.

All that done, she felt more in control.

Finally, exhaling deeply, she pulled back her shoulders and opened the door.

As if he'd been waiting for her, Damien stood at the end of the hallway, arms folded, overwhelming the space, blocking her way.

She started to take an instinctive step back but managed to stop herself.

Power cloaked him.

For a wild moment, before sanity plowed back into her, she wondered what it would be like to play with him.

In front of him, she stopped.

"You were there," he said. "At the demonstration."

She lifted a shoulder in a halfhearted shrug. "I missed the shuttle and had nothing better to do."

At the half-truth, he grinned.

How did he see through her so completely?

"What did you think?"

"You seem to know what you're doing."

"You were curious, weren't you?"

When she didn't respond, he continued, "You were wondering what it would be like to be in Susan's helpless, submissive position?"

After her experience with Todd, she'd told herself she'd never again be subject to a man's bigger, stronger demands. *And yet...* "Why would I? I can have a gorgeous man at my feet and tell him exactly what to do."

"Is that what you want?"

Catrina refused to consider his question.

"Or do you want a man who will concentrate all his efforts on pleasing you?"

"I have that now."

"Do you?" he countered. "Do your men give you the attention I gave Susan?"

"Of course."

"You ought to be taken to task for your complete lack of honesty."

She shivered. With a stubborn tilt of her chin she snapped back, "How dare you?"

"You looked down and to the left before answering." Then, in a softer tone, seducing her with his voice, despite the nature of their conversation, he continued, "When was the last time anyone cared enough to watch your movements so intently that they knew you were lying? Do all your relationships exist strictly on the surface? Do you crave something more? Deeper?"

Intimacy.

He'd asked the same damn question that she continually tried to outrun.

"Aren't you curious about what you're missing?"

"No."

"Another lie?"

She shook her head quickly. Too quickly.

He dropped his arms and took a step toward her.

"Damien…"

"You know the house safe word," he told her. "You can use it at any time. But you aren't going to, are you?"

Jesus. What the hell is happening here?

This close, his masculine scent and determination consumed her.

His blue eyes were as dark as a midnight sky. A tiny pulse in his jaw mesmerized her.

"Is your pussy wet, Milady?"

His words suffocated her, and she struggled to infuse her words with a dismissive tone. "From what? Being near you? Watching your little demo? Not at all."

Impossibly, he took another step closer.

"Shall I find out for myself?"

"No."

"Use the house safe word."

She should.

But she couldn't.

"Last chance, Milady." With exquisite care, he cupped her shoulders. "Tell me to stop."

"I…"

His grip was loose, and she could escape at any moment, yet the fierce, independent part of her was nowhere to be found.

He turned her slightly and backed her against the wall.

Then, ever so gently, he captured her wrists in one of his hands and pinned them above her.

Her chest rose and fell as emotions tumbled through her. She shouldn't want to interact with him.

But this seemed natural.

Right.

With the same kind of intensity that he'd watched Susan, he studied Catrina, as if searching for clues about what she wanted.

He touched the knuckles of his free hand to her throat.

She kept her eyes wide, pretending she wasn't affected.

Continuing, Damien skimmed down the center of her chest, bare skin to bare skin.

Then, unblinkingly holding her gaze, he traced beneath her breasts.

No one had ever showered her with this kind of attention, and it left her dizzy.

Even though she was covered by the material of her corset, her nipples responded when he moved over them.

There wasn't a part of her that wasn't aware of him.

"Open your mouth."

"Why?"

"Because I'm going to kiss you."

No.

While she started to protest, he dove inside her. She expected him to coax her. Instead, he consumed her.

He forced his way in, tasting of an intoxicating blend of persuasion and dominance, making her weak.

She was helpless to him.

Yes.

Damien insinuated a thigh between her legs, and despite her resolve, she began to rub herself against him.

The woman in her recognized his mental as well as physical strength.

The realization should frighten her.

But it didn't.

He was sure of himself, powerful enough for her to trust.

While he might demand that she hold nothing back, he wouldn't push her too far.

For a moment, he pulled back. "You're exquisite."

When he reclaimed her, he deepened the kiss.

She couldn't breathe. Couldn't think.

And suddenly she didn't want to.

Shockingly, an orgasm began to unfurl deep inside her.

A couple moved past them, but Damien never allowed his attention to wander.

On and on the kiss went, until she began to shake.

Gently, he released her mouth. "I won't be satisfied until you climax." He adjusted their positions, moving a hand between her legs to slip his fingers inside her thong. "Your pussy *is* wet, Milady."

She shook her head, and he laughed. It was a satisfied, rather than triumphant sound.

His focus entirely on her, he pressed a thumb to her swollen clit.

"I..."

"It's just you and me. I'll keep your secret. No one will have to know that you came for me."

Catrina had never known a desire so debilitating. Even if she found someone else or went somewhere to satisfy herself, it wouldn't be the same.

She needed *him*.

He made maddening circles on her clit, and he had one finger teasing her entrance.

"Do it," she instructed.

But she'd forgotten who she was dealing with.

"Ask." He shook his head. "And be grateful I'm not making you beg."

Beg?

Fuck you.

Relentlessly, the awful, skilled Dom kept her on edge.

"Shall I stop?"

Searching for self-control, she squeezed her eyes shut.

When she didn't respond, he stilled.

"Damn you, Damien."

"Ask for it, Milady. Tell me what you want."

She hated this. Loved it. "I want to come."

When he didn't change the tempo, she closed her eyes.

He allowed her the time and the space to wage her internal battle. Sensations assailed her, forcing her body to relax. She became a puddle of feminine hunger.

"*Ask.*"

Catrina was lost in the moment, in him. "May I come, Damien?"

"Look at me."

With a deep swallow, she did.

"One more time."

Much as she hated this, she understood him. He wouldn't let her escape or pretend she hadn't been aware of what she was doing. "Will you give me an orgasm?"

"The pleasure will be all mine, Milady."

He circled her clit and slid two fingers deep inside her pussy.

At the blessed relief, she cried out.

As he finger-fucked her, he continued to tease her clit.

Her legs shook with the force of his movements.

There was nothing sweet about this, and it was beyond hot.

"Is this what you want?"

But he already knew the answer because he studied her and responded to her reactions.

He changed his angle slightly, finding the sensitive spot inside her that no other man ever had.

With a whimper, she jerked against him.

"Come for me, Catrina."

He pressed his fingers against her G-spot.

Mindless of her surroundings, she screamed as the climax crashed into her. He helped her ride it, keeping his grip tight on her wrists, pressing her against the wall, supporting her body.

"So, so perfect," he said.

She screamed a second time, shattered.

Her body went limp, but she wasn't worried, he was there, holding her in a firm but tender grip.

It seemed like minutes later when she blinked and looked at him.

"Welcome back," he said.

"That was..." She clamped her mouth shut, desperate to be on firm footing again.

"Yes, it was. For me, as well."

She blinked. "I don't understand."

"I adore a woman who is so responsive. I appreciate you playing with me." He moved his hand from between her legs and straightened her thong and skirt.

"What just happened..." She pulled her wrists free from his grip. "It changes nothing."

"Maybe not for you." He tucked a tendril of her hair behind her ear, and she caught her own scent on him. "As for me, I'm intrigued. I want to know you on a deeper level."

His words terrified her.

Then she told herself he truly was a master in all ways. Which meant he used his words to great effect. "Not all women swoon at your lovely statements."

A flash of temper seared his eyes. "You know better than that."

"Do I?"

"I had a demo with Susan. I didn't say anything of the sort to her."

She hadn't stayed until the end.

"This was different."

"Was it?"

He took her hand and placed it on his crotch. "You tell me."

"So?" So hard. Big. Firm. She struggled not to be impressed or to let him know how much she appreciated him. "You have a hard-on."

"Were you born a cynic?"

With an exhalation, she shook her head. "Life taught me."

"I can teach you other things, show you a different perspective."

"Is that what this was about? *Proving* something to me?"

"Partially."

She recoiled.

How stupid to think, to hope, that he wanted her as a woman. "At least you're honest."

"The bigger truth is, I did that because I wanted to get you off, because I'm attracted to you."

"More pretty words, Damien?"

"Give me two weeks."

"What?"

"I'm challenging you. Spend two weeks with me, submit to me, see if the experience transforms you."

"I'm not sure this matters to you, but in case I wasn't clear earlier, hell fucking no."

"What are you scared of?" His tone was soft, challenging.

"Nothing scares me." *Another lie.*

"Then agree to it. You've got nothing to lose. You'll experience new things, get to spend a few days up here, have a chance to relax."

"Relax?" she scoffed.

"What would it be like if you could be yourself and let go, turn over control to someone else for a while?"

"I can't," she said, her heart thundering. That was as honest as she'd been with anyone, ever.

He inclined his head, showing he'd heard the fear in her voice. *Damn him.*

"Was it scary when I brought you off?"

She shook her head.

"When I made you ask for it?"

"No."

A woman on her way to the locker room continued by without disturbing them.

"I will demolish your barriers, Catrina."

A traitorous part of her wanted to say yes.

Instead, she met his gaze. His eyes were dark, probing. She was afraid he saw too much.

He brushed a strand of hair back from her face.

"I'm not a sub." She had to go before her resolve crumpled. "Thanks for the orgasm. My shuttle will be here soon."

He moved aside.

As she walked past, he swatted her, catching the bare flesh above her stockings and below her buttocks.

Shock stole her breath.

Then, fury blazing, she rounded on him.

Before she could speak, Damien had her against the wall once more, overpowering her with his scent, his presence.

The sting receded, leaving a tantalizing warmth that stunned her and made it impossible to weave coherent thoughts together. "That was unacceptable."

"Of course it was."

"I don't know who the fuck you think you are." Despite herself, she grabbed his shoulders and held on tight.

What the hell is happening here?

He leaned forward and brushed a kiss across her forehead before moving lower to graze her neck.

His gentleness surprised her, obliterating her defenses.

"Be at my place in Denver tomorrow night at eight," he whispered in her ear. "Just the two of us, Catrina."

"I can't." *I won't.*

"If two weeks is too frightening, start with one night. Eight o'clock," he repeated. "What could it hurt?"

Chapter Three

"You're out of your mind," Catrina told him.

The fact she was still hanging on to him and hadn't uttered her safe word proved that she was out of hers, too.

"Am I? Or am I offering what you secretly want?"

She maneuvered her hands to push him away. Budging him, she found out, was something that required his cooperation. Not having to deal with big, intractable men was another reason she liked being a Domme. "Out of my way."

"You're bossy."

"Assertive," she corrected. "Don't you forget it, mister."

With a smile capable of making her forget her own name, Damien stepped back.

Still trying to think rationally, she escaped.

Gregorio was in the foyer, his arms crossed as usual.

"I've got to get out of here."

He gave a sharp nod. "Of course."

After what seemed like hours, he returned with her coat and small handbag.

"I couldn't find the hatcheck girl," he admitted. "So it took me a minute."

Tension continued to tighten her stomach.

Then Damien — *damn him* — reappeared at her side to pluck her coat from Gregorio's grip.

"I don't need your help," she insisted.

"Regardless, you've got it." He moved behind her.

Struggle would be futile against this powerful Dom.

Instead, she shrugged into her coat.

"That wasn't so bad, was it?"

"Thank you." She forced the words through clenched teeth. "I've got it from here."

"Afraid not." He held up his hand. "I'm being prudent. It's snowing, and your boots aren't made for the ice."

"Does everyone get this kind of personal service from the owner?"

"It's okay to accept help, Milady."

For her, it wasn't. She'd been doing things on her own for so long that she wasn't certain she knew how else to behave.

"Think of me as your willing servant, if it helps."

"Right," she agreed.

Even Damien's lips twitched at the ridiculousness of the suggestion.

Gregorio opened the front door and said goodnight to a couple who were heading out.

"Well?" Damien asked.

He had a point. The weather was atrocious, and her footwear was meant for a club, not the ice.

Judging by the set of his jaw, this was a battle he intended to win.

"Fine." She placed a hand on his forearm.

Immediately she recognized her error.

With him, nothing was harmless.

Heat and strength radiated from him and through her. His effortless way of making her feel insulated and taken care of was both irresistibly sexy and unbelievably dangerous.

As he had with the other couple, Gregorio opened the door for them.

Bitter cold air nipped at her ears, making her shiver.

"You're welcome to stay," Damien invited.

She ignored him.

Dozens of lights outlined the flagstone path and silence shrouded them. For a moment she could believe they were the only two people on the planet.

Despite his dire warnings, the path had been shoveled, and a layer of salt had been thrown down, providing traction and melting the occasional snowflakes as they landed. "You'll say anything to get your way, won't you?"

"I'll say anything to spend a few extra minutes with you," he corrected.

He helped her into the backseat of the oversize and luxurious four-wheel-drive vehicle that served as tonight's shuttle. For this run, she was the only occupant.

"Take good care of her, Jeff," Damien instructed the driver as he reached across her lap to fasten her safety belt.

Once that was finished, he slid his thumb across the back of her hand.

A shiver that had nothing to do with the temperature danced up her spine.

"Tomorrow," he reminded her.

Before she could respond, he closed the door.

As the driver pulled away, she glanced over to see Damien still standing there, staring contemplatively.

"You must be important to the boss," Jeff observed, meeting her gaze in the rearview mirror.

"Not at all."

The man chuckled. "This could be fun to watch."

"Fun?"

"The boss doesn't like to be told no."

"He's going to hear it a lot from me," she replied.

"That's why it will be fun to watch."

Because his enthusiasm was infectious, she grinned.

He stopped at the intersection with the highway. "You're at the Lodge, right?"

"Promise not to tell Damien?"

"As if he wouldn't find out anyway, Milady."

"I'm sure you're right." Not that Damien cared enough to track her down, she was sure. "Yes," she confirmed. "The Lodge."

Jeff lapsed into silence.

Why couldn't Damien be more like him? Big, rugged, quiet, and happy to leave her the hell alone?

Though she collapsed against the luxurious leather, she couldn't relax. Damien's invitation played over and over in her mind.

After her broken engagement and the disaster with Todd, she'd vowed to remain in control of herself and her life. So why would she submit to the Dom of all Doms?

But damn...

Even though miles now separated them, every breath she took smelled of him, and her body was still seared from his quick spank.

Her cell phone rang.

"That will be the boss," Jeff said, glancing at her with an amused grin.

She dug the device from her purse and checked the display. "Aww, hell."

"I was right, wasn't I?"

Unfortunately. With a nod, Catrina sent the call to voicemail.

"You're only delaying the inevitable, Milady."

The phone lit up again.

"Sorry, Milady. I warned you. You matter to the boss."

With a deep sigh, she answered the call.

"I can't stop thinking about you," Damien said by way of a greeting.

The sound of his voice sent sparks of remembrance straight to her scorched skin. "That makes one of us."

He laughed. "Do you know how to tell the truth? Once you're at your hotel, you'll take a shower and masturbate to thoughts of me. You'll be wondering what a real spanking feels like."

"Absolutely not," she insisted, her words breathless.

"I should forbid it," he said.

Momentarily holding the phone away from her ear, she scowled. "As if I'd do anything you told me to."

"Well isn't that a conundrum? If you touch yourself, you'll imagine my fingers tracing your skin. If you don't play with that pretty pussy, you'll be following my explicit command. Oh, and, Milady…"

Keenly aware of Jeff's interest, she remained silent.

"Lick your fingers when you're done," Damien finished.

Without another word, the damnable man hung up.

A few moments later, she realized Jeff had parked beneath the hotel's portico.

At a jog, he climbed from the driver's seat and hurried around to open her door, offering his help as she stepped down.

Then over her protests, he escorted her to revolving glass doors.

"When the boss issues an order, *I* follow it," he said.

"Are you insinuating I should do likewise?"

"Oh, hell no, Milady. This is much more entertaining." He waited until she was inside before making a dash back to the sports utility vehicle.

In her room, she dropped her coat on the end of the bed before sitting on a chair to remove the tight-fitting boots. The cursed things might be gorgeous, but they hurt like hell. Her poor toes would be cramped for days.

Which would be another reminder of the evening...one that had turned her world upside down.

And if Damien had his way, they'd continue their exploration tomorrow.

She stripped and folded her clothes then placed them in her suitcase to make packing easier.

With that task handled, she headed for the bathroom and picked up a washcloth to scrub off her makeup.

Moments later, she was transformed back into her regular self.

No doubt the plain and ordinary Catrina would appeal to him a lot less than the dramatic diva she portrayed.

Which made her wonder... Away from the Den, what was he like?

Still pondering, Catrina turned on the shower faucet. As steam billowed in the room, his earlier words haunted her.

Damn him. He *had* caused her a conundrum.

She was aroused, and she didn't want to be.

With a deep sigh, she pinned up her hair, then stepped beneath the spray.

As he'd hoped, her thoughts were filled with images of him. She didn't want to play with him. And she most certainly had no intention of submitting to him.

But as she closed her eyes, she recalled the stunning shock that had rocked her when his hand had connected with her flesh.

The momentary hiss of pain had been replaced almost immediately with the white-hot heat of desire, making all her protests irrelevant.

Warmth from the water suffused her.

Focusing on her shower, she opened her eyes and reached for the bar of soap then made a lather. She slid her slick hands over her chest. Her nipples beaded, and her breasts were swollen.

Damn you, Damien.

With her lips pursed, she continued down her belly. She paused for a moment at her pelvis. Her pussy throbbed.

No matter how she justified things or what stories she told herself, the truth was, she didn't have sex as often as she would like. Far too often she used her trusty vibrator.

Right now, the idea of having Damien's cock inside her made her tremble.

Lightly, she skimmed her fingers across her pussy before continuing on. She didn't need another orgasm.

After finishing her shower, she dried off.

When she was finally in bed, sleep proved elusive.

Every five to ten minutes she'd sigh and check the time.

An hour later, she was frustrated that she tossed a pillow on top of the offending clock so she couldn't see the mocking numbers.

Because she had been restless, she ended up sleeping well past her normal time, leaving her discombobulated.

Across the room, her phone sat on the dresser, blinking at her, beckoning her over.

Unable to resist the impulse, she crossed the room to look at the screen.

A text message from Damien was waiting.

I hope you didn't steal an orgasm that belongs to me.

Her heart thundered. *Belongs to you?* The arrogance.

But if she were honest with herself, she'd admit the words sent a little thrill through her.

The words were part of the reason he was such a good Dom. If he behaved this way with everyone, that meant he started the seduction, the alluring mind-fuck, hours before he ever touched his submissive. Maybe she *could* learn a thing or two from him.

Still, she hadn't decided how to respond when a second text followed.

If you're a good girl, you'll be rewarded.

Ignoring both messages, she dressed and rode the elevator to the lobby restaurant in search of breakfast and a much-needed caffeine fix.

Unfortunately, the tall, black coffee didn't help. In fact, it flooded her system with nerves. The combination of that and no sleep left her jittery.

Then her phone chimed again, making things worse.

She looked at the screen.

Tonight?

A moment later, an address appeared on the display. If her guess was right, it was in a sprawling north-western Denver suburb, not too far from the foothills. Lots of land to go with the privacy and mountain views.

Catrina slammed the phone on the table, facedown.

Damn him for tempting her.

Preferring carbs over healthy eating, she ordered a waffle and slathered it in butter and maple syrup.

A number of people wandered into the dining room. Some, she recognized from the Den.

She was taking her final bite when Bradley and Master Lawrence strolled in, smiling at each other. They never looked in her direction.

Suddenly, unaccountably, loneliness rippled through her, leaving behind a gaping hole of emptiness.

For the first time since she'd made her lifestyle choices, she missed the intimacy that came with a relationship.

Something like I shared with Damien...

Shaking off the awful feelings, Catrina paid her bill then went upstairs to finish packing before heading back to Denver.

With the snow-covered mountain roads, the drive took an hour longer than it usually did, leaving her with far too much time to think.

When she was finally safe at her small but cozy Washington Park bungalow, she put away her clean clothing and tossed a load of laundry in the washing machine before going about her weekly chores.

Even after she was finished and hit the elliptical machine for a punishing forty-five-minute run, there were still too many hours left in the day before she could go to bed.

At loose ends, she wandered into her office.

She'd finished her monthly newsletter before heading to the Den, but she opened the document on her computer and proofed it a final time.

Then she pulled out manila file folders belonging to women she was meeting with the next day.

Her first appointment would be with her newest client, Jenny. The woman's husband had stunned her less than a week ago with the news that he was filing for a divorce. In the twenty-eight years the couple had been married, Jenny had allowed him to handle the bills and investing. When Catrina had met with her last week, Jenny had cried the whole time.

At times, Catrina felt as if her role were one of a counselor more than a financial advisor, but that was the part of the job, and she treasured it.

A little over five years ago, she'd been in similar circumstances…facing the unexpected and unwelcome end of a relationship and staring at the all-too-real possibility of financial ruin. Now, helping others navigate treacherous waters gave her life meaning.

An hour later, she closed the files and slid them back in the desk drawer.

She was at her desk, staring out of the window at a couple walking past, holding hands, when angst returned in a massive rush.

The rest of the afternoon and evening loomed.

Even though she didn't want to sit in front of the television all night, bingeing a show while eating a carton of ice cream, that was becoming a bigger possibility with each passing minute.

Sighing, she shoved her chair back from her desk and paced the hardwood floor of her still-to-be renovated home.

No light blinked on her phone, meaning Damien hadn't contacted her again.

Clearly he expected her to appear at his home, something she had no intention of doing.

A little while later, she wasn't as sure.

No matter what she focused on, she couldn't banish thoughts of him. Despite her resolve, he intrigued her.

Then her great internal debate began.

It couldn't hurt to see him.

But no good could come of it.

I'm not a sub.

But she did like to learn and grow.

Since she hadn't masturbated since she left the Den, sexual tension crawled through her. She hadn't deliberately followed his orders, yet she ached to feel his strong hands on her body.

Hells bells.

She didn't need *his* touch. Any man would do.

Which was a total lie.

Cursing her traitorous thoughts, she set up the coffeemaker for the following morning and programmed its timer. Still, it wasn't even five o'clock in the afternoon.

One thing was certain, she needed an outlet for her turmoil.

She telephoned a couple of friends, but no one was available to hang out.

As a desperate measure, she called Bradley. He begged off with an apology, saying he had to get ready for work the next day, adding in a sheepish voice that Master Lawrence had exhausted him.

That left only one option.

With confidence, she dialed her mother's number. Evelyn didn't answer until the third ring. With a gleeful giggle, she said she was going to a movie with a new beau.

My mother has plans? Then it hit her. "Wait. What? When did you get a boyfriend?"

"A few weeks ago. Milton. He likes to rock climb at an indoor gym. Can you imagine?"

"I'm having a hard time getting past the fact you're dating, Mother."

"*Yes!* Isn't it awesome?"

"Awesome?" She pulled the phone away from her ear and looked at it. "Sorry, who is this? I thought I was talking to my mom."

"I've got to go. Miltey will be here in a few minutes, and I hate to keep him waiting."

Miltey? In the background, her mother's doorbell rang.

"I'm sure you'll find something to do, dear. Give me a call later this week. Maybe you can meet him."

Without a formal goodbye, Evelyn hung up.

At times like this, that nasty, nasty internal voice turned up the volume, reminding Catrina she'd made the choice to shut herself off from intimacy and that there were consequences.

She informed her clients it was okay to trust again, even fall in love, as long as they made savvy financial decisions and didn't abdicate all their power. But she refused to take her own advice.

The clock on the kitchen wall indicated it was a few minutes past seven. She still had time to make it to Damien's house.

Catrina raked a handful of hair back from her forehead.

Who was she fooling? A man hadn't held her interest like this in years, if ever. In fighting herself and him, she was also fighting the inevitable. She could see him again and prove to herself that last night had been an anomaly.

After collecting a well-deserved orgasm, she'd wave farewell and never see him again.

Right?

Chapter Four

Nothing rattled Damien.

He owned half a dozen businesses and executed transactions in a handful of different time zones. Others came to him to solve their problems.

So why the hell was he wearing a path in the living room's hardwood floor?

Annoyed with himself, he checked his watch. Until this moment, he'd had no doubt Catrina would show up.

He'd expected her to be a few minutes late, but twenty?

Half an hour ago, he'd flipped the switch to ignite the fireplace, bumped the house temperature a couple of degrees, turned on the porch and path lights.

Afterward, instead of staring out of the window, he'd forced himself to return to his study to finish up an email to a potential client in Hong Kong. That had taken all of three minutes.

He'd flipped the lid closed on his notebook computer then tried to settle on the couch.

Once Catrina had left the Den last night, he'd been restless.

For the first time since his divorce almost a decade before, Damien had noticed how large his suite was, how big and empty his house was.

He'd ached to hold Catrina in his arms.

Not just any woman. Catrina, specifically.

There was something about her scent, the way she fought him, the way her eyes — the color of ground emeralds — glittered when she challenged him. And more, it was the way she tried to hide her vulnerabilities.

This morning, Gregorio had joined him for coffee and breakfast, and the two had spent hours in meetings.

But Damien had been distracted by thoughts of the lovely Domme.

Over the years, he'd interacted with so many subs that he'd become jaded.

If it weren't for demonstrations, he might never scene.

Which was why his attraction to Catrina intrigued him.

At the Den, he'd been aware of her scrutiny as he'd interacted with Susan.

When Catrina had vanished from the room before the presentation had ended, he'd suspected she'd been turned on by what she'd witnessed. The dampness of her pussy had confirmed his suspicions. She'd been aroused, even though she hadn't wanted to be.

Ever since, he'd been tormented by thoughts of her, recalling her soft, feminine sounds of pleasure and pain. He wanted to hear more, wanted to feel her pussy clenching his cock, wanted to inhale the scent of her hair when the luxurious strands spilled across his chest.

Damien hadn't been surprised when she'd ignored his text messages.

That she hadn't told him to fuck off meant she was interested.

That she hadn't replied at all meant she was conflicted.

During his drive back to Denver, he'd figured she'd show up at his home five to ten minutes late, making it clear she wouldn't willingly fall at his feet. Fifteen forced him to question his tactics. Twenty had made him nervous.

Now, as it edged toward twenty-five, anxiety gnawed at his insides.

As an avowed bachelor, he was unbothered by relationship issues.

Or at least he hadn't been until this dark-haired beauty had ensnared his attention.

At thirty-one minutes after the hour, the unmistakable beam of car headlights indicated a vehicle had turned into his cul-de-sac.

Fucking finally.

More relieved than he would admit, he exhaled before closing the blinds to ensure their privacy before exiting the house to meet her on the path.

With practiced patience, he folded his arms against the winter chill and waited for her even though she took her time turning off the car engine.

Slowly, she exited the SUV then hesitated for a moment when she saw him.

He inclined his head in greeting, though he wasn't sure she would notice his expression across the distance.

She turned up the collar on her coat before grabbing her purse and flicking the car door closed. Purposefully, spine erect, she walked toward him.

A few feet away, she stopped.

"I'm glad you came."

"I wasn't sure I was going to."

"Why did you?"

"I don't know," she admitted. For once, her answer seemed honest. "Curiosity, maybe."

"You've bruised my ego."

She tipped her head to one side and seemed to be trying to hide a smile. "You were imagining I was so overcome by last night's orgasm that I spent the last eighteen hours fantasizing about you?"

"A man can hope."

"Dreamer."

He moved a hand to his heart. "I fear that's a mortal wound."

"You'll survive."

He focused on the fact she had come, no matter her reasoning.

His next task was to convince her to stay. "Come inside."

Though he didn't need to, he tucked his hand beneath her elbow and guided her to the house, up the steps onto the porch, then he opened the door.

As she passed him, he caught a whiff of her just-showered scent, something tropical that reminded him of summer.

Her long, thick hair was piled atop her head, with some sort of butterfly-looking clip to hold it in place.

He closed the door behind them, locking out the elements and reality. "May I take your coat?"

After interminable seconds, she placed her purse on a nearby table.

He moved behind her to help her from the garment, then he hung it in the closet.

When he'd imagined her coming to his home, he hadn't known what to expect. Would she dress as a fierce and fiery Domme? Or would she wear a skirt that invited him to touch her?

But, as he was starting to learn, this woman was not predictable.

Damien loved seeing her at the Den with her dramatic makeup, false eyelashes, and bright lipstick. But this…? Other than a light brush of mascara, her face was bare.

Black jeans rode low on her hips, and a form-fitting sweater showed off her slender waist and the curve of her breasts. Instead of stilettos, she'd selected boots with chunky heels and metal buckles. Tonight, she looked more like a biker chick than a Domme fatale.

She sure as hell didn't look ready to submit.

Just how many facets were there to this woman? One thing was certain. He fucking itched to find out. "Something to drink?"

"Thanks, but no. I want an orgasm, and I'm here for it. Then I'm driving home."

"You're welcome to stay the night rather than go back out in the cold."

"Do you have a guest room?"

He winced. "Any more blows to my ego lined up today?"

She smiled.

This time, it was genuine, not polite like the ones she bestowed at the Den.

In that moment, he wondered how much of herself she kept hidden.

The more he saw of her, the more he wanted to uncover.

"I'll have something sparkling, non-alcoholic."

"Mineral water?" he offered.

"With lime?"

"Coming right up."

While he pulled out glasses and sliced a lime, she glanced around. "I like your home. Open concepts are wonderful." She wandered to the sliding patio door.

She moved aside the blinds to look outside. "Is that Standley Lake out there?"

"It is."

"I had no idea it was so big."

"Plenty of water skiing in summer."

"So you have a view of the mountains and the water?"

"Depending on the angle. And a covered patio," he said. "It will be chilly, but we can have coffee out there in the morning. Bald eagles nest out here."

She released the blinds and they swished into place as she turned to face him. A scowl was buried between her eyebrows. "I said I wasn't staying."

"Attempting to lead you into temptation."

"Anything to win?"

"Fair means or foul," he said, joining her and offering her one of the glasses.

Catrina shook her head. "You're honest."

"To a fault." He skimmed a finger down her cheekbone. "I like to touch you," he said. "Last night showed me how much."

She captured his wrist.

"You like it, too. I can see your heart beating, right there…" He continued lower, tracing the column of her throat.

Her breath caught.

"And the rise and fall of your chest tells me you're affected, too." He spread his hand on her sweater, above her breasts.

Though Catrina was a tall woman, she barely reached his chin. He wanted to wrap her up and keep her safe from the things that scared her.

She moved his hand aside then put some distance between them. "Your place isn't what I expected. I figured you more for an executive loft downtown." She rested her hips against a countertop. "Oh, no. Wait. I was wrong. This suits you fine."

"You're talking fast, Catrina." But he gave her the space she seemed to need. He pulled out a barstool and sat on it. She was here. For now, that was enough.

"You've got tons of privacy. Your subs can scream all they want without disturbing the neighbors. Why don't you lead the way?"

"I beg your pardon?"

"To your dungeon? Didn't you invite me here to get me naked and prove how susceptible I am to your charms?"

"Are you trying to piss me off?"

She blinked.

"Maybe you're annoyed with yourself because I tempt you, or you're unhappy that I've made you curious." He placed his glass on the quartz. "Perhaps you crave a taste of leather on your beautiful derrière and don't know how to ask for it."

"You're ridiculous." She pressed the globe of her glass between her palms.

"If you want to be over my lap, I'd be delighted to accommodate you. But you can't make it easy, can you? If you'd worn something more appropriate, I'd know you wanted to feel us, bare skin to bare skin. But know this, I'm not just going to rip off your clothes and give you an orgasm and send you on your merry little way." He moved his beverage to the side, sloshing the contents over the rim. "So answer my earlier question, Catrina. Why did you come?"

"Nothing better to do."

She really was trying to infuriate him. "Try again?"

"Look…" She exhaled. "I already told you why I'm here."

"Then go home and use a fucking vibrator if all you want is a random orgasm."

Color drained from her face.

"Be honest with yourself, Catrina, even if you want to lie to me."

Her hand shaking, she placed her glass on the counter next to his.

"What are you scared of?"

"Nothing."

Her answer was quick, too quick. "You're not afraid of the sexual aspect at all. In fact, you'd be happy to play with me as long as I got you off."

Her lips parted and she stood there, as if riveted.

"But you know I'm going to demand more from you than you want to give."

"Not true," she protested.

"Really?" He stood and pushed back the wooden stool. "I won't be satisfied with a few minutes together. I don't want to show you to my dungeon and force you to your knees, though at the moment, the idea does have some merit."

She flinched.

"That might send you scurrying, but it wouldn't frighten you. What terrifies you, though, is the idea that I want to get to know you. I want to know what keeps you awake at night, why you're scared of having something that isn't shallow."

"Don't give up your day job," she fired back. "You suck as a psychiatrist."

"Why do you need men to lick your boots?"

She rolled her eyes and countered, "Why do you need women to be subservient?"

"I don't, and they're not. Women are my equal."

"Please. I watched the demo you did with Susan."

"Then you noticed the way we interacted. You would have also been aware that everything I did was solely to meet her needs. Just as I met yours last night."

Catrina tucked her hands behind her.

To hide the fact they were still shaking?

"Just as I will meet them again tonight. If you're agreeable." He took a few steps toward her. To her credit, she straightened her shoulders. "Admit it... A BDSM relationship is about way more than getting your sexual kink on. It's about an exchange of energy, about being so focused on another person that their happiness becomes paramount to you. Your sub's experience matters more than your own."

"I get my subs off."

"Before or after they pleasure you?"

She looked away.

"I'm not criticizing you," he said. "Merely suggesting there's more to it than you realize."

She met his gaze.

"Have you masturbated?"

"What kind of question is that?" she asked, her voice delightfully breathless.

Damien knew how seductive the right sexual partner could be. That's why having her here meant something to him. "Since you didn't respond to my earlier text, I'm curious to know whether or not you followed my instruction."

"No." She cleared her throat as her cheeks flushed scarlet. "I didn't touch myself."

"I promised you a reward if you were good."

She swallowed deeply.

"You want it, don't you?"

Then she looked up at him.

Catrina, with her sudden shiver and wide, unblinking eyes was going to be a challenge...one he was looking forward to.

"I do indeed have a dungeon, one I want to show you. Before we get started, I want to know your safe and slow words."

"I'll go with halt, just like at the Den."

He nodded.

"And yellow."

"Now that's out of the way, I'll give you a choice... Shall I order you to strip for me? Or would you like to do it of your own free will?"

Chapter Five

Why did Damien make things so difficult?

It annoyed her to think he knew her as well as she knew herself. Maybe even better.

She'd spent the past five years locked away in a protective cocoon.

Damien, though, kept pushing, circling back to the questions he asked, never satisfied until she revealed everything he wanted to know.

"Since you haven't made a decision, I'll make it for you. Strip. Here, and now."

Her pulse stalled, and her thoughts splintered.

When she scened with her boys, she set the scene, named the time and place, and she was dressed for play when they arrived.

Standing in a man's kitchen and peeling off her clothes wasn't something she'd ever done before.

Damien confused her. Unlike last night, this wasn't a seduction, and he hadn't taken her to his dungeon, nor had he laid out any toys.

Except for what had already happened between them and the fact he'd told her to get naked in his kitchen, she could believe they were on a first date, getting ready to go to dinner.

"You're not shy, are you?" he asked.

When she didn't respond, he gentled his voice and said, "I would have never suspected. Take your time. But I will have you nude. Would you like some help?"

"Uhm..."

Once again, because of her hesitation, he made the decision for her.

Capturing her sweater, he tugged it from her waistband, then he pulled it up and over her head with a single, smooth move. Part of her hair dislodged and fell over her forehead and down her face.

She forced herself to breathe.

He stepped back, giving her some space, but not much. Clearly, he knew what he was doing.

Once he'd draped her sweater over the oven door's handle, he stood there, regarding her.

She crouched to remove her boots and socks, and he offered a steadying hand.

Though she was tall, she felt tiny standing before him in bare feet. She'd had no idea how unnerving facing a Dominant could be.

Though she respected the subs who scened with her, she marveled anew at their courage.

"Keep going, Catrina."

Hurriedly, before her thoughts could paralyze her, she removed her jeans.

Damien scooped them up from the hardwood floor.

Once she'd shimmied out of her thong, he extended his hand for that lingerie, as well.

Wordlessly, she shoved the skimpy piece of silk into his palm.

"You're beautiful."

Though he'd said the same to Susan, a husk vibrated his vocal cords, skittering awareness through her.

Next, she unhooked her bra and shucked the straps from her shoulders.

"Thank you," he said, accepting her final piece of clothing.

Catrina resisted the impulse to cover up. Instead, she drew her shoulders closer together, forcing her chest out.

"I turned up the heat before you arrived. Let me know if you're cold." He placed her undergarments on a stool. "Have you ever knelt for a man?"

He switched topics faster than anyone she'd ever known. It kept her off balance and from dwelling on any one thing for too long. "No." *Not willingly.* And she wouldn't be forced to ever again.

"But I'm warning you that I'm not about to start now."

"I can't and won't compel you to do anything. I respect everything you say and all your wishes."

His rich voice, thick and inviting, like whiskey warmed near a fire, hypnotized her.

"We can and should talk about anything that makes you uncomfortable. That said, it would give me great pleasure to see you kneel for me. As a courtesy, I'd allow you the rug."

As each moment passed, she fell deeper under his spell.

"The choice is entirely yours."

With that, he folded his arms and lapsed into silence.

At the Den and other places she'd played, she had watched submissives lower themselves with great care and elegance. And there had been a beautiful connection between Top and bottom.

"I thought this was about my pleasure?"

"It is."

She scowled. "You'll have to explain that to me."

How awful was this? Standing there, barefoot, naked, staring up at a breathtakingly gorgeous Dominant who wanted her to bend to his will?

"Going deep inside, releasing inhibitions, allows a sub to enjoy a richer experience."

"I'm not convinced."

As if he didn't care which option she chose, he shrugged. "Test my theory. Either way, you'll know what your submissives feel when they perform the act for you."

"Fine. I'll try it."

"Such a brave woman."

Like a true gentleman, Damien told her to move to the living room where a plush rug filled the floor in front of the fireplace.

Once again, he offered his assistance while she lowered herself to her knees.

Subs knelt for her all the time, and she'd never given much consideration to the surface. She was grateful for his foresight.

"How is it?"

She cricked her neck to look at him. "I really, really hate it."

"Then get up."

"What?"

"I meant it when I said I won't force you to do anything."

"But…"

"If you want to stop, do so." He folded his arms in his usual, unconcerned manner.

Maybe out of stubbornness, she remained where she was.

"What do you hate about it?"

"It hurts my neck."

"Fair enough. Anything else?"

"It's subservient."

"If you want to look at it that way."

She exhaled, not sure why she was still on her knees. But him talking to her, rather than walking away, made it possible. "What other possible way is there?"

"You tell me."

"Has anyone ever told you how frustrating you are?"

"Once or twice, perhaps." A tiny smile ghosted his lips.

This lighter side of him was endearing and allowed her self-consciousness to ebb. Because he treated it as if it were natural, it seemed that way.

This evening, she'd prepared herself to interact with a hardened Dominant. But his behavior was kinder than she'd been expecting, and her defenses began to crumble.

He stood with his denim-clad legs slightly apart. The leather on his boots was well-worn, and his belt looked supple, as if it were an old friend. He wore a short-sleeved, dark T-shirt that showed off his well-honed biceps. His muscular build was so damn sexy.

Sometimes he pulled back his longish hair and secured it, but tonight it was untamed, curling well below his nape.

She'd always thought of him as elegantly rough, but tonight, she saw a different side of him, patiently resolved.

Realizing he was waiting for an answer, she drank in his silent strength. After a full thirty seconds during which he said nothing, she hazarded a guess. "You asked me to kneel to ease my nerves."

"You're a quick study." He captured that stray lock of her hair and tucked it behind her ear. "You were nervous. I wasn't expecting that, so I changed my approach. The longer I allowed you to think about things, the more you'd be tempted to run. But you needed time to get comfortable with me as well as yourself and the dynamic of tonight's experience. I don't want you to overthink the moment. But there's more. I like to look at you. And yes, if you can relax enough to think about what I want and transcend your conflicting thoughts, you complying with my requests can bring us both pleasure."

He hadn't yet touched her in anything other than a casual way. There was no doubt he was earning her trust.

"When you're ready, I'd like you to sit on the peninsula." He pointed toward the kitchen area and the expanse of quartz with the barstools beneath it.

His request shocked her. Since he didn't appear to be joking, she rose and walked the short distance, aware of his gaze on her rear end.

She put her arms behind her and leveraged herself into position. Suddenly she wished she'd indulged in a glass of wine before leaving home.

"You look more spectacular than I'd imagined."

"You thought this up in advance?" she asked, crossing her legs.

"Oh, yes."

"You're a wicked man."

"You have no idea, Catrina."

Somewhere along the way, he'd stopped calling her Milady. Subtly, inexorably, he was asserting his power in a way she couldn't find objectionable.

"Please lie back and uncross your legs."

Catrina wrinkled her nose. "Are you planning what I think you're planning?"

"I hope so."

"I'm not sure about this."

"You can always refuse," he reminded her.

"No way."

"I didn't think you would."

"Don't gloat."

"Never, Milady."

Milady again. From him, it sounded more affectionate than a term of respect. But she didn't mind.

"You may be more comfortable if you remove that contraption from your hair."

She reached up, but halted when he asked, "May I?"

"Thank you."

He pulled out the hair clip, sending the tresses tumbling around her shoulders and down her back. "Doesn't matter which way you wear it," he said, "it's fabulous." He smoothed it to one side. "Now let's get on with it."

The quartz slab beneath her bare body was firm and cool, a startling contrast to the heat chasing through her.

"This is your reward for honoring my request not to touch yourself." He moved between her legs and parted her labia.

Though she squirmed, he didn't reprimand her. Nor did he command her to remain still.

When he placed his thumb against her clit, she lifted her hips scandalously.

"That's it," he said.

She wished she could see his expression, but he bent to lick her from back to front.

The pressure of his tongue nearly undid her. She cried out, already on the verge of climaxing.

"Come whenever you want."

It hadn't occurred to her that he might make her delay her orgasm. She oftentimes compelled her subs to wait, and Damien's words brutally reinforced the fact that, in coming here, she had ceded a certain amount of control to him.

All those thoughts vanished when he slid a finger inside her.

Desperately she dug her heels into cabinets beneath her as she tried to lift her hips even higher.

Her insides tightened and her juices flowed.

The combination of the way he simultaneously finger-fucked and ate her proved to be her undoing. "Damien!" She reached for his head and buried her hands in his hair.

In response to her urgings, he inserted a second finger inside her. She tried to sit up, or get away, anything.

He was wonderful and unyielding, licking her pussy, moving his fingers. This was one powerful reward.

Suddenly, she understood why Susan had looked at him with such awe. Being the focus of Master Damien Lowell's attentions was mind blowing. He seemed to have created a place where she could be herself and the rest of the world didn't matter.

She called out his name again as she tightened all her muscles in anticipation. Blood rushed in her ears.

Oh, my…

Her thoughts vanished as an orgasm washed over her — its engulfing energy more potent than anything she'd ever experienced.

Desperately gripping his hair, she screamed.

But Damien didn't stop.

"More," he said, his breath on her heated flesh.

"I… I can't." She meant it. The first had taken so much out of her, and she needed time to recover.

"Stop fighting me." He flicked his tongue back and forth across her clit, faster and faster, ignoring her gasping protests.

Impossibly, a second orgasm began to churn inside her. She knew she wouldn't be able to find relief, but she couldn't force her mouth to work long enough to say anything other than his name.

He stretched her wider, overwhelming her. Then he reached up to twist and squeeze one of her nipples.

The added sensation was enough, and she froze, forgetting to breathe.

He continued his relentless sensual assault, making her writhe from the exquisite combination of sensations, both pleasure and pain, until she spiraled into an abyss.

Time blurred.

She had no idea how long she lay there, but slowly she became aware that he'd removed his fingers and had stopped tormenting her clit.

An eternity later, she opened her eyes to see him standing there, broad, tall, steady.

While he was fully dressed, she was naked on his kitchen counter, splayed open before him, her labia swollen and exposed. Embarrassment made her lick her lips.

He helped her to sit up, then he removed his shirt.

She blinked. Did he want to fuck her on the countertop? "You can't be serious."

"I assure you I am." But one of his charming, deadly smiles played at the corners of his mouth.

Delighting her, he put his shirt on her then untucked her hair.

The black T-shirt enveloped her, and she snuggled into its warmth. The cotton was stamped by his scent, that of prestige and power, and she inhaled it deeply. She wouldn't tell him, but she had no intention of returning the garment to him.

"I need to keep you warm. I always take care of what's mine."

Yours? "But I'm not," she protested.

"You are. Get used to it. Warmer?"

"Thanks, yes."

His rugged handsomeness stole her breath.

She'd wondered what he looked like under his clothes, but the first glance of his bare chest exceeded her expectations. A smattering of hair arrowed downward to disappear beneath the waistband of his jeans. She was tantalized, aching to touch him.

He eased her down to the floor and held her close.

Looking up at him, she said, "I suppose I should take care of you now. Give you a blow job or something?"

"I'm not done with you yet."

"Oh. Right. You need to tie me up before you fuck me or something equally diabolical."

"You can relax. I don't typically beat women until the second date." He snagged both of their glasses.

Curious, she followed him into the living room and joined him on the couch that faced the fireplace. She tucked her legs beneath her and accepted her sparkling water. "This is an odd dungeon," she said.

"Building your anticipation."

"Uh, I'm good with never seeing it." Until tonight, she'd had no idea he had a sense of humor. That made her appreciate him all the more. "But I am puzzled as to what we're doing." What hot-blooded man wouldn't want to screw immediately after licking her cunt?

He faced her. "Talking."

"*Talking?*" She blinked.

"That's the most important part of submission. The physical connection matters, but I'm considerably more interested in your brain than anything else."

"I'm not sure if you're being serious here."

"Very much. When you fully offer yourself to me, it will mean you've shared your emotions, your fears, vulnerabilities. Everything."

She laughed. "Good luck with that. That's what I have my girlfriends for. I don't do that with men."

"You prefer they keep their place, under your foot?"

"That sounds harsh."

"But true?"

She took a sip and allowed her hair to fall forward to hide her expression. As he had earlier, Damien brushed back the strands.

"I'd prefer you to look at me when we talk."

She met his gaze and wished his eyes weren't that shocking shade of blue. He seemed to see into her, as if intent on prying out all her secrets. Despite the room's warmth, she shivered.

"When did you become a Domme? After a bad relationship?"

"So you became a Dom after a woman challenged you? You had to become a big, bad alpha male to prove something?"

Maddeningly, he kept his calm.

"I've always been a Dom," he responded, his voice as easy and well-modulated as it had been all evening. "There wasn't a moment or an event. It's not the same for you."

"What makes you all-knowing, all-seeing?" Desperately needing space, she scooted away from him.

"Because of the way you snapped at me just now."

"I didn't."

"Did I touch a nerve, Milady? I meant it when I said I want to know everything you've never shown anyone else."

"It's boring." *And private.*

"Your secrets are safe with me."

Because she believed what he said, and because she'd had years to recover, she decided to offer the barebones. "I was engaged once. Until he cleaned out the checking account we'd opened together." She tipped back her head. "We were saving for the wedding and for a house. Before he left, he maxed out my credit cards as well. And the worst thing about it…"

"Go on."

Damien hadn't tried to placate her or comfort her. He was simply listening.

"I freaking knew better," she finished. "Dad vanished before I was born, and my mother struggled her entire life, working two jobs to support us. I should have learned from her, but I didn't. I fell in love and was goo-goo starry-eyed." She slid her glass onto the coffee table. "Once was enough."

"It seems like a leap from a guy being an untrustworthy thief to you being a Domme."

"I decided I would be in charge of my life, make my own decisions after that."

"All of your relationships have been casual since then?"

When she looked at him, he shrugged and added, "You've been coming to the Den for several years. I've rarely seen you with the same sub."

"You're observant. I had one fairly serious relationship after my engagement ended," she confessed.

She sighed.

Even now, she hated talking about Todd. "I..." So she could carefully choose her words, Catrina hesitated. "He was nice enough, but boring, and so was the sex. So I suggested we mix things up..." How to explain what happened next? The change in him? The bruises he left behind? "I took charge, and he took exception."

Damien regarded her, as if waiting for her to go on, but instead she skipped to the next important event. "At a party, my friend Joann had one too many margaritas and was telling everyone I was single and deserved a man who would worship me. One of the men there offered to kiss my feet. We all had a great laugh about it, but it turned out he'd meant it. He was a submissive and he helped me explore my role. I took to it rather naturally." And it helped keep her emotionally insulated so she didn't get hurt anymore.

"And now you want to accept my invitation to explore the dynamic from the other side."

"Not really."

He quirked an eyebrow.

"I'm curious about interacting with you. For one evening. Nothing more." He didn't need to know that after she'd left him, she'd been restless and filled with angst. "I thought accepting your invitation would be fun." *Harmless.* And those orgasms had already made her trip across town worth the effort.

"How do you deal with one of your subs who continually tells you lies or half-truths."

She blinked. "I'm sorry?"

"It's a general question."

"My subs don't lie to me."

"Of course not. Your relationships aren't deep enough for that."

She opened her mouth to protest but closed it again. "That's a little unfair." But true. Which was part of the appeal of being a Domme.

"Theoretically, then," he said. "What would you do?"

The conversation made her squirm. "I don't know. Give him a spanking, maybe. Perhaps a chastity device for some time." She grabbed a pillow and hugged it to her chest.

"Do you suppose that would be effective?"

Before she could get defensive, he spoke again, "I would wonder about the reason. Is she being a brat and hoping to get in trouble? Some subs crave a punishment as a way to feel cherished. Or is my beautiful sub scared? Maybe trying to protect her emotions? Has she been dishonest with herself for so long that she can no longer recognize the truth?"

He couldn't be talking to her, about her…

Couldn't be.

But he was.

Damien was far scarier to her emotional health than she'd imagined.

"More than anything, I'd hope to establish the kind of relationship where she instinctively comes to me with issues and challenges. I'd want her to know I'd be there for her, that I was a rock in her life, someone she could turn to, no matter the crisis. After we figured out what was going on in a particular instance, I'd warn her that neither lies nor prevarication would be tolerated on that issue again, and we'd agree upon a punishment for any future infractions. I believe forthrightness is vital to a successful relationship."

"That's a nice hypothetical, Damien. In a long-term relationship, it might even work. But it's possible to have a scene without a relationship. You demonstrated that with Susan."

"Agreed. But I see them as two different things. As a Domme, if you understand the complexities, you can make a scene richer, deeper, more compelling for your partner."

"I'm here, aren't I?"

"But you weren't entirely truthful with me earlier." He held up a hand when she started to protest. "Before we have an argument, let me say this. Last night I mentioned that you look down and to the left when you're avoiding a question. If you have no need to protect yourself, you look me in the eye."

She didn't know whether it flattered or frightened her that his observation was so astute. Her mother had always known when Catrina was lying. Had she figured out the same thing Damien had? "We don't have a relationship, so I don't owe you anything."

"She said while looking me straight in the eye."

She blew out a breath. "You're insufferable."

"That was honest. So, would you like to answer, again, why are you here?"

"What I'd like is for you to mind your own business."

"When you're ready to tell me, I'll listen."

"Is this what you do to all your subs? Grind down their resistance so that they'll beg you to beat them just to get you to leave them alone?"

"You're on to something." Very deliberately, he put down his glass.

Then, before she knew what was happening, he had her over his lap, her bottom upturned and exposed. The pillow went flying. She kicked and struggled and protested. He trapped her legs between his then delivered a sharp slap to her right buttock.

She froze.

"Have you ever had a spanking, Milady?"

"I thought you didn't beat a woman until the second date."

"You're the exception to almost all of my rules."

As much as she was able, she twisted to look at him.

"I'll repeat my question, and this time I want an answer. Have you ever had a spanking, Milady?"

Chapter Six

"I'm not sure what you think I've done to deserve this one. I thought you talked about punishments in terms of a negotiation."

"This, Milady, is not a punishment."

"Then what the hell do you call it?"

"Pleasure."

"You have a warped version of the word's meaning. That freaking hurt, and it sure as hell wasn't fun."

"And yet here we are. And you haven't safe worded."

Damn him for noticing.

"You didn't enjoy that?"

"Hell no."

Gently, he caressed her buttocks with long, sweeping, repetitive strokes. Beneath his palms, her skin heated.

He ran his fingers up the insides of her thighs and tension eased from her body as her pussy dampened.

Last night, when he'd given her a smack, her physical turn-on had been instant. If she had thought about it in advance, she would have expected to be angry that he'd touched her. Instead, the intensity had added to her pleasure.

"Still think it's not fun?"

"This is acceptable, I suppose."

He chuckled. "When you're ready for your spanking, let me know."

"You may continue to massage me."

"I hadn't figured you for a brat, Milady."

Was that how she was behaving? Trying to goad him into taking the decision away from her?

But he wouldn't. "What do you want?"

Catrina was lost in a spiral of confusion. She was aroused, wanting more, and it seemed a betrayal of her ideals to ask for it.

Reminding herself this was a temporary arrangement, and that she'd already learned something, she said, "Go ahead and spank me, Damien." She tightened her buttocks in fear and anticipation, though she knew that oftentimes made the pain worse.

He didn't tell her to relax. Instead, he helped her to do so with a light, gentle touch. On top of his earlier massage, this felt wonderful, making it impossible to hold on to any tension.

When he increased the force, she liked it. Earlier, he'd given her a smack that hurt, but this couldn't be more different.

Though she found out what her subs liked and tried to deliver, being on the receiving end showed her, in a way that wasn't abstract, what it felt like. No wonder some of her executive playmates liked getting spanked.

Right now, her stress was melting away just like it did when she meditated or worked out.

"More?"

"Please."

When he continued, she added, "Spank me harder, Damien."

He did, but gradually.

He took the time to finger her after giving her a dozen or so smacks. She used her toes as leverage to rise up, silently seeking more.

Despite that, Damien didn't change what he was doing. She understood that he was delivering what she wanted, but at his pace, on his terms. Confounding Dom. But she had to admit, his way gave her a richer experience.

He varied the location, speed, and impact of his spanks.

"Surrender, Catrina."

She closed her eyes. The remaining parts of her hesitation were swept away as he continued the erotic dance on her flesh.

He teased her cunt and covered her legs and buttocks with blazing blows.

The more she went with it, the deeper she seemed to be swimming until an orgasm began to unfurl. She cried out his name, but the word emerged in a jumbled mess. She tried to move, but her legs felt lethargic.

"Do you want to come, Catrina?"

His voice seemed to come from quite a distance.

"Milady?"

"Yes," she whispered. "Yes. Please."

He drew moisture from her pussy and used it to insert a finger in her ass.

She whimpered.

He placed two more fingers in her heated core and moved in and out of both holes quickly, making it impossible for her to think. "Damien," she said.

"I've got you."

She expected him to ease up, but he didn't. Instead, he moved faster, purposefully.

Because he had her legs trapped, she was helpless, his prisoner.

Whatever he wanted to give or take, he could.

That she'd offered him this much control made her shudder. A single word would restore her power, yet she remained silent.

At his continued, persistent invasion, her stomach clenched. Emotions threatened to drown her, making it impossible to breathe.

"That's it," he coached her. "Come for me, Milady." He pulled out his fingers before reentering her in a single, forceful push.

She screamed.

His ruthless domination shoved her over the edge into a stunning climax.

The orgasm made her go rigid. Time and space collided.

Moments later, she shuddered.

"Damn, you're responsive, Milady," he murmured, easing out his fingers and turning her over.

Gently, he cradled her against his chest.

Because she was suddenly vulnerable, instinct urged her to push him away.

But when she started to move, he tightened his grip, stroking her hair and uttering soothing words that she couldn't quite make out.

He held her until her breathing became smoother.

She'd never been held after lovemaking. Not that this scene had counted as lovemaking, she reminded herself. So what was it?

She'd gone from college sex, to an abbreviated engagement, to a ho-hum sexual relationship with Todd, to being a Dominant. She gave comfort. She didn't receive it.

Damien kept his arms looped around her even when she straightened and put some distance between them.

"That was..." She tried to find words but was lost when she looked at him.

Damien's eyebrows were drawn together over his electric blue eyes, and he said nothing. No one had ever regarded her as intensely.

He cocked his head to the side, indicating he'd wait as long as she needed.

"It was different than I thought it would be."

"In what way?"

Trying to steady herself, she drew a few breaths. "This sounds ridiculous."

"I doubt it."

"Humbling."

He nodded.

"But also empowering."

"Perfect," he said. "The dichotomy. The yin and yang of submission."

Though she'd had no real idea what to expect when he'd turned her over his knee, she hadn't been prepared for her emotions to be as swamped as her body.

On some level she was concerned that he hadn't needed to cajole her compliance. Instead, she'd offered it. "My ass really does sting."

"Of course it does. It only qualifies as a spanking if it hurts."

That resolve-melting smile played around his mouth again.

Her heart warned her to run.

"That was a hedonistic beating, meant to arouse both of us."

"I'm the only one who got off."

"Doesn't matter. I get fulfillment from turning you on. That's what it's about for me."

She looked at him.

"As a Dom, *your* Dom...when you come, I am pleased. Giving is more important than receiving."

Although her ideas of domination were similar to Damien's, the execution of their scenes were different. Before one of her boys arrived, she would chat with him on the phone. She would find out what he wanted, and they would discuss their mutual expectations. After a scene, she would soothe her sub, dry any of his tears, tell him how proud she was of him, allow him as much time as he needed to dress in street-legal clothes, but she didn't sit in patient silence for this long while he made sense of the physical experience. Maybe Damien was right. Maybe she did need to experience this for herself.

"How are you doing?"

She was shattered. No matter how much time he gave her, she wasn't sure she'd be able to comprehend the emotional implications of them being together. "I need to go," she said, pressing away from him.

Surprising her, he helped her up. "Let's get your clothes."

She made small talk while they went into the kitchen. "Remain there," he said. "Don't get dressed."

He excused himself and went into the bathroom, and she heard water running.

This was awkward, standing in the middle of the kitchen, half-naked. She supposed it shouldn't bother her as he'd eaten her while she was spread on his countertop. He had a way of demolishing her inhibitions.

A moment later, he returned with a damp cloth. "Spread your legs, Milady."

She knew better than to argue.

He crouched to bathe her pussy and ass. She appreciated the attention but was becoming more and more desperate to make her escape. "Thank you," she said, when he nodded his satisfaction.

Aware of his gaze and wondering if her buttocks were bright red, she first pulled on her thong, then her jeans before tugging on her socks and stuffing her feet into her boots. She knew he noticed how much her hands trembled.

When she started to pull off his T-shirt, he said, "Keep it."

Back in the foyer, she shoved her sweater and bra into her purse. With a half-smile that felt as fragile as her control, she dug out her keys.

"I'll take those."

"Uh…"

"Milady, I'm not going to try to keep you here. I wish you would stay. And you're welcome to. But if you're intent on leaving, then I'll warm up your car while you put your coat on."

Put that way, how could she refuse, even if it prolonged the goodbye? She dropped the keys into his palm.

He pulled on a fleece jacket over his bare chest. *Damn.* No matter what he wore, he was a good-looking man. After turning up the collar, he headed outside.

Catrina shivered when she closed the door behind him. And it had nothing to do with the sudden gust of cold air that had swirled around her.

She heard the car engine start, and she shrugged into her coat before she could change her mind about leaving.

When he returned, a few snowflakes clung to his midnight-colored hair.

"I'll walk you out," he said.

Survival instinct warned her to run…now.

"Send me a text when you arrive home," he said.

"I'll be fine. The drive is short, and the roads aren't all that—"

"Don't push your luck, Catrina." His words were tight with tension. He captured her chin and tipped back her head. "I didn't ask for a call. Just common courtesy. I'd prefer to tie you to the foot of my bed and keep you there until morning. So I think a text is a hell of a compromise."

She sucked in a breath. The image that kaleidoscoped through her mind terrified her. "You wouldn't do that."

"Of course not. That's far too uncivilized."

Relieved, Catrina exhaled.

"I'm not an ogre. I'd handcuff you to the headboard."

The look he shot her was indecipherable, and she couldn't determine whether or not he was joking. "I need to go." *To save myself.*

As he'd promised, he walked her to the car.

As she slid into the driver's seat, he leaned in and said, "You'll think about this interaction a lot. You'll relive it. And after you have, you'll be curious."

His voice wrapped around her, heating her.

"You'll wonder what else there is and what you're missing," he continued. "You liked the spanking. Maybe you didn't want to like it, or it offends your sensibilities that you enjoyed it. And we can talk about that. But the fact remains, you want more. You want me to fuck you as much as I want to be inside your hot pussy." He paused, but he didn't give her time to object. "You know my number. Call it anytime." Damien stepped back, started to close the door, but then hesitated. He captured a fistful of her hair, looped it around his hand to draw her head toward him, then finished with, "I meant it when I told you to text when you get home. If you don't, Catrina..."

She wanted to protest but couldn't find the words.

"I will give you a spanking you won't like and will always remember. Am I clear?"

She nodded.

"I didn't hear you," he said softly.

"Yes, Damien." She needed to escape while she still could, before she begged him to let her stay.

Hell.

He was right. As he'd spoken, a hundred different ideas tumbled through her brain, and it was as if she could feel his cold, steel cuffs around her wrists. "I understand," she said.

He angled her head back a little more. Then he placed a light, gentle, full-of-promise kiss on her mouth before he released his grip.

"Drive safe, Milady."

Without another word, he closed the car door.

She pulled away, hands shaking, grateful she could drive without conscious thought. She looked in the rearview mirror. He remained where he was until she lost sight of him.

As she drove, Catrina clutched the steering wheel, and the tension in her grip made her shoulders ache. Damien Lowell disturbed her in a way no other man ever had.

He made her question everything she knew — or thought she knew — about relationships, and worse, about herself. Being a Domme gave her a huge sexual kick. Mostly, however, she now admitted that it was about staying in control.

What she'd just experienced with Damien had demolished that.

She'd enjoyed letting him take the lead. She'd liked the hot orgasms. And the spanking had aroused her. Afterward, as she'd snuggled into his arms, it had been as if the outside world no longer existed. Her fears and worries had vanished.

When she'd been younger, more idealistic, she'd thought that it was possible for a man and woman to become partners and support each other. She'd been a romantic, even though she'd seen her mother's constant struggle for survival.

Tonight, he'd been supportive, wanting to know her inner thoughts and feelings. She'd glimpsed what it might be like to have someone to turn to. Part of her wanted to accept what he was offering.

She shook her head to clear it. Life had taught her to put away foolish, impractical notions. It might take all her resolve and determination, but she would do exactly that.

When she arrived at her cold, dark condominium, she sent a one-word text.

Safe.

With her insides tied up in knots, she didn't want to say anything more.

Instantly, her phone chimed.

I enjoyed having you here. You know how to find me.

He'd told her she would want more, that she'd wonder what she was missing. And she was terrified to the tips of her toes that he might be right.

It was better to keep distance between them. Lots of it. Lots and lots of it.

The question was, how did she plan to do that?

* * * *

Confounding, frustrating, annoying-as-hell woman.

Damien shoved away from his computer at the Den. Damn it. He'd looked half a dozen times, but he hadn't seen Catrina's name on the weekend's reservation list.

With a sigh, he strode to the window and stared at the expanse of pine trees and snow-covered ground.

It had been almost two weeks since she'd been to his house.

As he'd requested, she had sent him a text that night, letting him know she'd made it home safe. Since then, he'd heard nothing from her.

He'd known the abbreviated scene had challenged her emotionally.

Fuck.

Challenged her?

Who was he kidding? It had challenged *him*.

Her body language had indicated that she'd enjoyed what they'd done.

Perhaps a bit too sure of himself, he'd told her she'd want to explore further. But more, he'd hoped that they'd connected in a way she'd never imagined possible.

Their time together might have been short, but he'd held her. She'd told him about her fears and offered him a glimpse inside her carefully constructed defenses. There'd been no doubt she'd taken tentative steps toward trusting him.

She'd captivated him, but that wasn't enough. He wanted the feeling to be mutual.

Because she'd let him in, he'd anticipated she might panic. He'd have been delighted, but surprised, if she had contacted him right away. He had expected her to take a couple of days to think things through, maybe as long as a week.

But this...? He was beginning to wonder if he'd misjudged the situation, and her.

"Boss?"

Damien looked over his shoulder. Gregorio stood in the doorway, scowling.

"I knocked twice," Gregorio said.

Turning, Damien waved the man in. "Is the reservations system working correctly?"

"As far as I'm aware," Gregorio replied. "Are you having problems?"

Damien shook his head.

"Aha."

"Aha, what?" Damien spread his legs and folded his arms across his chest, matching Gregorio's stance.

"Things become clear."

"What the hell does that mean?"

"This makes three weekends in a row that you've been here. You're hoping to see someone specific."

"Don't you have work to do?"

"No. Really. Everything's set. I can listen to your woes for at least an hour."

"Out."

"You've got it bad."

"Are you hoping to get fired?"

"This is serious," Gregorio said. "If you're talking about sacking me and taking care of all of this yourself, you're not thinking straight. We need the good stuff."

"I might beat your ass."

"Would that help you?"

Damien took a seat behind his desk.

The two had been friends for years, and the question was sincere. Gregorio knew Damien's moods as well as Damien did. And if Damien needed the release, no doubt Gregorio would expose his back.

Without an invitation or permission, Gregorio crossed to a sideboard and opened a door. He slid aside a supposed-to-be secret panel and removed a crystal decanter of alcohol Of course, in typical fashion, the man had gone straight for Damien's private reserve. Brandy this time.

Gregorio tugged out the stopper then slowly poured a small amount into two separate snifters. He returned to slide one across the desktop toward Damien.

"We've been through a lot," Gregorio said, taking a seat. "Relationship breakups…"

Including Gregorio's shocking divorce.

"Several new business ventures and one spectacular failure."

Damien didn't need to be reminded of that. Making the cover of a respected Wall Street magazine because of a bankruptcy still gave him nightmares.

No matter how many successes he'd had since, his portfolio had been tarnished.

"But I haven't seen you like this before."

"Like what?"

"Smitten," Gregorio clarified.

Fuck that. "Men don't get *smitten*."

"Fair enough. *Obsessed*. Mistress Catrina?"

"How — ?"

"My brilliant deductive reasoning skills." Gregorio crossed his long legs. He grinned. "Susan was here last week with a new guy. You were cordial to them both. To my knowledge, you haven't played with anyone other than Mistress Catrina recently."

"No one should know about that."

"The tension between the two of you when she left that night was like electricity in the air. And since she hasn't been back, I can't think of anyone else whose name you'd be looking for on the reservation system. Yep. There's no one else you'd be smitten by, well, I mean if you were smitten — which you're not — since men don't get smitten."

"Do you want to shut the fuck up now?"

"Oh, hell no. I'm just getting started."

Gregorio grinned, pissing Damien off even more.

He held his glass in his palm, warming the brandy. The ritual itself helped settle him.

A minute later, he brought the snifter closer and swirled again, releasing more of the alcohol's aroma. As always, he appreciated the sight of the liquid clinging mysteriously to the inside of the glass.

A few seconds later, he took a sip. The liquid gold tasted of smoke and fruit, and it warmed on its way down.

"Good idea?"

"Indeed."

Gregorio took a small drink. After closing his eyes, he made an appreciative sound. "This stuff can make anything better."

"Especially when it belongs to someone else and you didn't have to pay for it," Damien shot back wryly.

Gregorio nodded his agreement. "Especially then."

Following Gregorio's lead, Damien pushed away from the desk and relaxed against his chairback. He realized this was the first time in two weeks that he'd managed to release any tension without first spending an hour at the gym.

"So, you played with her outside of the Den."

"Mind your own business."

"More than once?"

"You know goddamn well I'm not going to answer that."

"Have you called her? Or are you waiting for Mistress Catrina to fall under your spell? Wait. No. Holy shit..." Gregorio uncrossed his legs and leaned forward. "Unless you subbed for her."

Over the top of the snifter, Damien regarded his second-in-command he shrugged.

"Never mind that." Undeterred, Gregorio continued, "She subbed for you, which meant something since she's a Domme and sometimes shows up with multiple pets. And now you want her to become a sub for you. So, let me guess. You issued an ultimatum. You want her to do things on your terms. Ergo, you can't give in and call her."

"Ergo? No one really uses that word."

"You have been waiting for her to come to you. Only she hasn't. And that means this is a unique situation for you." He took another drink then said, "How'd I do?"

"I'm relieved you'll be able to get a job as a psychic advisor when I fire you."

He expected Gregorio to be at least a little chastened.

Instead, the man all but crowed. "Damn. I'm better than I thought."

"It's time for you to get back to work," Damien said.

Gregorio grinned and raised his empty glass in a silent toast before leaving the office and closing the door behind him.

Contemplatively, Damien ignored all the screens demanding his attention, and instead, stared out of the window.

With the frost on the trees, it looked fucking cold. And since the atmosphere was so dry, he doubted it would snow. Now, knowing Catrina wasn't planning to attend, he wished he'd stayed home. He had no desire to interact with anyone. And if he remained in his suite, he knew he'd brood.

Another sip of the brandy warmed his insides. In selecting the beverage, Gregorio had made an excellent choice.

Right now, it annoyed the crap out of Damien that Gregorio had been right about so many things.

After Damien had finished the drink, he forced himself to go through Gregorio's plans and projected revenues for the upcoming month. Master Niles' former production company was requesting to expand their usage of the Den's facilities. And Gregorio had proposed buying an adjacent lot so the facilities could add onsite lodging to the five-year plan. Or at least a stable for pony play. Damien wasn't sure if Gregorio was serious about that one, or whether he'd added that line to see if Damien was paying attention.

An hour later, music blared, all but shaking the empty snifter still on his desk. Tonight's theme was retro-dance party. He couldn't wait to see what attendees came up with. Teased hair and leg warmers? No doubt some would celebrate with high-protocol standards they no longer observed.

He hadn't anticipated, though, that Gregorio would hang a disco ball from the living room's vaulted ceiling.

How the fuck am I supposed to endure this?

Chapter Seven

At five o'clock the next afternoon, Damien again checked the reservations list which worked great, thanks to the work of Brandy, their tech genius. Because snow hadn't fallen, at least ten more people had signed up. Catrina was not among them.

Two hours later, Damien had watched all the television he could tolerate. He'd finished his work and cleaned out his email inbox. Despite a shower, he was unable to settle in with a true-life crime story that had, until recently, engrossed him.

Restlessness churned at him. He tossed aside the book and strode to the closet. Telling himself he might as well be useful and meet with some of the potential new members—anything was better than dwelling on Catrina—he dressed in business attire and strolled downstairs.

After last night's craziness, bright colors, thundering noise, outrageous outfits and big hair, this event was subdued. Gregorio had put together an elegant mixer.

Low-key jazz oozed from the sound system. No one had to shout over the band to be heard. Waitstaff moved throughout the area with fruity, non-alcoholic beverages made from sugary ingredients he would never touch.

He chatted with a few people in the living room, answered questions about membership and various activities and gave one Dom some tips on dealing with a beautiful but very saucy sub.

Then, seeing Gregorio was occupied in the kitchen with the caterer, Damien excused himself. He went downstairs to check on the play area. The Den employed a number of House Monitors, men and women who knew the rules and enforced them to keep everyone safe. Regardless, Gregorio and Damien tried to make themselves as visible and available as possible.

He wandered down the hallway, looking in on all the private rooms, checking in on the participants. It had been a long time, years even, since he'd availed himself of the Den's facilities for a personal scene.

Until now, he hadn't missed it.

But at this moment, the idea of having a woman spread before him in beautifully bound supplication, helpless and writhing in expectation...

Damien inhaled sharply.

Maybe he should seek out one of the house subs to slake his sudden need.

In the open area, some couples sat at tables. A small group of Doms stood in a circle. One put his booted foot on his kneeling sub's shoulder. The position appeared uncomfortable for both of them.

Another's sub was seated cross-legged on the floor.

After nodding toward the group, he walked to the bar for a glass of sparkling water.

That's when he saw her.

Catrina was alone, seated at a high-topped table, swirling a straw in her drink.

The hell was she doing here?

"May I get you anything, Master Damien?" a house sub inquired.

"No. Thank you, Mary."

She was a relatively new employee, having been hired to replace Brandy, who Master Niles had stolen away and never returned. Even though Mary was tall, willowy, available and agreeable, the idea of taking care of his needs with anyone other than Catrina vanished. Truth was, even if she hadn't shown up, he wouldn't have scened with another sub. No one but her would do for him.

She watched him over the rim of her glass, tracking his every move.

"May I join you?" he asked as he neared her table.

"Please."

Though he'd seen her on numerous occasions over the years, the more he knew her, the more there was to uncover. Tonight, no pretty man knelt by her side. In fact, there wasn't a leash in sight.

As was usual for her when she attended the Den, her makeup was startling. Her eyes appeared enormous, more luminous, thanks to false lashes. Her red-colored lips were full and pouty.

She'd left her hair loose, though a large clip held a chunk of it back from her face and showcased her stunning cheekbones.

By any standard, her black dress was demure, but fabulous. The square-cut neckline covered her breasts but revealed her collarbone and an alluring glimpse of her cleavage. Previously he hadn't played with her nipples much, but now he itched to explore all of her.

"Nice event," she observed as he sat.

"Quite," he agreed.

"I heard last night was a little different."

"I looked on the dessert table when I was upstairs. There isn't a single orange cupcake in sight."

"Orange?"

"They were a complement to the neon pink ones, I'm told."

"Sounds like fun. I love big hair and hoop earrings. I'll be here for the next eighties night." She moved her straw through the ice cubes in her glass. Her filmy shirtsleeve fell back, and he noticed her white wristband.

Gutted, he stared.

Any hint of ease between them vanished.

To avoid confusion, when a guest checked in for the night, they were issued wristbands. Doms and Dommes wore red ones. Tonight, she wore white, which meant she was heterosexual and looking to scene...as a submissive.

I'll fucking kill anyone who touches you.

He took hold of her hand.

Leashing his temper, keeping his voice low and well-modulated as he said, "You're full of surprises."

"I decided to accept your challenge and try to submit." Unblinkingly, she met his gaze.

Damien rubbed his thumb against the flutter of her pulse.

Did she know she was flirting with danger?

"To you, Damien."

"Of course it would be to me." Her words should have soothed him, but they didn't. "This is my domain. And I wouldn't permit you to play with anyone else."

She met his eyes. "You'd stop me?"

"My house. My rules."

"That's a little…"

Arrogant? Possessive? Unreasonable? All of those things.

Catrina brought out intense reactions in him that he wasn't sure he appreciated. "I'm not interested in a single scene with you." He wanted so much more.

"I understand. That's why it took me so long to reach a decision."

"What convinced you?"

As if hypnotized, she stared at the small circles he made with his thumb.

He stopped rubbing and captured her chin to tip her head back slightly. "No hiding."

"Maybe you can help me learn to be a better Domme. Alternatively, perhaps the experience will leave me unchanged."

No fucking chance.

"But there's only one way to know. And…"

He waited.

"I'm curious." She shrugged. "I liked what happened at your house. And the fact I can't stop replaying the events shook me up. Worse, it made me question everything I've assumed over the last few years. Part of me wants to pretend it never happened. But the truth is, I'm also intrigued. It took me a long time to reconcile my different thoughts and feelings."

As much as he wanted to say something, he remained silent.

With a soft sigh, she went on. "How can I be a strong, independent woman, but then enjoy being in your arms after you spank me? I've spent years depending on only myself. The bigger question to me is…do I even want to consider a change?"

"Why not?"

"I've never met a man who was worthy of trust."

Damien winced.

For a moment, she stared into the bottom of her glass. "And I like my life."

A full thirty seconds passed before she met his gaze.

When she did, her eyes were wide, honest. She placed her hands on the table, palms up. "It meant something when you said you'd always want your subs to come to you. I'll be honest. I thought that was a line. Or maybe a nice fantasy. The more I thought about it, the more I thought it sounded like friendship."

"Or a partnership?"

"Don't push it, mister."

He grinned. Now that she was near and not planning to see anyone but him, the tension that had gripped him for two weeks seeped away.

"So I decided I'd talk to you about it and see what we could work out." She wrinkled her nose. "Damn. And as much as I hate to admit it, I've already learned a thing or two from you."

"I'm honored you'd say so. It's mutual. I've learned not to assume what you're thinking. And I'm honing my patience skills."

"Oh, Damien…" She batted her eyelashes. "You've only just begun."

"I accept your challenge."

Catrina cocked her head to the right and more seriously added, "I want to find out what I don't know."

"It will be an adventure for both of us." Wanting connection, he began rubbing her wrist again. "I want two weeks of your time. When can you arrange to be away from work?"

Her chest rose as she drank in a deep breath. No doubt this was becoming more real to her. So he continued his reassuring touch.

"I work from home, but I have to meet with clients periodically."

"We should be able to manage that," he said.

"My customers matter to me. I won't abandon them." She brought her chin up.

"I'd never ask you to. The things that matter to you matter to me. So let's figure out a schedule. Are you amenable to working from here? Gregorio can set up an office for you."

"Your house isn't an option?"

"I promised you an experience. Being up here qualifies. It's a long way to Denver, but the distance isn't insurmountable. And I'm happy to drive you back and forth."

"The house and surroundings *are* gorgeous."

And he had all the equipment he could possibly want. "Let Gregorio know what you need. I assume you have a notebook computer that you can bring? We have a satellite connection you can use for email."

"As long as I can get online, I'll be fine. I can pack all my files in a box."

"How many hours a day do you need for work? I won't have you tied to my bedposts all the time."

"About that..."

He remembered her having a similar reaction at his house to his threat. "Scares you?"

"Yeah."

"You have a safe word." He paused. "But I'm hoping you'll eventually trust me enough to surrender."

His soon-to-be sub arched one of those sexy dark eyebrows. "I might agree if I tie you up a time or two."

"Sorry, Milady. Not happening."

She tugged her hand away from him.

"Talk to me, Catrina, always. About everything. We can resolve anything as long as we keep the lines of communication open."

"That all makes sense. And it's great. In theory. But I'm not good at it. My first response, always, is to protect myself."

Because no one else ever has?

Damn it to hell.

In this moment, she seemed delicate, vulnerable.

He'd always seen her as larger than life, a dominant, powerful force. Of course she still was, but her open, hesitant side made protective instincts roar through him. "Not all people are trustworthy." He stilled his finger over her pulse point. "But I promise I will work to earn yours, every day, every moment."

"Let's start with one week," she said.

Damien shook his head. On certain things, he was willing to compromise. On others, he'd remain steadfast. The trick for him was in knowing which to choose when. "Two weeks is hardly enough time for you to explore what it means to live and breathe submission. A month would be better."

"As you just said, not happening."

"I never thought it would." He fingered her wristband. "You wanted to start tonight?"

"Yes. But I wasn't sure what your reaction would be since I didn't call or make an online reservation."

He would have waited forever.

"I didn't want to presume too much, and..." She paused. "I was a bit afraid of being rejected." She shrugged fatalistically. "If that happened, I would have traded it back in for a red one."

"Now that I have you here, Catrina, I'd like to keep you."

"I wasn't planning on staying."

And he didn't plan on letting her go.

"Maybe next weekend? I didn't bring any toiletries or even a change of clothes."

"Jeff can pick them up."

She blew out a shaky breath. "You have a solution for everything."

"Only the things I truly want."

To her credit, she kept her gaze on him, and she didn't look away, even though he noticed her shift uncomfortably. "As for clothes," he added. "You won't need many. I intend to keep you naked."

"Sounds cold."

"I'll turn up the heat. Anything else you want to discuss before I take you to a private room and make you scream?"

* * * *

Catrina's mouth dried.

Over the last couple of weeks, she'd played out a dozen scenarios in her head. She'd show up and he'd reject her. Or he'd frown and scold her. Best case, he'd fall at *her* feet. Still, she hadn't been prepared for this Damien, tender and simultaneously unyielding. It scared her when she thought of how easily she'd fallen under his spell.

His touch reassured, his voice soothed.

Sexual desire knitted her insides when he was close.

Earlier, she'd watched him come down the stairs. The first sight of him had stolen her breath.

As was his custom, he wore all black.

This evening, though, his clothes had a more refined cut, and the fabric seemed richer, as befitted the elegance of the night. His trousers were tailored, his wing-tipped shoes polished. His sweater, she guessed, was cashmere. He looked every inch the owner and master of the place.

He'd swept his gaze over the gathered crowd, but he hadn't noticed her. He'd nodded toward several guests before continuing confidently down the hallway to check out the private rooms.

Everything about him oozed success and confidence.

She'd slipped over to the bar and secured a diet cola, knowing she needed to occupy her hands and her time until he saw her.

And she'd known the moment he had.

When he'd locked his gaze on her, she'd shaken, as if electricity had zapped down her spine. Courage had almost deserted her.

The way he'd moved toward her, with undeterred purpose, proved how much he wanted to dominate her.

And damn it, she'd spent far too long denying the obvious. She wanted him to.

A sub had interrupted him for a moment, and Catrina had been momentarily afraid he would be needed elsewhere.

But he'd continued toward her.

Drawing on skills she'd learned in a college acting class, she'd pretended to be relaxed. She'd swirled her drink, thinking it was a metaphor for what was going on inside her.

And now that the rules were in place, he stood and offered his hand.

It was more than a polite gesture, she knew. It was his first demand. He was claiming her in one of the Den's most public spots — for everyone to see.

After only a moment's hesitation, she placed her palm against his, accepting his strength as she slid from the high stool.

"Milady." He nodded, indicating she should precede him down the hallway.

His courtesy surprised her.

He could have instructed her to follow him. Part of her wondered if he might ask her to crawl. She should have realized that nothing about him was predictable. "Any particular room?" While each was furnished with a counter, sink and a few toys, none were identical.

Because a production company rented space here, she'd heard that a storage area existed, containing an amazing array of furniture and contraptions.

With enough notice, almost every fantasy could be fulfilled.

Some rooms had no doors so that participants could be watched by anyone who wandered past. Others could be sealed off, except for a small observation window. All scenes were looked-in on at some point by either Gregorio, Damien, or a designated House Monitor.

"Last one on the right is vacant."

She'd never been down that far, and she wondered what he had in store for her.

Gregorio intercepted them on the way. "Enjoying the evening?" he asked, his arms folded across his imposing chest.

She detected a hint of a tattoo on one biceps.

The Den's second-in-command glanced between Damien and Catrina, obviously taking in their body language.

"It's okay to ask her if she's willing," Damien said dryly.

Gregorio nodded. His pirate-like earring glinted in the dim light, and his bald head made him seem all the more imposing.

"Please give us a moment, Boss."

With a sigh, Damien stepped aside.

When he was out of earshot, Gregorio asked, "Are you under any undue pressure, Milady?"

The exchange hit her as strange, but she appreciated that Gregorio wasn't afraid to challenge Damien and that Damien was willing to follow his own rules. "I'm here of my own free will."

"And you know the Den's safe word?"

"Halt," she said.

"I'll be looking in on you." He cocked his head in his boss's direction.

"You're not invited," Damien said when he rejoined them. "She's mine."

Gregorio grinned. The expression was quick, as if he were satisfied in a very personal way. "I never thought otherwise, Boss."

"Please prepare an office for Catrina on the second floor."

Gregorio dropped his arms. "Private?"

"Adjacent to mine."

"By when?"

"Monday morning. I have plans for Catrina tomorrow."

"I take it our meeting is canceled?"

"Not at all."

Gregorio frowned.

Obviously, Damien confounded everyone around him.

"Consider it done, Boss. Milady, please, if I can be of service, let me know."

"Enough," Damien said, the word a growled warning.

Without saying anything further, Gregorio pivoted, then vanished into shadows.

With Damien's fingers possessively resting against the small of her back, Catrina continued down the hallway.

As they neared the end, he reached over her head to push open the door.

She missed a step as she crossed the threshold.

Nothing could have prepared her for what she saw.

A gigantic spool-looking contraption dominated the space. Though she didn't know what it was called, she knew two ways it could be used. And in either case, she'd be completely helpless to him.

He placed his fingers lightly at her spine again and nudged her forward.

She swung around to face him. "I'm not a masochist."

"Not yet," he said.

Her knees wobbled. "Damien…"

"I was teasing you," he said softly. "I won't do it again."

She appreciated that.

Slowly, she moved closer to the torture device while he closed the door.

It made a tiny *snick* as it sealed, and her spine went rigid.

"It has no lock," he said as if he'd read her fear.

Of course she knew that. For the protection of subs, few doors at the Den had locks. In her small panic, she'd momentarily forgotten.

"Milady, I'll never ask you to do something that will cause you bodily harm."

She glanced over her shoulder.

"I'll release you anytime. You have a safe word."

Which meant he fully intended to affix her to the cursed thing.

Catrina was learning that her thought process was more dangerous than anything he could do to her.

He walked across the room to stand in front of her. "We'll go as slow as you need."

She could ask for a different room or to play in a more public space.

But she wanted to trust him.

Gently, he took hold of her shoulders.

"I mean it."

At the table, he'd run his thumb over her wrist, back and forth, as well as in small circles, helping keep her calm. Until tonight, she'd never fully comprehended the power of a Dom's touch.

Even though she rubbed her boys' heads, ruffled their hair, ran a finger down their cheekbones, stroked their cocks to the point of distraction, and even imprisoned their faces so she could make eye contact, the situation with Damien was different. More profound. He fully intended to form a bond that drew her closer to him, deeper under his spell.

Suddenly, Catrina was terrified that she might never want to get away.

"What will it be?" His voice was low, hypnotic, as he went on, "Do you want the full experience I can offer you? Or do you want to go home wondering how great tonight might have been?"

After glancing at the contraption, she looked back at him. "I don't…"

Chapter Eight

Taking in a shaky breath, Catrina closed her eyes.

Refusing to look at the wheel, she instead focused on Damien and drew strength from his reassurances, the behavior she'd seen from him over the years, and her small experience with him at his home. "I mean... Yes. I want this."

The light of approval that flared in the depths of his eyes was the only reward she'd ever need.

So very softly, he squeezed her shoulders. "I won't let you down."

Let me *down?*

The truth was, she didn't want to disappoint him.

Still holding her, offering his unspoken strength, he asked, "As we proceed, what would you like me to call you?"

Honestly, she hadn't thought about it. Her mother referred to her as 'my Cat.' Some of her closest friends had nicknamed her Trina. Clients and friends used her given name. "Catrina is fine."

"Do you object to me calling you Milady?"

She tilted her chin and met his gaze. "As long as you're not saying it in a way that mocks me."

"I know how much this took for you. I will never underestimate it, and I will always treat you with the reverence you deserve. Your being here, what you're offering me, is a gift. I will cherish it, and you."

She glanced away, but she felt his gaze on her. Relenting, she met his eyes once more. "Thank you," she said simply.

Even if the words were as difficult as the concept was foreign, respect went two ways. The words nearly lodging in her throat, she asked, "And how should I address you?"

"Damien is fine. Though I would enjoy the formality of Sir."

She sank her teeth into her lower lip as she considered his response and her subservience. Common courtesy, she understood, as did he. But calling him Sir meant she was well and truly acknowledging him as *her* Dom.

After releasing her shoulders, he asked, "Will you strip for me?"

They both knew it wasn't a polite question.

Since she'd been naked for him one other time, this should be easy enough.

So why am I struggling?

She removed the clip and the weight of her hair spilled down her back. Then she grabbed the hem of her dress and pulled it upward, over her head.

As he had done at his house, he held out a hand for the items.

"Black shelf bra. Nice choice."

"Thank you."

An eyebrow quirked, he regarded her.

"Thank you, Damien."

"You make some classy choices, Milady," he said, taking in her stacked heels, garter belt, stockings, and a wisp of fabric that counted as panties. "Please continue. I don't want you hiding anything from me."

Shaking a little, she shook off her shoes, leaving them tipped over on the floor. Then she took her time unfastening the garter's clasps before rolling down the stockings.

When he growled impatiently, she hurriedly removed the rest of her clothing.

"I might keep you in a ski parka," he complained. "It might be the only way I survive this. You have curves in all the right places, Milady."

His approval carried her nervousness away.

Always considerate, he placed her discarded clothing in a neat pile on the counter.

"Would you like to know what we're going to do?" he asked when he returned. "Or would you rather it be a surprise?"

Every word he uttered had power. "Surprise me." Knowing what was coming might build fear.

"In that case… Over the spindle."

Her mouth dried. "I was afraid that was coming."

"Are you flexible enough to be on your back?"

"I think so."

He helped her into place.

The piece was big enough to make the stretch more comfortable than she'd expected.

"Make sure everything's okay before I attach you."

Her hair fell down behind her. But as long as she didn't try to lift her head, her neck didn't hurt. That had its own disadvantages. It made it harder to see what he was doing.

Her feet didn't quite reach the floor, but her calves rested against the wood, supporting her lower body.

"It's fine, Damien."

"Good. Then reach your arms back," he said, crouching near her.

"Uhm... Maybe I should have said I couldn't do this position."

"You would have wondered what you were missing."

"It's a little unnerving to think how well you know me already."

"Milady, your expression gives away everything."

He secured her to ties she hadn't before noticed. Keeping a close eye on her, he tightened the bonds. "Your movements are nicely restricted?"

She tested their strength. "They are."

After placing a gentle kiss on her forehead, he smiled. "You're doing well."

His approval shot arrows of pleasure through her.

"For my security, I'm going to fasten your ankles."

Her legs were parted, which meant her pussy was exposed to him.

Now that she was helpless, her pulse raced. Damien was fully dressed in street wear, not even club attire.

She wished she could see him better but being facedown would have been worse.

Since her vision was restricted, her hearing seemed more attuned than usual. His footfall echoed, and she guessed he was walking toward the counter. *For a condom?* "Are you going to fuck me?"

"Do you want me to?"

"If it's part of the scene."

He said nothing.

The sound of a squeak indicated he'd opened a cupboard door. His expensive shoes ricocheted off the room's tile floor as he returned to her.

"I like to look at you, my pretty little submissive."

She opened her mouth to protest but then closed it again. Right now, she was assuming that role.

"That's right," he said. "*My* pretty little sub."

Though she knew what he expected her to say, she couldn't respond.

"You know I can do anything I want to you."

Catrina closed her eyes.

"Breathe."

As her mind raced, she considered using the house safe word, but his reminder chased the fear away.

The truth was, he could only do what she wanted.

That was the magic of the power exchange.

"I've been thinking about your nipples, wondering how much tension puts you on that edge between pleasure and unendurable pain. Have you ever had them clamped?"

"No."

"Then we'll start with some tweezers."

"I thought I told you I didn't want to know what you would be doing to me," she said, wrinkling her nose.

A few moments later, he was standing above her, and she was looking upward, scant inches from his crotch.

Suddenly she wished he were naked.

With great intent, he leaned forward to capture her right breast.

Wanting to get lost, she closed her eyes.

As he feathered a thumb across her nipple, he increased his pressure, making her sigh deliriously.

"And how's this?" he dug in his fingertips just a little more, and she whimpered.

Immediately, he backed off.

She drew a grateful breath, but he repeated the squeeze. Before she could yelp, he'd backed off again. His touch was light as he skimmed his fingers back toward her nipple.

For a moment, he did nothing.

Then he touched her ever so gently. "Good?"

"It is."

"And this?" He increased the intensity of the pinch.

"Fine," she responded.

He tugged.

She arched toward him as much as her bonds would allow.

"You're okay with quite a bit of pressure, it seems."

"I like that." As much as she hated to admit it, he was right about so many things.

"You're getting turned on?"

"*Yes*," she reluctantly admitted.

"Is your pussy wet?"

Did he have to be so sensual? "It is," she whispered. "Yes, Damien."

"How about both nipples together?" He pinched and pulled and rolled them between his thumbs and forefingers.

"God, yes!"

"Would you like to come already?"

"Yes, yes, yes." She strained, trying to lift her hips, silently begging him to bring her off.

"I think it will be more intense if you wait."

"I don't want to wait." She tried to meet his gaze, but he was infuriatingly focused elsewhere.

"You'll be okay." His tone was reassuring in a way that did nothing to lessen her dismay.

He leaned over to affix the clamps.

"Damn!"

He adjusted the pressure.

"The tighter I make them, the hotter you seem to get."

"Damn you." She was on fire. "I want an orgasm."

"Oh, Milady, you'll get more than one."

Her clit felt swollen, and her whole body tingled.

"If I'd had any idea how you'd react to me, I'd have tied you up and dragged you in here a very long time ago."

"You've got me now," she said, barely able to form the words. "Make it worth my while."

"Challenging me again, Milady? Hoping I'll rise to the bait?" He chuckled.

Damien continued to master her as he chose, not how she wanted.

Not knowing what would happen next magnified her reaction.

Leaving her helpless, aching, wanting, he crossed to the far side of the room.

Before she was ready, leather strands landed on her belly. She gasped.

"Red is definitely your color."

With gentle strokes, he crisscrossed her tummy, her breasts, flicking at the rubber tips that gripped her nipples. He didn't vary the impact much, and the rhythm helped her to relax.

After long minutes, sighed as she surrendered to the lash, to him.

"Are you doing okay?"

"Mmm."

"Is that a yes?"

"Yes…" She almost added Sir because it seemed natural. But for her it wasn't.

"Ready for more?"

"I think so."

"You always have your safe word."

Damien took a step back then made bigger motions, gently landing on her pussy.

She strained and moaned each time one of the broad strands caught her most tender flesh. The leather scalded her from the inside out.

"I can't… I can't…" She thrashed her head.

He continued until her teeth chattered.

Nothing seemed to exist beyond the thunder of her heart, the ragged sounds of her breath and the reality of his leather caress.

If he were her sub, she'd grab hold of his head and drag him between her legs, compelling him to eat her until she came with a scream.

But movement was impossible, and she could no longer think.

"That's it. Let go."

Of what?

He seemed to be everywhere, and when he squeezed one of her breasts while flicking her clit, she understood.

Instead of straining against the bonds, desperate to get her needs met, she relaxed, allowing the smooth wood beneath her to take all her weight.

"Excellent."

She closed her eyes. When each lick landed, she breathed into it.

Instead of wanting the scene to end, she wanted it to last forever.

Sound receded.

Nothing existed but the moment, the sensation of the flogger and its delicious, stinging pain.

Then, suddenly, she became aware of…nothing.

Before she could react, Damien licked her pussy.

Sensation flooded her, and she screamed her pleasure as she came.

But he didn't stop.

He reached up to flick her nipples where the clamps seized them, then he licked and sucked, fucking her with his tongue, conquering her.

"Damn. Damn, *damn!*" She orgasmed once more.

He lifted his head and gave her a couple of sharp slaps with his hand, then laved away the hurt.

Impossibly, she came again.

Until him, she'd never had multiple climaxes, even when she'd been masturbating with a really powerful vibrator.

"I want you for myself," he said.

She wasn't sure she could endure anything more.

"You're perfect, Catrina."

He loosened her legs then cautioned, "Move slow." He rubbed her skin, bringing some circulation back.

Softly, she sighed.

Though she gave her subs aftercare, she hadn't known just how wonderful it truly was. In future, maybe she'd spend a little extra time with her subs. The high after a scene like that was stunning, and the figurative distance to the ground was vast. Already he'd taught her that a gradual return to normal was better than a fast one.

By slow measures, he loosened the nipple clamps. She appreciated his consideration. Removing them quickly could be more painful.

He caressed her breasts then sucked the tips, easing her pain.

"Thank you," she said.

"Your manners are very pretty."

She'd expressed her gratitude unthinkingly, rather than intentionally because it was his expectation. Now she understood her subs better, too.

"I want you to take your time," he instructed as he unfastened her wrists. "I'll help you to sit up."

As she moved, she winced.

Even in that short length of time, her muscles had stiffened.

Damien moved to the side of the spindle.

She expected him to offer a hand, but instead he supported her head and back as she wriggled forward.

"Stay there," he said when she was sitting. He made little circles on her shoulders to help loosen the tightness.

Even without her saying a word, he seemed to know what she needed.

"Your body is a lovely shade of red."

"It feels well used."

"Not quite. But close." He helped her to stand and held her so close that his erection pressed against her, and she inhaled the scent of his crisp masculinity. His arms were both strong and gentle. A tiny part of her brain betrayed her, whispering that it was okay to lean on him and drink in the comfort he offered.

But that would be dangerous to her equilibrium.

"Time for part two of your lesson."

"I hope it's as good as this one. I hate to be disappointed."

"I have a gag the perfect size for that smart mouth," he said easily. And he meant it. He went to the far side of the room and returned with a penis-type gag.

"I…ah…was joking." No way could he really mean to put that in her. Bravado deserted her. "I thought you wanted your sub to come to you and discuss things and that you'd agree on a punishment beforehand. You said that. Right?"

"You were testing me."

"Ah, I was teasing, Damien. Really."

"So what would you do with a sub who was disrespectful?"

He kept some distance between them, but since he was dressed in business attire and she was wearing nothing but the stripes from his flogger, she was at a disadvantage.

As tall as she was, Catrina wasn't accustomed to feeling tiny next to anyone.

Why had she taken a sensual moment between them and painted it with a smart-ass comment? Maybe she should be grateful he was giving her a moment to explain. "I'd ask him what had compelled the behavior," she said, remembering their discussion at his home.

Unable to help herself, she allowed her gaze to flicker to the penis gag.

"Let's give it a try, shall we? What compelled your behavior, Catrina?"

The way he said her name… This time there was no husky purr, and she didn't like the harshness in his tone.

Digging deep, she found an honesty that surprised even her. "Nerves," she replied. "I liked the spindle, and I didn't think I would. I enjoyed the flogging, and that caught me off guard." Her nerves were frayed, and she took a breath before continuing. "Even though you were generous enough to give me a number of orgasms, I'm still restless." She lifted her hands then let them fall again. "All of this is so new and unexpected."

Since he was still waiting, head tilted expectantly to one side, she glanced at the floor before adding, "I apologize for my bratty behavior."

"You drove an intentional wedge between us."

"Yes," she admitted softly.

"Hoping to piss me off."

"I seem to do that a lot." She wrinkled her nose. "But this time, I promise, it wasn't intentional."

"Go on."

"It was a way of protecting my turbulent emotions."

"Oh, Catrina..." This time, understanding echoed from his voice. "I appreciate your honesty and the courage it took."

She could mainline his approval. "Thank you..." Breathlessly, she whispered. "Sir."

Fuck me. He lowered the gag.

Damien leaned forward to capture her mouth with a kiss that left her reeling and even needier.

When her knees wobbled, she grabbed his wrists for support.

By insulating herself, playing with her boys and sending them home hours later, she missed out on this kind of interaction.

Finally, he ended the kiss, leaving her lips swollen.

"I want you to be who you are." He fisted a hand in her hair and pulled back her head. This Dom amongst Doms offered no quarter, as he imprisoned her gaze with his searing blue eyes. "I want to know the real you, the woman you really are, not sub, not Domme, but the whole, complete person you are when you're not frightened."

At his terrifying words, a chill lanced her.

"Your quick wit is part of your personality, one I enjoy. But question your own motivation, Milady. Are you being funny? Or are you trying to drive me away?"

The column of her throat was exposed to him.

Although he still held the gag, he placed the pad of his thumb in the hollow of her neck.

Damien — with his searing insights — humbled her.

"I'll know *you*, Catrina. Nothing less."

Trapped, unable to avoid his scrutiny, she nodded.

"Tell me you agree."

"I'll do my best." Or face the penis gag, she supposed.

"For now, that will do." Slowly he released his grip on her hair, but he held her shoulders until she regained her balance.

"Back to my earlier question. When one of your boys misbehaves — when you are sassy — what should happen? After the conversation?"

"A spanking," she said quickly. "If I say something disrespectful, I think you should spank me."

Wolfishly, he grinned. "Nice try."

"I'm not sure I understand."

"There isn't a single misbehavior that will earn you a spanking, Milady."

"Oh?" She blinked. "Why?"

"When you're over my lap with your bare bottom upturned, I can only think of bringing you off. Trying to spank you would torture me."

"How so?"

"Since the first time I had my hand on your bare skin, I've thought of little else except you and doing that again."

The way he said it, with a rich husk, made her believe he was serious.

"The gag it will be, then."

She glanced at it. The penis was enormous. Just the threat of it made her pull back.

"Incentive to behave?"

"Or keep my mouth shut."

He traced her upper lip with a finger. "Turn *to* me with your fears."

If he had any idea how difficult that would be...

"I'll try." She offered nothing else. No false promises.

"You may put on your dress and shoes as we go through the public area. I'd prefer you naked and gagged, perhaps even leashed."

His casual threat made her world tilt. But then the rest of his sentence shocked her. "Wait. We're leaving this room?" When she needed another orgasm? The man was a monster.

With a grin, he leaned in closer. "I've got more in store for you, Catrina. Much, much more. And now you're curious. Aren't you?"

Chapter Nine

He fetched her dress and held it while she wriggled into it. "You make an excellent ladies' maid," she said.

"When the woman in question is you, the pleasure is entirely mine. But keep in mind, you won't have it on for long."

While she slipped on her shoes, he tidied the room and sanitized the equipment before gathering her undergarments.

"You could put those in your pocket," she said when he opened the door. Silk, satin, and lace dangled from his grip.

"I could."

But he didn't.

Which meant everyone in the club would guess he'd had her naked.

Upstairs, on the main level, they garnered a couple of curious glances.

Long-time members knew she was a Domme, so seeing her with Damien must have been a shock.

No one was more surprised than Catrina herself at the turn of events.

When she'd checked in earlier and asked for a white wristband, the house sub at the door had called Gregorio over. He'd clarified she knew the meaning of what she was doing.

"This is better than any fireworks on the Fourth of July," Gregorio had said before personally fastening the white strip into place.

Then she'd gone to the basement to stand at the bar, wondering what Damien's reaction would be when he eventually spotted her.

Would he be happy? Pissed that she'd ghosted him?

Her musing had been interrupted when a Dom she often conversed with had joined her. As if it were an ordinary exchange, he'd started to chat.

When he'd finally noticed her wristband, he'd momentarily fallen silent before nodding tightly and inviting her to scene.

This evening, she'd planned to submit, but only to one man.

And if what Damien had said earlier was correct, she'd saved herself and the Dom from a very unpleasant scene with the owner.

Because of the exchange, she'd moved from the bar to a table where she'd be less approachable.

"We'll continue up to my quarters," Damien said.

"Oh?" Like many people, she'd wondered about the off-limits parts of the Den. There were bathrooms upstairs that were available to guests, but a sealed door prevented entrance to the rest of the second story, which also meant his private area was inaccessible to guests.

Gregorio was leaning against the balustrade, and he pushed away when he saw them approach.

"The production company could use you as a model," Gregorio said to her. "Your height shows the spindle off to its fullest effect."

"How long did you fucking watch?" Damien asked, voice tight.

"The whole time."

"And by that you mean?"

"Thirty seconds. No longer. Just enough to be sure everything was okay." He held up his hands. "Promise."

She'd be the first to admit she didn't know Damien all that well, but his behavior seemed unusual.

"We'll see you tomorrow."

Gregorio nodded.

"Milady? Shall we?"

She started up the stairs, and he was right behind her.

Not much longer, he'd pressed his finger to a keypad that opened a door.

Moments later, she was inside an office area, and they were sealed in silence…such a shocking departure from the thumping noise of the club's music.

In front of her was a vast open space. Off to her right was a wall of windows, complete with a set of French doors that presumably led to a deck.

An enormous desk loomed in front of her. "Yours?"

"It is."

Like she expected, there was no mess. The surface was bare, except for an empty brandy snifter.

He rounded to the far side of the desk to deposit her undergarments on a chair. Then he put the blasted gag on top.

She shuddered. "I hadn't realized you'd brought it."

"It was more than an idle threat, and the reminder is visible."

As well as effective.

Do you forget anything?

He opened a drawer and pulled out a remote control which he aimed at the wall behind her.

She turned, surprised to see dozens of images, each showing a different place on the property. Guests were exiting vehicles, checking in at the front desk, milling in front of the hearth, heading down the stairs or onto the back patio. "Command central?" she asked. "Unless you have serious voyeuristic tendencies?"

"As of tonight, I'd rather participate than watch." He pushed a button, and the pictures vanished.

To her left, there were two cubicles, each separated by a thick sheet of glass that was etched with a mountainscape of an eagle soaring above a peak.

"Your choice," Damien said. "They were both prepared for you."

She chose her words with care. "You expect me to work here?" *With you nearby?*

"There's someplace you'd rather be?"

"Anywhere." When he'd said that Gregorio had been instructed to ready an office for her, this hadn't been what she was expecting. She'd thought there'd be walls between them, doors...distance. "I'll never get anything done if you're so close."

"I'll shackle your foot to the desk."

Catrina wrapped her arms around herself. "I'm not sure whether or not you're joking."

"I'm not."

"That's what I'm afraid of." She'd played with him in private, been to his secluded house in the Denver area, yet nothing had felt more intimate than this.

"Would you like to see the third floor?"

Your domain.

A place she'd heard nothing — not even whispers — about.

He gave her the code to open an opaque glass door that led to another set of stairs.

When she arrived in his private suite, she paused.

The space was breathtaking with its soaring windows and ceilings and glossy hardwood floors that were covered with numerous throw rugs. A couple of tables were strategically placed, and a chair sat near a leather couch. Both faced the television atop the gas-burning fireplace.

To the back of the apartment was a small kitchen, complete with coffeemaker, refrigerator, sink, stove, and microwave oven.

"I feel like I'm at an exclusive hotel."

"That was my designer's intent. I don't always want to go downstairs for my coffee, and when I'm up here, I prefer my own deck for my first cup."

Catrina might never want to leave. "You're not a morning person?" It astounded her how little she knew him, and how much she was about to learn.

"I prefer some quiet time before I engage with others. Let me finish showing you around."

The luxury continued.

Not surprisingly, he had a well-equipped gym as well as a small study lined with books and a cozy-looking leather chair.

His bedroom had an enormous walk-in closet — unlike anything she'd ever seen. In addition to multiple built-in dressers, it contained numerous shelves and lots of rods.

A quick glance revealed how fastidious he was.

Dozens of pairs of black slacks hung next to dress shirts and suit coats. An entire selection of ties was arranged in an acrylic drawer, apparently grouped by color. His shoes were tucked into individual cubbies.

A ridiculous number of belts hung from a rack, and the idea of the leather connecting with her bare butt made her back out of the closet.

"Everything okay?" His lips quirked.

Once again she wondered if he were a mind reader. "Fine."

"Plenty of room for your belongings when you come to stay."

Why do you keep me on edge like this?

Shoving aside his question, she took in the main room.

A king-size bed faced a window, and two nightstands had artistic antler lamps on their surface. His spa-like bathroom was tiled, with double sinks, a soaker tub, and a shower big enough for two.

"I want you to be comfortable here. Ask for anything you need." He met her gaze. "Except privacy."

"Do you spend all your time coming up with words to terrify me?"

"Of course not."

He backed her up until a wall stopped her.

"No?" she asked.

"I also think about the dozens of ways I'd like to fuck you."

Her pulse turned thready.

He took a step away. "There's a box of condoms and a bottle of lube in a basket in the linen closet. Fetch them."

He left her behind in the bathroom.

For a few seconds, she remained rooted in place before she shook her head to clear it.

Did he finally mean for them to have sex?

Since she was ready to crawl out of her mind, she sincerely hoped so.

Because everything was so perfectly organized, she found the items exactly where he'd said they were.

Taking breaths to calm herself, she walked back into the bedroom, but he wasn't there.

Following the soft strands of light jazz, she walked into the living area.

"Very good. Now place them on the mantel."

He'd turned on the fireplace and dimmed the overhead lighting, bathing the room in a soft glow.

Lord of all he surveyed, Damien was seated in the chair, an ankle propped on his knee.

As she followed his orders, he never took his gaze from her.

Had anyone ever paid this much attention to her?

When she played with her subs, she gave each her entire focus, but she truly didn't spend hours thinking everything through, the way he clearly did.

As she slid the belongings where he indicated, she realized there were no personal effects in sight, no pictures, no knickknacks. Had there been any in his office? And she didn't recall any in his bedroom.

Clearly he'd left everything the way the designer had arranged it. Catrina struggled to resist the sudden urge to clutter things up, shake him up as much as he unsettled her.

"It's really different up here," she observed as she faced him. Secluded, and except for the music, eerily quiet, with no sounds from the outdoors reaching her.

"I like my privacy. And I want you to have the freedom to scream all you want."

Her breath nearly strangled her. "You do enjoy challenging me."

"It's time someone did."

And they were barely getting started.

"Come here, Catrina." He stood and extended his hand, a gesture that looked like an invitation, but she recognized as a command.

On unsteady legs, she complied, stopping a couple of feet in front of him. He took her shoulders and drew her even closer, closer than was comfortable for her.

He released one of her shoulders and moved his hand to her face where he tipped back her chin. "Your next lesson begins now?"

Her tongue seemed too big for her mouth. "And the subject?"

"Concentrating, fully, on pleasing your Dom. We'll start with you getting naked, we'll continue with you undressing me."

Catrina had watched his scene-setting demonstration that evening at the Den.

Now she recognized he'd merely offered a glimpse at the weapons in his arsenal. His tone seduced her. The way he touched her sent her pulse reeling. Even the music added to the atmosphere, seducing her.

It was the way he used his tone and words, however, that stirred her imagination in a way that could have been an art form.

Though they hadn't been sexual, she was already dazed.

"Proceed," he said, releasing her.

Locking her knees so she could remain upright, she took a step back.

As she had earlier, she removed her dress. He nodded toward the nearby couch, and she draped the material over the back.

"Keep your wristband on. I like what it symbolizes. Oh, and leave the heels on for now."

"Such a male, Damien," she observed.

"Turns out I'm an ass man. Much as I loved seeing you displayed on the spindle, I'd like to put you over it the other way, just for my edification." He sat. "Start with my shoes."

It was one thing for a man to kiss her feet, it was another to be at his.

She considered crouching, but that would give him a glimpse of her pussy. So that left kneeling as her only option. "Too bad you're not wearing boots. I could straddle your leg to get them off."

"I'll wear a pair tomorrow."

Bastard probably would, too.

She knelt and untied his laces before removing his shoes and socks.

He stood. "I'm at your mercy, Milady."

Since she was on her knees, it made sense to also remove his belt.

Which would be so much easier if his dick weren't engorged.

But that she had that effect on him thrilled her.

After fumbling with the buckle for several seconds, she finally managed to get it undone.

"Wish it had taken you a little longer."

She looked up at him.

His grin was equal parts diabolical and pleased.

She tugged the leather free and rolled it up before placing it on top of one of his shoes.

For a moment she considered removing his pants. But when he lifted his hips, her mouth would be mere inches from his cock.

Ignoring the way his lips twitched at her internal debate, she stood.

Leaning in, she removed his pricey sweater.

Lord have mercy.

She'd thought he'd looked imposing while fully dressed in his own-the-world business attire. Now, he was devastating.

Clothing only made him appear civilized.

His glorious body was honed to perfection.

Unable to help herself, she took in his impossibly broad chest and chiseled biceps. His six-pack abs were well-defined, absolutely taut without an ounce of excess flesh.

Judging by the definition in his thighs and calves, he didn't concentrate all his workout efforts on just his upper body.

She'd never seen a man so gloriously rugged. "Damn," she whispered before she could stop herself.

"Glad you approve."

To distract herself, she tossed his sweater near her dress, pretending not to notice his wince.

"That deserves a spanking."

Yes, please. "I'll be more careful in future." *A lie. Total and complete.* Did he see through it? See what she suddenly needed from him? "Will you stand, Damien?"

While he did, she kept her gaze on his chest. Anywhere but on his very-obvious bulge.

She unfastened his trousers and allowed them to fall down. Thank God, he had on underwear, even if the fabric was tented. "Boxers, Damien?"

"I like my balls loose," he said. "But wool can chafe. I can wear something else if you prefer?"

"No," her response was instant.

"What do you like about them?"

"The way I can reach my hand inside the front." Like she did with her boys. Though he was nothing like the men she ordinarily played with.

"Do it."

"I…" She was accustomed to being in charge, giving or withholding pleasure. From her years of experience, she was comfortable handling a cock, stroking it, tying a leash around it, even placing it into a cage.

But this…

She wasn't sure how to proceed.

"Be my good sub."

Trying to ignore the fact she was shaking, Catrina closed her hand around him.

"Talk to me."

He'd been so approving of her. How could she be any different? "Silky." Gently, she slid her hand back and forth. Then, as he responded, she tightened her grip a little. "I love how thick it is." *Thick? Enormous.*

And no doubt he intended to dominate her with it.

A few strokes later, he clamped his hand around her wrist. "That's enough."

She was accustomed to making that decision. Most times, it was a couple of seconds before he spilled.

"I'm in charge."

With an exhalation, she looked up and met his deep, beautiful eyes.

"I know this is unique for you. Maybe even a challenge."

As he'd said, he was in charge. "It is."

"Remove my boxers."

With a tight nod, she did as he said.

"Remain as you are," he instructed, leaning down to place the undergarment with the rest of the clothing.

"Play with your nipples," he instructed.

"They're already sensitive from your clamps."

"All the better."

Aware of his heated scrutiny, she rolled the tips between her forefingers and thumbs.

"Harder. I want you fully aroused."

Lowering her gaze, she squeezed and tugged.

"That's better." He took hold of a handful of her hair, and she whimpered a little. "I want you to look at me. See my reaction, how much I cherish your obedience."

Compelled, she had no choice.

"Now play with your pussy. But don't come."

Often, she'd do that while masturbating one of her subs. So the self-consciousness she experienced while standing in front of Damien stunned her.

"Should I repeat myself?" Growled menace wove through his question.

"No!" Immediately, she fingered herself, sliding back and forth between her pussy lips.

Fire flared in his eyes, driving her on. "Slick already?"

"Very," she confessed.

In the absence of any other instruction, his hand still fisted in her hair, she continued on, getting damper and damper.

"Now finger-fuck yourself."

No one had ever made these kinds of demands, and she loved it.

With a small moan, she dipped inside.

"I can smell your heat."

"Yes." Impossibly, she who didn't believe herself capable of multiple orgasms was already on the verge of another rocking climax.

Her whimpers became moans.

All embarrassment disappeared as need built. "Damien."

"That's my sub," he whispered encouragingly. "Play with that gorgeous pussy."

As the edge neared, she moved faster and faster, jerking her hips, trying to get better angles, more pressure.

She stopped caring how tight he held on to her, and she closed her eyes. *So close...*

"That's enough."

Enough? No. Not even...

"Catrina, stop!" he snapped, clamping her wrist.

Blinking, she froze.

"I expect instant obedience."

"But—"

He pulled her fingers from her pussy. "Lick them." He raised her hand to her mouth.

On the verge of frustrated tears, she made an exaggerated show of sticking out her tongue to clean off the tangy dampness.

"Sexy," he said. "I like the added sound effects. Been watching some of Master Niles' videos?"

When she was done, she dropped her hand to her side.

"As I mentioned earlier, I know this is a unique experience for you. You're not a person who lives and breathes submission. You generally make decisions, decide how scenes progress, I'm being more patient than I normally would." He pulled her head back a fraction of an inch. "Don't think that I'm not noticing your lack of immediate compliance." After releasing his grip, he continued in a gentler tone, "Magic happens when you get out of your own head, like you did when we played downstairs. You know it. I know. Our arrangement is only two weeks. Yield, Milady."

She didn't respond.

It was one thing to strategically prevent her sub's orgasm. Yet it was completely different to be on the receiving end, experiencing sharp pins-and-needles sensations between her legs at his horrible denial.

Desperate to alleviate some of the stress, Catrina pressed her thighs together.

"That won't help."

As always, he was right. In fact, her efforts seemed to make her neediness worse.

"I'll always ensure you're taken care of. Your satisfaction is mine."

At this moment, with frustration crashing into her, she figured he never intended to let her come again.

"But because you're trying to circumvent my decisions, you're going to be punished."

She gasped.

"Place your hands at the small of your back."

Questioningly, she scowled at him.

"Would you like them secured in place so that you're not tempted to disobey me?"

What the hell did he have in mind?

"You may want to take me up on that. Because I promise you, Catrina, I'm going to make the next ten minutes some of the most miserable of your life. Ones you'll never forget…"

Chapter Ten

"Last chance to have me cuff you. Evey time you don't do as you're told, I'll start the timer over. You won't be offered this favor again."

Being cuffed is a favor?

This side of her Dominant terrified her.

"Time's up."

Her mouth dried.

Damien placed his hands on her shoulders and backed her up against a wall. "Hands behind you."

As slowly as she could, she moved into position.

Not that stalling would help.

Her punishment wouldn't start until he decided it did.

And they had all night.

"Spread your legs as wide as you possibly can and bend your knees."

What the hell are you thinking?

"I love having you helpless, at my mercy."

"That makes one of us."

"We can add the gag to the punishment, if you want."

Determinedly, she pressed her lips together and shook her head.

"Good choice."

She bit back an instant, smart-ass retort.

"Keep in mind, ten minutes. You'll endure every second."

Do your worst. Thank God she was smart enough not to utter the words aloud.

"Open your mouth."

Hesitantly, she did.

"Get them wet."

Damien stuffed two fingers in her mouth, deep. Fighting back her gag reflex, she sucked and licked in a frantic attempt to placate him.

"What are you not going to do?" he asked when he was finally satisfied and had removed his fingers.

"Move my hands from behind me."

"What happens if you do?"

His questions were logical, a perfect way to be sure she couldn't later pretend she'd misheard or misunderstood his instructions. Even as she acknowledged his technique, she hated that he was using it on her. "The timer starts over." On whatever diabolical teaching method he'd concocted.

"And why are you being chastised?"

Fucking get it over with already. "For trying to steal an orgasm."

"So what's the best kind of learning tool I could use here?"

Color drained from her face.

Denial. "You wouldn't."

He grinned. "Keep your knees bent. You're going to be wide, wide open to me. Everything you have to offer is mine. And I will take it."

The possessiveness in his words rocked her.

"Now..." He lowered himself to his knees. "Shall we begin?"

He'd already spent an impossible amount of time tormenting her emotionally. God, what a mindfuck. The man truly was a master.

"Waiting for an answer."

"Yes, Damien. I'm ready." To get whatever the hell is going on here over with.

"Very well." He instructed his whole-house computer to set a timer for ten minutes.

Shocking her, he lowered himself to his knees.

Then he parted her labia and pulled back the hood of her clitoris.

She jerked.

"That was only a couple of seconds, Catrina. You'll do well to remember how you're supposed to behave."

Heaven save me.

Leaning forward, he licked between her feminine folds.

"Oh!" The gnawing sensation that had been eating at her since they were in the dungeon plowed into her, a hundred times stronger than anything she'd ever experienced.

He licked and sucked, eating her, bringing her close to the edge only to immediately back off, ratcheting her desire skyward.

On and on he went, inserting a finger inside her to find her G-spot while he relentlessly teased her ultra-sensitive bundle of nerves.

"Damien!"

"Hmm?"

"I can't…"

"Can't?"

"Do this for ten minutes." *I'll spiral out of control.*

This time, he didn't respond.

Instead, he worked his free hand behind her rear in order to bring her pelvis a little farther forward.

Gradually, he inserted a second finger. Using both, he fucked her hard, driving her mad.

Everything in her tightened in anticipation of the orgasm that was going to rip through her when…

He stopped.

Completely, pulling out his fingers, easing back his head, leaving her shaking.

While she recovered, he stood and dropped a kiss on her mouth.

She tasted herself on him, and the scent of musk in the air screamed intimacy like she'd never known before.

"You've got another eight minutes to go."

Eight more minutes?

Meaning he wasn't finished yet? "I've learned my lesson, Damien." *No trying stealing orgasms. At least for the two weeks. Unless I'm alone.*

"Maybe so." He shrugged. "But I'm enjoying this."

She'd never had a man tell her he enjoyed eating pussy. Her former fiancé had done it on a fairly regular basis, but she'd suspected he'd done it because he felt it was a requirement.

His cock jutting proudly in front of him, Damien crossed to the bedroom, only to return with a set of clamps draped over his palm.

Having her pussy tormented was bad enough. Adding nipple stimulation would make the intensity ten times worse.

Giving thanks for each moment that ticked by without him touching her, she watched him lower the bars to loosen the tension on the clamps.

But when he placed the first, desire arced straight to her pussy.

"Did you like that, Catrina?"

"You know I did."

"That's the only reason to do anything to you. Because it turns you on."

When her second nipple was pressed between the vinyl protectors, he tugged on the chain, and it took all her self-control to remain in place.

"Well done. I'd hate to reset the timer."

Why did he get to tell lies when she didn't?

Again, he knelt. "Where was I?" He parted her labia.

And then, awfully, he captured the chain for her clamps.

"Oh!" The bite of pain was nearly enough to push her over the edge by itself.

She should have known that his short respite was more calculated than anything.

"Remember your position."

He licked her, dampened a finger, then slid back inside her.

Within seconds, he was fucking her with his hand as he ate her pussy and tugged on the clamps, using enough force to distend her nipples but not enough to dislodge the little tormenting device.

Then he looked up at her and used his mouth to wet a finger on his other hand. That could only mean...

In anticipation, she tightened her buttocks, even though she knew that would only make his inevitable penetration more difficult.

Damien continued to eat her until she was delirious, her shoulders slammed back against the wall, and then he worked his large finger inside her tightest hole.

"You are all mine."

He'd vowed she would be, but she had no idea how much he'd meant his words.

Relentlessly, as time dragged and she teetered on the precipice, he finger-fucked her pussy and ass as he made love to her with his mouth.

And every time she almost tipped over into the abyss, he stopped.

How could she have had no idea how dreadful being edged truly was?

But he wasn't finished with her.

Lifting his head, her temporary Dominant captured the chain once more, this time with his mouth.

"No... Please."

He drew back slightly, shooting darts of sensation through her sensitized nipples.

It was *almost* enough... "Damien!" Over and over she cried his name, begging to be allowed to come.

But he wouldn't yield.

Desire was a physical hurt.

"You're almost there, aren't you?" Letting go of the chain, he pressed his tongue to her clit again.

Lost in her delirium, she bent her knees and leaned forward, grabbing hold of his head to grind her pussy against him.

Instantly, he stopped his movements and looked up at her with a terrible, terrible grin.

"Tut, tut, Milady. Seems we need to reset the timer."

Tears of frustration—as well as from his denial—flooded her eyes.

"For our next go-round, you may want to consider asking to be secured."

She wasn't sure she could endure another moment.

"You did surprisingly well," he told her, brushing away a tear, then removing the damnable clamps. "I'll be right back with you."

His voice cheerful—and annoying as hell—he canceled the timer.

In the bathroom, water ran. Then, as promised, he returned, with a washcloth, a tie, and a square box.

After placing two of the items on the coffee table, he gently dabbed her face, then the rest of her body that was now covered in goose bumps.

Showing some compassion, he swept her off her feet and carried her to the couch, where he sat with her in his lap. Beneath her, his cock was hard and demanding. So he was suffering, too. *Good.* She hated to be in this alone.

Without trying to get his needs met, he wrapped her in his arms and held on until her body warmed.

Minutes later, with a sigh, she allowed herself to completely relax.

"That's better."

Did that mean her awful punishment was over?

"Are you ready?"

So much for her unspoken wish.

Leaning forward, he picked up the tie and dangled it in front of her. "I can give you this, but it will extend your time to eleven minutes."

She pushed away from him and looked at him, her mouth open from shock.

The light in his eyes was raw.

When he'd done the demo with Susan, Catrina had thought him to be considerate and gentle.

But he was pushing her to absolute limits, and maybe past them.

"Your choice. Of course, you're free to refuse."

An extra sixty seconds so that she remained in place? Since she'd already failed once, she nodded.

After helping her to stand, he used the strip of gray silk to tie her wrists behind her.

But surprising her, instead of positioning her against the wall, he stood, lifted her again and placed her on her back on the leather couch.

Narrowing her eyes, she asked, "What are you up to?"

"Something you'll enjoy."

Catrina wasn't convinced. After what they'd already shared, she was certain his plan was not in her favor.

She studied him as he picked up the box and lifted the lid.

"Damien…"

He pulled out a U-shaped vibrator.

Instinctively, she pressed her legs together. "No. No."

After removing a small, packaged wipe from a pocket, he cleaned the toy.

"Have you used one of these?"

Since the cost was prohibitive, she had yet to splurge, though she'd looked at them online and had one on a wish list. If the reviews were to be believed, this little thing offered the ultimate pleasure, though it was designed to be used with a partner. "No."

"You'll like it."

That was what she was most afraid of.

"This version comes with a remote control." He pressed a button several times, running through the vibe's settings, from an occasional pulse, to holy-mother-of-God speed.

Hardly daring to breathe, she prayed he didn't select that one.

No way was she going to survive the next eleven minutes.

After turning off the device, he teased her again to ensure she was wet, then he tucked the flat end inside her, against her G-spot.

Could the world please open up and swallow her whole?

Then he bent the silicone into place so that the fat head rested on her clit.

When he turned it on, it shook for a fraction of a second.

Maybe, just maybe, she had a chance of holding on. On that setting, the thing could prove more annoying than exciting.

"Are you ready?"

"The clock isn't already running?" she demanded miserably.

A moment later, he started the timer.

Damien stood over her, and she couldn't look away from his glorious cock.

For what had to be five minutes, as she grew more and more restless, he stood there, slowly stroking himself.

She admired his control.

Pre-cum glistened at the tip, and he swiped it off, and transferred it to her lips.

Grateful for any distraction, she licked away the saltiness. "Yes…"

"That was fucking sexy, Catrina."

She never remembered being excited to taste a man before. But with him, she couldn't get enough.

Would he continue, ejaculating in her mouth, or on her?

She'd never experienced that, either. The idea, though, made her ravenous.

Still pleasuring himself, he leaned over to tweak one of her nipples, making her jerk. Maybe because he'd clamped her earlier, she was more sensitive than usual.

"You liked that."

It wasn't a question. *He knew.*

"And this…" He bent to suck the same one into his mouth.

Whimpering, she lifted her hips.

Too soon, he pulled away. *"No."* Good thing her hands were behind her. She would have grabbed hold again, wanting more.

Leaving that nipple beaded and wet, he moved to the other, driving her mad.

"How much time do I have left?"

"No idea."

Everything he did seemed calculated to drive her out of her mind.

"Are you desperate to come yet, Catrina?"

Yes. "Please."

"That's good. Hang on just a little longer."

Afraid he'd say that, she squeezed her eyes shut.

Reassuringly, he smoothed strands of hair back from her face. "I know you can do it."

Catrina wished she had half as much faith.

"Shall we mix things up?"

Mouth parted, nerves slamming into her, she met his gaze. Right now, this was maddening, but not awful.

"Uh..." How should she respond? What would a trained sub say? "This is working fine, Sir."

"Is it?" He pushed the thick part of the vibe harder against her clit.

She gasped.

"The little pulse won't make you come, will it?"

Until now, it had been more annoying than anything.

Now...

"This... It's torture."

"Not yet, it's not."

His brand of torment had been going on forever, a punishment that didn't fit her crime. Her orgasm had lasted thirty seconds, maybe a minute at the most. And if he weren't as skilled, she wouldn't have come at all. Essentially, this was all *his* fault.

This time, she was smart enough to keep her thoughts to herself.

"Let's see how you react to other settings."

"As I said, this is fine. Honestly." Then, hoping to convince him, she added, "I mean, this is just right, *Sir*."

"You're exquisite, Catrina. Utterly exquisite." He smiled in a way that did nothing to reassure her. "And clever. Fortunately for you, I have plenty of experience with subs who are trying to appeal to my kinder nature."

"Let me guess, you don't have one?" *Why did I say that?*

"When it comes to this? To you? No."

Another pulse went through her, and she jerked.

"At some point, you may appreciate it."

I'm not convinced.

He set the device to a low, steady hum that was much more intense.

She wiggled, trying to get away.

"You'll want to make sure the vibrator stays in place."

That was the last thing she wanted.

After about twenty seconds, he increased the speed.

"God, no!" Her body instinctively seeking pleasure, she lifted her hips in a vain attempt to have the thing satisfy her. Even as she did so, her rational mind screamed at her to fight off her reaction.

"Much better."

"In your opinion."

"A little more difficult to remain in control?"

"Almost impossible," she admitted.

"That's what I was hoping for."

A few seconds later, he turned down the intensity enough for her to exhale.

Then he crouched next to her, inserting a finger inside her drenched pussy to press against the flat part of the toy.

"Since it's meant for two people, you'd usually be wearing this while we were having sex. So this" — he demonstrated — "would be firmly against your G-spot."

Desperate for the alarm to signal, she writhed.

"How's that?"

She was spiraling, no longer capable of speaking.

Continuing the torment, he adjusted the speed to the highest setting.

Twisting her fingers together beneath her, she gulped in air.

No longer able to focus, she gyrated, all-but fucking his finger and the vibrator.

And every time she was a fraction of a second away from satisfaction, he'd change what he was doing. "Please." Over and over, she pleaded with him.

Finally, when she could take no more, the timer rang.

"You did it. Excellent, Milady."

He turned off the device and removed it from her, leaving her clit pulsing and swollen. Her body shook from cold, and sobs tore from deep inside.

Damien had left her completely humbled, her body weak from unfulfilled desire.

Without her being aware of what was happening, he dried her between her thighs and helped her to sit.

After unknotting the tie, he rubbed her wrists, pausing for a few seconds on a pulse point. Then he encouraged her to roll her shoulders.

Afterward, he sat and pulled her onto his lap and draped a blanket around her. Beneath her buttocks, his cock was stiff.

He'd made her suffer, but maybe he was experiencing some anguish of his own.

At least she hoped so.

Against her ear, his heart pounded a reassuring rhythm, helping her reorient.

"How was it?"

"Awful."

"That bad?" His tone held no sympathy, and she deserved some.

Because she wasn't looking at him, she found the courage to say what she meant. "Worse than that."

But the lesson had been effective. As a Domme herself, she had to respect his technique. No way would she ever attempt to come without his permission again.

"You may want to thank me, Catrina."

Maybe she'd misheard. Her head was stuffed full of cotton wool, and her brain didn't seem to be firing correctly yet. "Thank you?"

"For my attention."

His expectations were high if he expected gratitude for what he'd forced her to endure.

Complete lethargy claimed her, but she lifted her head as much as she was able, trying to see if he was serious.

His jaw was set in an uncompromising line.

He meant it.

"I could have required a fifteen-minute session. Maybe twenty."

She tried to escape, but he tightened his grip, imprisoning her.

"Another demonstration, perhaps?"

Frantically she shook her head. "Thank you, Damien," she managed. "You were quite thorough." That much was true, even if she didn't appreciate his efforts.

"You're very welcome."

Against the humor in his voice, she ground her back teeth together.

"Now that you're almost warmed up, would you like to know what's next?"

Next?

Chapter Eleven

"When you're ready, fetch the lube and a condom."

Even though he'd given her a few more minutes to recover than she'd expected, the pins-and-needles sensations continued to chase through her body.

Still, she was willing to pay almost any price, as long as it ended with a climax.

Slowly, she slid from his lap and made her way to the mantel.

"You have one fine ass, Milady."

She glanced over her shoulder. "Thank you, Sir." This time, the word rolled more effortlessly from her tongue.

"I can't wait to fuck you in it."

Her mouth dried.

She had little anal experience, but what she'd tried, she'd enjoyed.

But having Damien's massive cock inside her?

That, she wasn't sure of.

Her hands now trembling, she picked up the items and faced him again.

He was watching her, his hot gaze evidently never having strayed from her body.

Slowly, she returned to him.

The sound of her shoes seemed to ricochet in the silence, which was a good thing. At least it covered the sound of her thundering heart.

She placed the items on the coffee table.

"You'll be putting the condom on me."

She often performed that act for her boys. In fact, she loved doing it. She could tease and prolong, never letting them know what to expect. Keeping her sub guessing was one of her favorite things to do.

Damien wasn't asking her to do anything she didn't normally do, but her frame of mind was different. Interesting how the same act could be submissive or dominant, depending on her attitude.

He stood and nodded toward the floor, silently indicating she should kneel.

Thankfully, he offered a hand to steady her while she lowered herself before him.

"And you'll be using your mouth to put the condom on me."

"What?" She tried to look up at him but couldn't see anything past his ridiculously large cock.

How in the hell was she supposed to follow his order?

"Quit thinking so much." He spread his legs.

If only it was that easy.

She placed the bottle of lube on the floor then fumbled the small foil package a couple of times before finally managing to get it open. Then she checked to be sure she had the condom positioned correctly. "Are you serious that I can't use my hands?" she asked.

"I'm sure I don't need to repeat myself."

She used her mouth and her tongue to unroll the confounding thing.

"Think about how much you're pleasing me," he instructed, cradling her head in his palm.

After drawing a steadying breath, she continued, attempting to make the act as erotic as possible for him.

"That's it."

When she touched her tongue to the underside of his cock, he jerked toward her. Noting and loving his reaction, she added a little more pressure before pulling away and repeating what she'd done.

Keeping her hands curled on her thighs, she worked the latex lower and lower while returning to caress his most sensitive spot.

"If you're this skilled at doing that, I should have you give me a blow job every morning."

Not that her jaw would survive that.

As she got the condom almost in place, she began to gag. Her eyes watered, and his cockhead touched the back of her throat. Using her hands would help tremendously.

"Almost there." A few seconds later, he said, "Good."

She pulled back, and tears spilled from her eyes.

"You make an excellent sub, Catrina." Gripping her upper arms, he helped her to stand. "Make no mistake. You are *mine*."

His cock pressed into her stomach, and he kissed the top of her head.

Damien's tender touches would be her undoing.

"I'm going to fuck you from behind. You'll be clear who has mastered you, Milady."

Catrina was so far gone that she didn't take exception to what he said.

"Brace yourself on the back of the couch."

Yes.

She wanted this desperately.

With his assistance, she got into position.

Shocking her, her pussy instantly dampened.

The way he looked at her, touched her, let her know how much she meant to him created a dynamic she'd never had with anyone else.

"You're wet for me."

"Yes."

Still, he toyed with her until she all but danced and whimpered, desperate for his possession. "Take me, Damien."

She sighed when he guided his cockhead toward her, and she lifted up onto her toes to allow him greater access.

"Damien."

"Patience, Milady." Slowly, surely, he entered her, resisting her when she wriggled her hips backward. No matter what she tried, the annoying-as-hell Dominant remained in total control.

Finally, he clamped her hips in his strong hands, holding her steady while he drove into her.

She cried out when he was up to his balls in her pussy.

"That's it. Scream for me."

It was almost impossible not to with the way he fucked her, pulling out, thrusting in, filling her completely.

Her breaths became ragged.

"Hold on a little longer."

She was not certain that was possible.

Trying to comply, she gripped a cushion, seeking purchase.

His claiming was full. Complete.

"Wait for it."

Catrina dragged in gulps of air.

All of a sudden, he stopped moving.

He pulled out, and she turned her head. The curtain of her hair made it difficult to see exactly what he was doing, but she heard him squirt lube onto his hand.

"I'm not sure I'm ready for that."

"When I fuck your ass, Catrina, I'll make sure you are."

She let her head fall forward again. So far, he'd given her nothing she couldn't handle.

He inserted a slick finger in her anus.

Can I do this?

Knowing what to do, she forced herself to breathe, and she swayed gently, allowing him access.

"Now a second."

She gasped. The insertion more than doubled the feeling of being stuffed full.

While she tried to adjust to his sensual act, he slid his dick back in her heated pussy. Her body shook as he simultaneously pounded her front and back. "Oh my God, Damien!"

Reality blurred as an impending orgasm — unlike anything she'd ever known — flared in her. She wasn't sure how longer she could last, no matter what he demanded.

Then he reached around her to pinch her clit, and she screamed.

In a sensual wave, the climax crashed over her.

She bucked and cried, but as always, Damien was unyielding, riding her, forcing her to accept everything he offered.

Then, with a vicious curse, he dug his fingers deeper and called her name as he came.

The absolute force of his possession shattered her a second time.

The relief of finally being allowed to orgasm was short-lived.

Once the physical release subsided, its awful, implication-filled emotional residue clobbered her.

"Was the wait worth it?"

He gathered her hair and held it back, then he stroked her nape.

She'd never experienced anything so profound.

He'd devastated her, yet she ached to turn to him for comfort. How was she supposed to sort through everything that had happened between them?

When she'd decided to see Damien again, she'd be intrigued, curious to experience the things she put her subs through, but nothing could have prepared her for the stunning reality.

"Catrina?" he prompted.

Her first reaction was to fire off a smart-ass comment, but she was so out of control she couldn't think of anything.

"*Catrina?*"

Words didn't exist to explain what she was going through. "I…"

Quickly, he withdrew his spent cock and eased out his fingers before helping her up and turning her to face him. "Talk to me."

"I'm good." It was a lie, but one to protect herself while she sorted through her emotions.

"Let me draw you a bath."

"Shouldn't I be doing that for you?" Until now, she hadn't considered that he might expect her to cook and clean for him. Wasn't that part of what a sub was supposed to do? What did she really know beyond a Friday or Saturday night hook-up?

"I'm self-sufficient, Milady. I don't need a housekeeper or personal chef. And I know my way around the grocery store. I even know how to operate all household appliances."

"It's unnerving how you do that. Read my mind." *See through me.*

"Wish I could say that I had that kind of talent, but your face is expressive. You frowned after asking your question."

He picked up the blanket and draped it around her again.

Snuggling into the softness, she followed him into the bedroom, and he invited her to select one of his T-shirts while he went into the bathroom.

"I thought you wanted to keep me naked."

"Most of the time," he called back over the sound of running water. "But I also don't want you to catch a chill."

Willing her hands to stop shaking, Catrina opened one of the drawers and selected a T-shirt from the bottom of the pile. She went with a soft, well-worn one, something that spoke of comfort.

After leaving the garment on the end of his bed, she joined him in the bathroom, where he'd discarded the condom and was just finishing washing his hands.

As he'd promised, the bathtub was filling with water, and inviting steam rose from the surface.

Before getting in, she hesitated.

"Something wrong?"

"I lost my hairclip."

"I'll be right with you."

She wound her locks into a makeshift bun and piled it atop her head. The fix wouldn't last long. And before it fell, he came back holding the clip triumphantly.

"I wasn't sure where I left it."

"Found it tangled with your stockings," he admitted. "May I?"

She bent her head while he placed the clip. "You're hired."

"I could happily do little things for you all day."

Their eyes met. "Are you serious?"

"Yeah.

Damien showered while she soaked.

Sharing the bathroom like this was unique for her, and she lay back and enjoyed the warmth and the fact he was so near.

Suddenly drained of energy, she relaxed and closed her eyes.

Since their first scene in the dungeon, he'd turned everything Catrina thought she knew about D/s relationships upside down.

The way he'd edged her then fucked her consumed her energy and left her utterly drained.

"Next time, I'll shower before you drain the water heater," he said.

Realizing she'd been lost in thought, she opened her eyes as she sat up.

Damien had wrapped a white towel around his hips. His raven-dark hair curled at his nape. Beads of water clung to his torso. Was there anything sexier? "I should apologize," she said, "but this feels too wonderful for me to be sorry about your cold shower. I'm afraid my muscles would have been sore without the bath."

He grinned. "I have an on-demand heater. My shower wasn't cold. You can take as many baths as you want, as hot as you want them."

"I may take you up on that."

He grabbed a towel from the linen closet and wrapped her in it when she climbed out of the tub.

Although they hadn't spent a lot of time together, she was already expecting him to hold her and give her a kiss, which he did after releasing the clip from her hair. The dichotomy he represented fascinated her. Strong and tough yet soothing and responsive.

In the bedroom, she reached for his T-shirt.

"I'll keep you warm," he said, plucking the material from her fingers and tossing it back where it was.

He was willing to go to bed this early? "We're spending the night together?"

"There's no sense in you driving home."

Why hadn't she thought this through?

She wasn't sure she even had the energy to drive back home or ask Jeff to give her a ride into Winter Park where she could find a hotel room.

"I'd like you to stay."

Her breath caught. Unaccountably, she wanted to be near Damien.

Her reaction shocked her, left her a little uncomfortable.

She always sent her boys home, so this was unique to her. Being in his bed, his arms…?

"You've behaved well enough for me not to cuff you to the headboard. And definitely well enough not to make me tie you to the footboard."

"You wouldn't."

He shrugged. "No?"

She should know not to second-guess him. Maybe he meant it, or perhaps he was just teasing. Either way, he kept her off-balance. No doubt he did it intentionally.

"Never forget I'm a Dom, Catrina."

How could I?

* * * *

"How was your lesson?"

"My...?" Catrina wiggled her upper body to better prop her bare shoulders against the headboard as she regarded Damien over the rim of her coffee cup.

Earlier, he'd awakened her by wafting the steam near her nose.

After he'd helped her to sit up and adjust the blankets around her, then he'd turned over the brew before heading for the shower.

She'd taken a sip and sighed in bliss. He'd made the coffee the way she liked, which meant it was strong enough to dissolve a spoon, and the bitterness had been tempered by the addition of a dollop of cream.

She wasn't sure how long he'd been up. Long enough to dress in a pair of jeans and — God help her — nothing else.

Even if he hadn't reminded her of the sex they'd had last night, the first sight of him would have brought it back. "I thought you weren't a morning person," she said, stalling, changing the subject, not really wanting to talk about what had happened.

"I was thinking of reinforcing it if you hadn't learned it well."

"Uhm...I'm good with that."

He sat on the edge of the bed, near her. *Too near.*

"Are you?" he asked.

Knowing he wouldn't be satisfied unless she gave him some input, she chose her words with care. "As you told me, being on the receiving end is much different than planning the scene."

"Being subject to someone else's whims?"

Angling her head, she looked at him. He'd certainly made his point about her trying to circumvent his command, and yet…

Being edged like that was the perfect punishment.

And the entire time, he'd been completely engaged with her. A spanking would have been faster and easier, for both of them.

Instead, he'd been creative, and she would always remember the way he'd watched her, ensuring she remained balanced on the brink of an orgasm but without actually climaxing.

His skill at reading her was awe-inspiring.

He'd shattered her so completely she was still picking up the pieces.

"Catrina?"

"This is definitely a learning experience. A growing one."

"Anything specific you want to discuss?"

"Maybe later." *Maybe.* "I'm processing it myself."

"Just say the word."

"Thank you."

But he didn't move. Instead, he remained in place, contemplating her.

"I woke up craving your pussy."

Her heart slammed into overdrive.

"Holding you, letting you sleep because you seemed exhausted, even though that was the last thing I wanted. I had a hard-on most of the night."

Had she ever known a man this revealing?

"After we scened, I took you from behind. This morning I want to watch your face as you cry out my name."

She sucked in a breath.

"You screamed last night."

"I didn't." Her hand shook so hard that the coffee sloshed.

With great deliberation, Damien moved to capture the drops with his thumb and pressed them against her lips.

Breathlessly, eyes wide as their gazes collided, she opened her mouth to lick off the sweetness.

It was a reminder of their temporary relationship and the sensual dynamic that existed between them. "I'm sure I didn't," she protested as she struggled for normalcy.

"You most certainly did. Your cries, the way you whimpered my name... Sweetest music I've ever heard."

A shudder rippled through her.

Years ago, she'd longed for this kind of interaction with a man.

But her life had changed so much since then.

"More coffee?"

Grateful for the reprieve and a chance to reset, she finished her last sip, then handed over the empty cup. "Please."

Before leaving the room, he pulled on a body-hugging athletic top.

When she was finally alone, she slipped from beneath the blankets to hurriedly donned the T-shirt she'd found in his closet yesterday.

Though it was long enough to cover her buttocks, it offered no protection against him or his potent demands.

Sounds of his strong footfalls reached her, and she dove back into the bed and drew up a sheet.

Two weeks.

Had she really agreed to that? Could she survive it?

In less than a day, she'd endured things she'd never dreamed possible.

And the orgasms, when he finally allowed them...? He'd left her completely destroyed.

Last night, after her bath, she'd been drained.

Then when he'd turned off the light, she'd held herself rigid, afraid she wouldn't be able to find sleep in the bed of the man who'd Dominated her and given her an exquisite taste of submission.

But that was the last thought she'd had until she'd been awakened by the tantalizing scent of fresh-brewed coffee.

Moments later, he returned, and every part of her vibrated with awareness. Shocking her, just the sight of him aroused her.

His gaze on her in his ultra-focused way, he crossed the room.

"Take as much time as you want and need to relax. Have a shower, a bath. Sit outside in the sunshine if you want."

And then...?

He offered her the coffee cup.

"Find me in my study when you're ready. I have plenty in store for you."

Their fingers glanced off one another's as she accepted the offering.

"Such as...?" *Do I even want to know?* If he answered her, would she spend her time terrorized? But if he didn't respond, her imagination might run away with her.

"I'll tell you this much..." He leaned forward to tuck sleep-tousled hair behind her ear. "If you're able to walk straight when I'm finished with you, I will have failed you."

"I..."

"Get yourself ready, Catrina. But don't take too long. If I have any hint that you're stalling, things won't go well for you..."

Chapter Twelve

What do you have in store for me?

Without another word, he left the room.

Playing with him had already taught her that he meant every word he said.

Her hands shaking even worse than before, she took a big gulp from her cup, wincing as the heat scalded her mouth.

Once she recovered her equilibrium, she dashed into the en suite, pausing with surprise when she noticed he'd laid out a brand-new toothbrush for her.

After finding a washcloth in the linen closet, she scrubbed off her remaining make up. Her fake eyelashes would last a few more days, or maybe she'd remove them at home.

Since she'd had a luxurious bath last night, she settled for a quick shower.

Then, unsure what to expect, she wrapped the towel around her tightly then walked to his study.

Since he was studying his computer screen, she gently knocked on the doorjamb. Instantly, he swung to face her, sweeping his gaze over her.

"Oh, Catrina. What you do to me."

Awareness flooded the space between them, and she fought back an instinct to kneel.

Where did that come from?

"The siren of my dreams."

"I…"

"Wait for me." He stood. "Put a condom on the nightstand."

When she nodded, he continued. "I'll give you five minutes, and then I expect to find you on your back on the side of the mattress, knees over the edge, legs spread as wide as you can get them."

She resisted the temptation to wrap her arms protectively around herself.

"Be naked, which is always my preference for you. Any questions?"

"No." Again, the word Sir hovered around her.

"Five minutes," he reminded her. With a tight nod, he returned to work.

Dismissed, she exhaled and went in search of the condoms, finding them where they'd been last night, on the hearth.

His demands made it impossible for her to keep her thoughts clear, and she had to concentrate hard on what he'd said.

In just under the allotted time, she lay back, naked.

He kept her waiting, and she was sure he did it on purpose to let her mind race with possibilities.

Such an effective tool — one she'd have to remember with her boys.

But suddenly, as cool air drifted over her body, her old life seemed so very far away.

With her eyes closed, she drew in a few steadying breaths, then attuned her hearing to listen for him.

Despite hearing nothing, she remained exactly where she was.

"What a good girl."

Catrina blinked.

How had he entered without making a single noise? And how long had he been there? "Do you have a camera in here?"

"No. Our bedroom is a sanctuary. When we're in our suite, I will share you with no one. It seems I'm a very selfish man."

Unaccountably, his response pleased her. She wanted to be special. For this to mean something…as much to him as it did her. "So that means you were standing there, watching me."

"I warned you there'd be no privacy."

He took a purposeful stride toward her.

"Part your labia, Milady. Use both hands."

Trembling, she took hold of each pussy lip and pulled it back.

"Keep your legs right where they are while I spank your pussy."

Oh, God. "But—"

"Do you need a spreader bar?"

"I'll stay in position."

"See that you do."

When he was in front of her, he abraded her clit, making her jerk against him.

"Sensitive."

Frightened was more like it.

Nothing but the sounds of their combined breathing disturbed the atmosphere. Even though she'd been wet as she waited for him, apprehension had taken hold.

"Don't move."

Obeying was difficult, but she kept her hands in place.

He pulled back the hood to expose her clit.

Unable to help herself, she tightened her buttocks. He didn't reprimand her, and he didn't do anything else for a long time, just kept her there, exposed in the most terrifying way.

"Concentrate on pleasing me as I discover your secrets."

Her heart raced, but she remained where she was.

He touched her clit with a fingertip that was warm and damp. His touch was kind, at odds with what he'd said.

Then, never taking his gaze from her pussy, he gave her a couple of swats.

Shockingly, they were gentle enough for her to exhale with relief.

The next few aroused her.

The following half dozen made her cry out.

"More?"

Before she could formulate an answer, he delivered open-handed, hard slaps.

"Fuck! Damn it." She tried to pull her hands away so she could protect herself, but he brushed them aside.

"How does it feel now?"

As the pain receded, she throbbed with need.

"Tell me what you want."

Shamelessly she tried to lift herself toward him. "I need you, Damien. Put your cock in me." She writhed, silently urging him to hurry.

"So pretty, all swollen and red."

"And I'm wet."

"You like having your pussy spanked."

He licked her, soothing the burn, exciting her even more.

"Don't you?"

"Yes!"

"Are you forgetting something?"

What? Desire held her in its relentless grip.

He gave her another few swats, more painful than the others.

Screaming, she tried to escape.

"What are you forgetting?"

She'd trained so many subs. This shouldn't be this difficult for her. "Thank you. Thank you for the pussy spanking, Sir." The comparison of the two made her appreciate the first one. Remembering her manners would save her a lot of pain in the future.

"Much better. Now put your hands above your head."

Did this mean he wasn't going to do that any longer?

"Do you need to be tied?"

She studied his face, trying to read him. "How should I respond? Are you going to punish me if I touch you?"

"This morning? No."

"In that case, I'll try to keep them in place."

Momentarily, he left her to put on a condom.

Then his large, throbbing cock was at her entrance.

"Yes, please."

"I love it when you use your manners."

But instead of taking her, he moved his shaft across her pussy, teasing her with it.

"After that spanking, this is too much."

"You're thinking about yourself," he pointed out.

He was right. She was at such a fevered pitch, she was no longer considering him. "Yes, Damien," she said. Her resolve to concentrate on his pleasure lasted for a whole three seconds before she lifted her hips to envelop him as he thrust forward. "Yes," she said around a gasp.

"Look at me."

She opened her eyes.

His face was only inches from hers. His blue eyes had never seemed so compelling, and she couldn't look away. He placed her wrists one on top of the other and encircled them with one of his hands.

"You can come after I do."

"Not sure I can wait that long."

"It'll be two days before I let you climax again if you don't follow my instructions."

With the way he'd edged her, she knew he meant it. "You're dastardly."

He grinned, and it made him even more intimidating. "I could screw you for the rest of the morning, Milady. And I might."

"Please don't." She was already fighting back an orgasm with every breathing technique she'd ever learned. The way he held her and fucked her blazing cunt had her teetering on the precipice.

Damien used his free hand to play with her nipples, driving her mad.

She was desperate to close her eyes, certain it could help break the bond.

"Look at me," he reminded her.

Instead of arguing, she kept her gaze fastened on him, drinking in strength from the set of his jaw.

"That's it."

She met his surges and whimpered with each one.

"Beautiful," he said. "So beautiful in your surrender." He released her wrists and pushed a thumb against her clit.

"Damien! Damien," she pleaded.

"Legs around my waist."

The change in positions gave her a moment of respite, but ultimately it put him deeper inside her.

"*Now.*" He impaled her then jerked inside her a few times, his ejaculate pulsing from his body.

Using her calves as leverage, she ground out her own orgasm, sobbing as she splintered from the inside out.

Her Dominant was there for her, holding her, murmuring words she couldn't make out, a hand feathered in her hair.

"You're absolutely perfect," he said approvingly when she turned her face to look at him.

Every time they were together, she fell deeper under his spell.

Will I be able to save myself?

"Quite an apt student."

Striving for lightness, anything to deal with what was happening to her emotionally, she responded in kind. "My teacher provides plenty of motivation, though it might be fun to stay after class."

"If you need extra instruction, you're more than welcome to stay after class." After easing out of her swollen pussy, he repositioned her on the bed, with her head on a pillow. Then he pulled a sheet up around her. "Rest for a minute." He joined her, pulling her into his arms. "I'll drive you to Denver today."

With a frown, she stiffened, then she pushed away so she could look at him properly. "I'm capable of making the trip by myself. I do it all the time. Or you said Jeff could pick up a few things for me?"

"I gave him the day off."

Did you?

He'd given plenty of hints that he was possessive. And she was becoming certain he meant it. "If you go alone, you'll spend too much time inside your head and freak out."

"I don't *freak out*," she protested.

"No? Then what's happening right now?"

His radar was keen, and he saw too much—her fluttery pulse and the way she wrung her hands together. "Okay." Her next breath was a little ragged. "Maybe I am." Then she amended, "A little bit." Then she sighed. "This—*you*—has been a little overwhelming."

"Which is why we need a reset. We should enjoy the day together."

She narrowed her eyes at him. "A reset? What are you talking about?"

"How about we leave here in half an hour, have breakfast at my favorite restaurant on the way to Denver? Relax a little. Get to know each other."

It sounded suspiciously mundane.

No kinky stuff during the meal or the drive?

Being in a BDSM dynamic with him was something she understood.

But hanging out with the gorgeous, somewhat mysterious man as a friend…? That was something she didn't know how to deal with. Getting to know him more intimately might come with devastating consequences.

To save herself, she needed to keep him at a distance.

"Don't overthink this."

How well he knew her.

"I'll be right back."

He left the bed and returned a minute or so later with a warm washcloth that he used to bathe her pussy.

His exquisite aftercare melted her.

"Can you be ready to leave in thirty minutes?" he asked. "Or do you need a little longer to get ready?"

Fortunately, she had a change of clothes in the car, but only lipstick and mascara in her purse. "Maybe a little longer? I need the bag that's in my car, and I'd like a bath, or at least a shower."

"I'll handle it." He confirmed the location of her keys—in her purse in the coat-check area. "Take your time."

Catrina was chin-deep in bubbles and hot water when he popped his head inside the bathroom to tell her he'd left her belongings in the closet.

"Though I'd prefer that you wear your corset and those thigh-high boots."

Shaking her head, she grinned. "Always thinking sexy thoughts?"

"Can't get them out of my mind when you're around."

Maybe he said that to all the women he engaged with, but she still grinned.

In under forty-five minutes, she was wearing a pair of jeans, ankle boots with chunky heels, and a soft sweater.

He walked into the bedroom, and her mouth watered.

Not surprisingly, he was in black. But his jeans snuggled him like a lover, as did his Henley. Confounding man had left the top few buttons open, seeming to invite her touch.

Leaning against a wall, he took her in. "That might be even sexier than the corset. You're as hot as hell, Milady."

So are you.

His hair was severely brushed back, and its thick length was secured by a strip of leather.

And his leather bomber jacket...?

He was so masculine that she ached to be on her knees for him.

Forcing aside the unwelcome thought before she could act on it, she said, "Ready."

Downstairs, he helped her into her coat, then they spent less than half an hour on the road before arriving at a rustic mountain lodge near Winter Park. Not only was the place cozy with its wood beams and blazing fire, it had soaring windows with breathtaking mountain views.

Skiers and snowboarders were excitedly talking about the fresh powder and lack of wind and discussing the runs they were going to get in. A few others were talking about backcountry conditions while locals scanned their phones or glanced at the silenced televisions.

Though the place had a short wait list, they were quickly seated at a table next to a window, maybe because he came here a lot. Or the host had a crush on him. With the way she greeted him and smiled while dismissing Catrina, she was willing to bet the woman liked him.

Damien ordered steak and eggs, with a side of salsa and half an avocado. Almost no carbs.

No wonder his physique was so incredibly sexy.

After scanning the menu, she opted for *migas*, the house specialty. She'd never had them before, but they sounded delicious, three eggs scrambled with jalapeños, green chilies, tomatoes, gobs of cheese, and tortilla strips. And happily, it came with a side of hashbrowns. "I need my energy to keep up with you," she said while biting into a banana walnut muffin, one of the offerings in the complimentary breadbasket.

The food arrived, and he finished his meal a few minutes ahead of her. "Impressive," he said, nodding at her nearly empty plate.

"Now I'm ready for a mocha," she said, when she forked the last bite of potatoes from her plate. Not that the muffin hadn't been dessert all by itself. But she still craved more caffeine.

"We may need to hire a cook if you're going to consume a couple of thousand calories at every meal."

She raised one of her eyebrows. "Perhaps I shouldn't exercise so much."

"Eat up."

She grinned and raised her juice glass in his direction.

They walked to a nearby coffee shop where he ordered an Americano and she scored their largest mocha before they returned to the car and started back toward town.

"You're a great chauffeur," she said. He was a competent driver, not hyper-aggressive, but assertive, giving her tons of confidence.

His sedan was all luxury, with heated leather seats and individual temperature controls for the driver and passenger sides.

Her side was ten degrees warmer than his.

She sipped the extra-chocolaty beverage while he told her about his business ventures and gave her the history on how the Den had come about. He and his wife had both been avid skiers, and she had a large extended family.

Margot had wanted a large home for family retreats, holidays, reunions. And since the house could be rented for a premium during the winter season, it was a solid investment.

"You were married?" she asked, putting the drink in the cup holder. How had she never heard that juicy piece of gossip?

"Didn't last long."

"I had no idea. What happened?"

"Nothing," he said. "It was unremarkable. Margot and I married. Things didn't work out. We went our separate ways. End of story. No great devastation that left me emotionally crushed."

"Quit holding out."

He slid her a glance, and his eyes were darker than she'd ever seen.

"We started dating when I was in grad school, then we got married a year or so later." His grip on the steering wheel was light yet competent as he negotiated a hairpin curve while climbing Berthoud Pass. "I got a job at a private equity firm. Getting married seemed like the next logical step. But I was at least as fascinated by money as I was with my wife, and I worked a lot of hours, including weekends."

Catrina turned in her seat to face him. "What happened to the marriage?"

"Aside from the workaholic husband? Things fell apart when she realized she didn't want to be my sub anymore."

"Wait. What? Sub? You left out whole chunks of the story."

"Frustrating, isn't it?"

At his pointed question, she collapsed against the seatback. "I get it."

After a few seconds, he relented. "A bunch of us frat brothers flew to a friend's bachelor party in Vegas. We went to a BDSM club. It was my first visit, and I was hooked. I'd known I had Dominant urges, but until that night, I didn't have a term for it. My girlfriends had just thought I was an overbearing jerk. They were probably right."

"You bossed them around?"

"And ordered them to suck my dick while I pulled on their tits." He had the good grace to wince. "I'm not proud of it."

"Now you make women beg for the privilege."

"I hope my technique has improved over the years."

"Yes." Heat rushed through her as she recalled the ultimate, crashing satisfaction he'd given her. "I can say it has."

"It didn't come easily. I joined a BDSM club out by the old airport. At a demo one evening, the instructor suggested Doms try switching roles. I wish I could say it was my idea, but one of my subs told me I should give it a try."

"Sounds as if you had a rough go of it, ego-wise."

"When you're told your sexual tactics are in need of improvement? But she was right. Getting a swipe from a cane taught me that I should be a bit more careful with how I wielded one."

She shuddered. Canes intimidated her. It was part of the reason she didn't use one unless her boy requested it. "Was the sub Margot?"

"No." He glanced her direction. "I met Margot at a concert, and by then I was upfront about my lifestyle and what it entailed. The idea of doing something scandalous thrilled her, at least initially. After we were married, she didn't find it as exciting. She was bored and restless because of the amount of time she was spending alone. And being my slut princess every night when I got home close to midnight lost its appeal. She found someone less demanding and more available."

"I wonder how that's working out."

"She misses it."

She studied his profile. "How do you know that?"

"Ran into her recently at a dinner party."

The information swam through her mind. And was there something more there, a hint of possessiveness that she didn't have a right to? "You haven't seen each other in...years? And the two of you immediately had a discussion about BDSM?"

"She brought it up."

"That's surprising."

For a brief moment, he took his gaze from the road to flick a pointed glance in her direction. "I don't scene with married women, unless their husbands are there. And her fourth husband, Larry, has no intention of letting her anywhere near me."

"Fourth?"

"She's still looking for something she can't find."

"But knowing she obviously still thinks about you, can you blame him for being jealous?"

"He's a retired pro wrestler. Could still pile-drive me straight into the ground."

"Ouch." The ridiculous image made her laugh. "I'd stay away, too. Seriously, no lasting repercussions from the divorce? You haven't remarried."

"No need." He paused before adding, "I have my businesses. And I'm fortunate to enjoy the company of beautiful women."

When the unwelcome envy slithered back in, she shoved it to the back of her mind where it couldn't bother her.

They had a superficial, two-week deal. Nothing more.

Her life was full, with her career and men who wanted to worship her.

Clearly, she and Damien were both enjoying their lives.

Still, she couldn't resist saying, "Seems a little superficial, maybe even lonely."

"We all make our choices. And everything comes with consequences, Catrina."

She crossed her legs. The man had a way of saying things that made her see her own life, as if he were holding up a mirror in front of her.

"There are times when I'd prefer the company of others. That's part of why I have the Den along with a circle of close friends. I've no desire to marry again."

"I thought you performed Julia and Master Marcus's wedding ceremony."

"It was an honor to do so."

Before she could ask another question, he held up a hand to stop her and added, "Don't get me wrong. I understand why some may choose to do so, and I respect all of those reasons, especially the legal and financial ones. But once was enough for me."

"You were hurt?"

"Loss is never an easy thing." He shrugged.

They both lapsed into silence, and she contemplated what he said. A few minutes later, she asked, "If I'm understanding correctly, you two bought the mountain property Den as second home?"

"Correct."

"How did you end up with the house?"

"Gregorio had..." He paused before continuing, "borrowed the place while we weren't using it."

What hadn't he said while he carefully chose his words?

"And he thought it might have business potential, so I bought out Margot's interest. For considerably more than actual value."

"But it meant so much to her."

"She actually bought something in Aspen."

He must have made her a hell of a deal.

"The place is much better suited to her personality."

Catrina had visited the fancy alpine ski town once, during the summer. Her usual syrupy, chocolate-laced drink was three times the price she paid in Denver. And even at sale prices, she hadn't been able to afford to shop in the town's beautiful stores. Window shopping, however, had been a blast, even if the cost of parking had also been prohibitive.

"The Den turned out to be a solid investment," he said.

"It's a big place when you're there alone."

He acknowledged her statement with a short nod.

"You don't miss having someone to share it with?"

"As I said, there are trade-offs."

More curious than ever about the enigmatic man, she focused on his profile. "Are you afraid of falling in love again?"

"That seems like a romantic question, coming from you."

"Ironic, isn't it?" She shrugged.

"In answer to your question… Afraid? No. Truth is, I was never in love to begin with."

His answer took her aback. "Never?"

"As I said, getting married seemed like the next logical step. I cared for her deeply. I was committed to her. Ultimately that wasn't enough for either of us. Anything beyond affection never entered the equation."

"You don't believe in happily ever after?" she persisted.

"I haven't thought about it much, but no. I suppose not. You?"

She'd much rather ask questions than answer them. "I used to."

Damien allowed the silence to grow and stretch, waiting for her to go on.

Uncomfortably, she shifted.

Because he'd been forthcoming, how could she be less so? Besides, the clock had already started ticking. In less than two weeks, they'd go back to their previous relationship. She'd be a Domme at his club, nothing more.

The thought hurt, even though it shouldn't.

"Years ago, I was engaged, and I believed that we were partners in everything. So I supported his dreams. That's what couples do, right?"

With his infinite patience, he didn't respond. Instead, he waited.

"He rewarded me by clearing out my checking account and vanishing."

"Jesus." He winced. "You didn't deserve that."

"It helped me become the person I am." She wrinkled her nose, wishing she hadn't learned the hard way. "And then I had a long-term boyfriend. We were not exactly..." She sought an explanation that wouldn't reveal too much, but that was honest. "We didn't connect in the bedroom."

"The issue was him."

The force in Damien's tone made her blink.

"You're amazingly responsive, Milady."

She appreciated his loyalty. "At the end, he took exception to my attempt to...liven things up." Catrina stopped short of telling him the rest...that she'd seen a horrible side to Todd that she hadn't anticipated.

"There's more to it." He nodded to her wrist that she was absently stroking.

"Yeah. Like I said, he didn't appreciate my efforts." Even now, the memory embarrassed her, and she didn't like to replay it. "Reacted badly."

"An understatement?"

"You might say that."

"Did he hurt you?"

How did Damien manage to see so much, read between the lines. "Nothing that required the cops or anything." The bruises had healed in less than two weeks, but the emotional pain lingered. "Maybe I should have let him know what to expect. If I'd known then what I know now..."

"I've seen you with your boys. I'm betting whatever it was, he overreacted."

"Maybe." The same thing she'd wondered. "But he caught me off-guard, and I never wanted to experience anything like that again, so I told him to pack up his stuff and get out."

"And...?"

"He had a few choice words for me." This part was awful, too. "I probably deserved them." Though she hoped never to be called those vile names ever again.

"Lines of communication need to be kept open."

"Agree."

"Physically hurting your partner because you're pissed is never the right response."

"Which is one reason I like BDSM. Rules are clearer. Expectations are set."

"No messy emotions, right?"

She would have agreed with that assessment…until she met Damien.

And now, everything inside her was topsy-turvy.

When they neared the city, she directed him to her bungalow.

"Nice area," he said.

"Yeah. I love Wash Park. Great for people-watching. Lots of dog walkers, coffee shops, boutiques, and lunch places."

"Are you hungry again?" His lips quirked into a half smile.

"No," she fired back. Then, maybe not smartly, she added, "I haven't burned any calories."

"I'll rectify that situation." Because they were at a stop light, he turned to look at her with smoldering eyes. "In fact, let's get started right now."

"Now?" Her echo emerged as a high-pitched squeak.

What did he have in mind, and why could she never resist the opportunity to say something smart, instead of keeping her mouth shut?

"No time like the present. Unzip your jeans."

"Uh…"

"Are you going to make me repeat myself, Catrina?"

Chapter Thirteen

"This will be much worse for you if you don't do what you're told."

His tone dripped with seriousness.

"But people might see!"

"Final warning."

Never in a million years had she even considered behaving this way. And now she was prepared to do what her Dom demanded.

Fingers shaking, she followed his command.

"Now masturbate."

Before the light turned green, he reached into the back seat and grabbed a blanket that he placed over her lap.

"Thank you."

Trust.

She should have suspected he wouldn't have done anything to truly humiliate her. But her belief in him deepened even further.

Every day, she learned something more from him.

"Now masturbate yourself. Don't come. Otherwise you'll think I went easy on you last night."

Is this really happening?

"Get on with it."

Trying to give directions while he drove was about impossible.

Maybe because he'd forbidden her to orgasm, she was breathless in under five minutes.

Damnably, he continued past her street to prolong her agony. "Oh, Damien."

"Problem?" His grin was as wicked as his tone was curious.

When she was whimpering, breathing hard, he finally pulled into her driveway.

"Keep your hand where it is." After turning off the engine, he walked around to her side of the vehicle to open the door. "Now..." He leaned in, blocking any sight of her and stealing oxygen that she needed to breathe. "Let me lick your fingers."

Her heart thumping, she locked her gaze on him and did as he said.

"So damn delicious." Slowly he released her. "You may zip up."

It took some maneuvering, but she finally managed to put herself together.

"Shall we?"

Once she was capable of moving, she pulled the lapels of her jacket tight against the early afternoon chill.

Because her hand was still trembling, she fumbled with her key.

"May I?" He reached around to help her.

"Thank you."

When they were sealed inside, she tried to see her house through his point of view. Considering how he lived, this wasn't anything special. "As you can see, I'm still working on it. A little at a time."

"I see why you bought it. Lots of potential. Fabulous location. And it's big."

"It takes a lot of my time," she agreed. "And money."

She shrugged out of her coat and accepted his, hanging both in a closet. "It's an investment, but I got it for a bargain-basement price."

"Solid thinking," he said. "I approve. Mind showing me around?"

The kitchen was the first room she'd remodeled. She had quartz countertops, top-of-the-line appliances, and she'd installed a window over the oversize sink.

"Great choices."

"The heartbeat of the house, right?"

"Or the bedroom," he countered, making her reel once more. "Nice backyard."

"Much better in summer when I have potted plants blooming and the trees have leaves."

He followed her into the living room.

Here, the hardwood floors were dull and splintered. "On the to-do list," she said. As was, eventually, building shelves to hold her knickknacks, photos, and her dozens—maybe even hundreds—of books. As it was, every surface was covered, with items stacked on top of one another.

Next up was her office.

"Nice job in here, too."

"This was the easiest room. Not a lot of trim work, and the floors were in fairly good shape since the previous owners had used it as a guest room. While I'm here, I might as well grab my files and computer."

Catrina didn't excuse her clutter.

She was a creative thinker who left notes and ideas in every corner.

He held a large pink tote steady while she filled it. "What do you do, exactly?"

"I'm a financial advisor." She tossed her favorite pen on top of the folders. "For women."

"A job choice you made after your former fiancé wiped out your bank account?"

"You were listening."

"To every word you say."

And he did a great job at adding the pieces for a more complete picture. "After I recovered from the shock, I used his betrayal as motivation." She met his gaze. "I dug out, working two jobs. One of them was at night and weekends as a server to restore my savings. Then I figured out what I needed to do in order to open my business. Now I specialize in helping others to rebuild or carry on after the loss of the primary earner. It's estimated that ninety to ninety-five percent of women, at some point, will be solely responsible for their finances. So understanding, planning, and literacy is really important."

"I admire you. You took something painful for you and used it for good."

"Wasn't just for me," she admitted. "My mom, too." She smiled at the memory. "She was my case study. If you can get your mother to listen, you're doing okay. She's always believed in me, but to do what I said with the small amount of funds that she did have... She made a plan, set some objectives, read a whole bunch of prospectuses, did some research on her own. She's still a few years away from being able to retire, but I got her to double the amount of money she thought she might need."

"Impressive."

"Most times, women are not prepared for the shock of their loss, and then you throw in retirement funds, or lack thereof, debt ratios, bills…" She shrugged. "I get most of my business through referrals, and I have a group that meets monthly where women set goals and share their frustrations, help one another with strategies."

"Different approach than I've seen men use."

"Turns out the sexes are different, Mr. Lowell."

He arched a dark, sexy eyebrow. "Are they indeed?"

She put her computer in a backpack, grabbed her phone charger then led the way back to the living room. Part of her couldn't believe she was going to do this.

"I want to see your bedroom."

"I'm just going to throw a few things in a bag," she said when he placed the tote near the front door. In his hand, it didn't look at all feminine. Ignoring his statement, she added, "You're welcome to watch television or have a drink while you wait. I have beer in the fridge."

Not surprisingly, he followed her. "Where do you keep your lingerie?"

She sighed and pointed to the dresser. "Third and fourth drawers."

"Grab your suitcase."

Since there was no point in arguing, she did as he said.

He selected a few items and tossed them on her bed. "Shoes?"

Never had anyone packed for her before. "In my closet."

He added a pair of stupid-high sandals to the growing pile.

Surrendering to the inevitable, she gathered her toiletries from the master bathroom while he started going through her street-safe clothes.

"When you play with your subs, do you go to their place, or do they come here?"

"They come here."

"Where do you play?"

Catrina knew where this was going, and butterflies danced in her tummy. "The other bedroom."

"Do you want to show me?"

"That's..." She hesitated.

"Private? Your domain?"

"Yes."

"Is it important for you to keep it that way?"

With as turned on as she was...

"The choice is yours. No matter what you decide, I will one hundred percent respect your decision."

He wound his fist in her hair and brought her in close for a scalding kiss.

When he ended it, she wondered if she could deny him anything...

Damien's cock throbbed.

Catrina, gorgeous, innocent, and skeptical, appealed to him on so, so many levels. Her eyes were as green as they were revealing.

And with her face being devoid of makeup, she hid nothing from him.

All her concerns lay exposed in the depth of her eyes.

Unwilling to push, he proceeded with caution. Being dominated in her own space had to seem strange. "We could try...stop anytime it was too uncomfortable."

"I..." She twisted her hands together. "Yes."

Making this easier for her, he acted, picking her up and tossing her over his shoulder.

"What are you thinking?" She squealed around a laugh. "You'll break your shoulder carrying me."

"I could do this all day, Milady. And I might." He swatted her upturned derrière.

"Damien!"

Undeterred by her little kicks, he strode to the end of the hallway.

He carried her past a beautiful black screen that hid a kneeling bench. The gorgeous piece appeared to be an antique. Carved from rosewood, if his guess was correct. In addition to an angled velvet-covered pad, the narrow upright part had ornate scrollwork along with a thick, velvet rest for elbows.

Perfect.

Treating her like the princess she was to him, he gently placed her on the floor next to it. "Take off your shoes, please."

She hesitated.

"Something wrong?"

"I don't know." She shook her head. "You'll think my brain isn't firing on all cylinders."

"BDSM brings up a lot of things for participants."

"I guess..." She tipped her head back to look at him. "This makes it... I don't know. More real."

Quietly he waited for her to continue.

"At the Den, even your quarters, allowed me to compartmentalize this better. Sceneing there is expected. Right? But this is where I'm in charge and plan what happens."

"That makes complete sense."

At his reassurance, her shoulders relaxed. In relief?

"I think I want to try."

"Safe word anytime."

Slowly, she nodded before removing her boots.

"I know this isn't easy. And I appreciate you."

"That helps, Damien. Thank you."

Her approval would fire his Dominant dreams for weeks. "Now the rest of your clothing."

He offered his hand for support, and she accepted.

Within minutes, she was radiant in her nakedness and vulnerability.

And he was fucking humbled.

"When you're ready, please put your hands behind your head and spread your legs."

"Are you... Are you going to inspect me, Damien?"

"I am."

Hardly breathing, she continued to look ahead.

"You doing okay?"

"Struggling to know how to act."

At the Den, he'd taken charge, kept things moving. This was more like a scene he'd have with someone he was in a long-term relationship with.

Forcibly he reminded himself this was a temporary arrangement.

All he wanted to do was give her the total experience of submitting.

Nothing more.

"Are you tempted?"

"To?" She looked at him.

"Cast your gaze at the floor."

"No." The word was all-but a breathless whisper.

"As an acknowledgment that I'm your Dom."

This time, she didn't respond at all.

But as he circled her, she lowered her head.

Had anything ever turned him on more? "Lovely, Catrina."

He stopped in front of her and trailed his fingers down her chest, between her ribs, down her stomach.

Even though she was silent, she trembled at his touch.

Slowly, very slowly, he continued on, moving lower, until he parted her feminine folds.

She jerked.

He loved the way she reacted to him.

"Slide yourself back and forth over my finger."

After a slight hesitation, she nodded. "Yes, Damien."

With her eyes closed, she moved her pelvis against his hand.

"That's it. Pretend you're fucking it."

"I—"

"Don't think. Let things flow between us."

Catrina worried her lower lip.

After a few seconds, she began to gyrate her hips.

"That's it."

Within thirty seconds, she bent her knees a little, no longer held herself as rigid.

"Beautiful." He slipped a finger into her heat. "Keep moving."

With a moan, she complied.

In that instant, she'd managed to let go of her thoughts and surrender.

There was nothing more sensational than this moment.

"Come for me, Catrina." Because of her trust, she deserved it. And so much more.

"Damien…" Opening her eyes, she grabbed hold of him for support.

Then, rising on to her toes as he found her G-spot, she again called out his name.

"Take it."

Whimpering, she came, and he wrapped an arm around her waist to support her as her body crumpled. "So perfect."

He pulled out his finger and gathered her close, never wanting to let her go.

Because she was still shaking, he picked her up and carried her to a chair where he sat with her in his lap.

"I didn't know I could come this many times," she told him a few minutes later, her cheek pressed to his chest.

"We're consuming some of those calories so I can take you to lunch later."

"A man after my heart." She smiled up at him.

Am I?

When her breathing returned to normal, he said, "Ready to try the bench?"

She looked at it, then back at him. "You could just give me another dozen orgasms?"

"And I will."

Fire banked her eyes.

"But the next ones you'll have to earn."

"Spoken like an evil Dom."

"Is there any other kind?" he replied.

He eased her from his lap and ensured she was stable on her feet.

"Are your toys in the closet?"

She nodded.

"Anything off limits? Reserved for certain subs?" If she were his, he'd take her shopping for implements he'd never share with anyone else.

"No. My boys generally bring their own if there's something they prefer."

"Anything in particular you want to try?"

"Quite frankly? No. I've never given it much thought."

"Mmm. No curiosity at all?"

Red seeped into her cheeks. "I bought all of them for a man's tougher hide."

"I think you'll find yours is much less delicate than you might imagine."

"I was afraid you would say that." She tightened her ass cheeks.

He crossed to the closet and found all of her toys arranged in order.

Within seconds, he pulled out a flogger then selected a cane. When he turned back to her, she was kneeling as he'd instructed.

She looked exquisitely beautiful, her knees on the red velvet, her elbows on the top rail, her palms pressed together, with her long hair flowing around her.

He'd always thought she was beautiful. But now she took his breath away.

Her submission—no matter how temporary—was an incredible gift, one he'd forever cherish.

If he had his way, he'd keep her on that thing forever. "Ever felt a cane?" he asked quietly.

Her eyes widened.

"It can be vicious, leaving a terrible mark." He paused. "But it doesn't have to be. You no doubt have subs who desire varying degrees of intensity."

"Of course." Her voice wavered.

"I've played with subs — male and female — who find they love the cane more than any other toy."

"I'm skeptical."

"Timing and arousal and location all factor in. Certain body parts are more sensitive than others. And of course, the way it's wielded matters more than anything."

"I'm not sure I'm buying what you're selling, Damien." Her gaze was riveted on the thin, reedy piece of rattan.

"You have a safe word if you don't want to try it."

"It's a long drive back to your place, and I want to be able to sit comfortably."

Watching her squirm the whole way would be its own, sweet reward.

"And I'm sure you'll want to play again over the next two weeks."

"A persuasive argument." He grinned at her very submissive ploy. "But one that won't work."

"I'm curious enough to try, but I'm saying yellow before we even get started."

"Fair enough."

"Let's get this over with."

"My pleasure." And he intended to make sure it was hers, too. After brushing aside her hair, he kissed her nape.

With a sigh, she relaxed a little.

"I'm going to start by flogging your back."

"I thought…"

"I wouldn't attempt the cane with you being so worried or without warming you up."

He moved all her hair across her left shoulder, and softly said, "I'm marking you as mine, Catrina."

She interlaced her fingers so hard that her knuckles whitened.

He trailed the broad, thin strands over her exposed skin. "What would you do to relax an uptight sub, Milady?"

"I'd keep talking to him," she said. "And I'd start easy."

"Would you?" Slowly, he used the flogger on her, allowing it to fall with a gentle sway. "How would you know if your technique was working?"

"His breathing would change. He may perspire a bit..."

"Then what?"

"His muscles wouldn't be quite as tight. So I'd be able to actually see that he wasn't as nervous as he had been."

Her grip began to loosen.

Since her skin was starting to appear dewy, he made his hits more random, across her back, her buttocks, even her feet. He took a step back so he could get more leverage on his swing to give the blows more impact.

She allowed her head to fall forward a little.

"You're doing well, Milady." *You're mine.* Surrendered.

When she was completely relaxed, he switched out the flogger for a cane and quietly told her he'd done so.

With the tip, he tapped the soles of her feet.

She curled her toes and her body tensed.

"Nothing unexpected or that you won't enjoy." Leaning in, he skimmed her neck with kisses. At the Den, she'd wanted to be surprised, but he wouldn't do that to her today.

"Oh..."

Part of him wanted to scoop her up, carry her to bed, and fuck her hard.

Instead, he moved back again. "On your gorgeous behind."

She tightened, then intentionally loosened her muscles. Only then did he lay a few light stripes across her buttocks.

"Uhm. Ah..."

"Too much?" But he was guessing it wasn't.

"I..."

"You?" he prompted. He continued his strokes, not adding a lot of variety.

"*Like.* Like this."

Impossibly, his cock hardened even more. This woman, beautiful in all ways, thrilled him. He yearned to hold her, cherish her. "Keep trusting me, Milady."

"Yes..."

"Your feet?"

She wiggled her toes but didn't protest.

With the lightest of motions, he struck her soles.

"Oh..."

He stroked between her thighs, and she obediently parted them.

Her pussy was wonderfully damp. "Would you like to come for me?"

She didn't respond, but she shifted against his hand, silently imploring him.

He gave her his full attention, smiling when she wiggled and moaned.

"Damien, Damien, Damien." She didn't pause, making his name sound like a chant.

Stopping what he was doing, he used the cane three more times on her reddened butt cheeks, making her writhe before he set down the rattan and dropped to his knees behind her, fingering her pussy, playing with her clit, satisfying her as completely as she deserved.

Less than two minutes later, sobbing, she came, drenching his hand with her climax.

After removing his hand, he soothed her, kissed her.

And when she started to shake, he picked her up from the bench and carried her into the living room. He shoved aside a blanket and several magazines before sitting on the couch and pulling her toward him.

Cradling her tight, he stroked her hair and uttered soothing words, cherishing her.

"That was…"

Curious, he waited.

"Amazing."

Her answer, along with the way she'd reacted to his physical domination, turned him on. This woman, independent and strong, yet so trusting in his arms, was starting to get to him.

She twisted slightly to look up at him. "If you'd have asked me if I was willing to try that, I would have refused. I had no idea the cane could be so stimulating or so wonderful."

"I hope to open a whole new world for you."

"You've already started."

A few minutes later, she excused herself to dress while he washed up and put her playroom back in order.

Before leaving, he gave the kneeling bench one last, fond glance.

Maybe he'd buy one of those for his own personal collection.

One thing was certain, two weeks with her wouldn't be enough.

When they met up in the living room, she'd secured her hair with a ribbon. The jeans clung to her hips, and she wore the same sexy boots.

Beneath her sweater, he made out the sight of her erect nipples. "No bra?"

"I figured you prefer it."

If it didn't kill him.

From across the room, her phone rang, and she found her purse to dig out the device.

"Anyone important?"

"It's my mom."

"You're allowed to talk to her." He grinned. "Unless of course you've misbehaved and I've shoved the penis gag in your mouth."

She gasped.

The phone rang a third time, and she turned her back to him to answer.

While she said hello to her mom, he carried her bag and backpack to the car and waited for her with the engine running.

A few minutes later, she locked the front door and knotted her jacket's belt as she walked. Every action she took radiated class and seduction. With the way she moved and her confidence, she could be a fashion model on a Paris runway.

She slid into the passenger seat. After closing the door, she turned to look at him. "Uhm…"

"Is there a problem, Catrina?"

Chapter Fourteen

"I hope not."

He waited.

"It seems we're having lunch with my mom and her new boyfriend."

"We are?" He watched her until she fastened the safety belt, then he eased away from the curb.

"Yeah. Sorry. I couldn't get out of it."

"I'm looking forward to it. Where are we going?"

"There's a brew pub at Denver west. Steaks aren't bad."

"You're hungry again?"

"You would be, too, if you'd been beaten."

"Good point." The farther west they drove on I-70, the quieter she became. He slid her a quick look. "Everything okay?"

"Yeah. Fine."

"It's okay to talk about it."

"My mom's getting married."

"Congratulations?"

"I've never met him."

A little lost by the conversation, he asked, "Is that a prerequisite?"

"You don't get it," she said, staring straight ahead.

Rather than argue, he suggested, "Enlighten me?"

"This is so out of character for my mom." Catrina was silent for so long that he thought she might not answer. "They've known each other less than six weeks. In fact, until recently, I didn't know she was dating. I don't know anything about him. Hell, she can't know anything about him. And they're already shacking up."

"Meaning, they're living together?"

"You say that like it's okay." She scowled.

"She is an adult, I presume. Of sound mind?"

"I thought so, until this."

Wondering why it suddenly felt as if he were navigating a minefield, he asked, "What's your concern?"

"I wish she'd slow down, make sure she's making wise decisions."

"You're assuming she's not."

"Whose side are you on, anyway?"

"Yours." He took her hand. "Always."

Catrina reclined her seat a little. "She made a disastrous decision with my dad."

"That was at least twenty-five years ago, unless I'm mistaken." He waited until she nodded to confirm his guess. "Other than that, does she have a bad track record?"

"No. She's dated a little, and she's had some long-term relationships. But that doesn't mean I like this. What if he's a gold digger?" She drummed her fingers on the dashboard. "He's probably trying to take advantage of her. You know, one of those men who drain women and then dump them."

"I don't blame you for being concerned."

"Really?"

He exited the highway at Colfax. At a red light waiting to turn left, he flicked his thumb across her fluttering pulse.

"It's just sudden. Do you think I'm overreacting?"

"No. I think you care. I think you want her to be as cautious as you'd be."

"Thanks for that."

The light turned green, and he accelerated. "Does she know I'm with you?"

"Yes. You're a business associate whom I've known for a few years. We see each other from time to time. Nothing serious."

"That works." He nodded. "Close to the truth."

"Better than telling her you made me strip and kneel before caning me then using your fingers to get me off."

"Good call." They exchanged grins, and he saw her vulnerability beneath her tough-girl exterior. He wanted to see that more and more.

Her mother and boyfriend were already seated at a table with large mugs of beer on the table when Catrina and Damien arrived.

"When did you start drinking beer?" Catrina asked with a scowl after introductions were performed.

"I've developed quite a taste for it," Evelyn said.

"So fast?" Catrina kissed her mother on the cheek but limply shook Milton's hand. Damien pinched her ass before they sat down. "Behave," he warned against her ear.

Catrina shuddered, but she didn't protest.

Evelyn, bursting with enthusiasm, started talking about their upcoming wedding plans. The woman surprised him in some ways. Both she and her daughter were tall and slender, but Evelyn was as outgoing and vivacious as Catrina was reserved. It made him double his determination to break through her shell, prove the world wasn't an unsafe place.

The server dropped off menus and silverware then nodded when Catrina ordered red wine. Damien took Milton's advice and asked for the house amber ale.

"Traitor," Catrina whispered.

"Brat," he responded with a smile. Then he looked at Evelyn. "When's the big day?"

"In three months," Evelyn said.

"Three *months*?" Catrina repeated.

"The chapel isn't available any earlier than that."

"Any earlier? You just met," Catrina responded. "What's the rush?"

"Young lady, I assure you we don't have to get married," Milton said with a grin.

Catrina's eyes widened.

"Miltey! *Behave!*" Evelyn scolded, but she ruined it by laughing, and the two clinked their beer glasses together.

"So will it be a large wedding?" Damien asked.

"Small," Milton said. "Several hundred guests or so."

Catrina straightened her spine.

"He's kidding, my Cat," Evelyn hastened to reassure her. "We're only inviting those closest to us."

"How did you meet, anyway?" Catrina asked.

The engaged couple looked at each other, then Milton nodded.

"Miltey and I met online."

"Oh my God." Catrina's face drained of color. "Mom? Don't you know how dangerous that is?"

"Of course I do." She scowled. "I joined an online group that has a page where you can ask about men you're interested in. It's called Date Him or Dump Him? Let me tell you, the stories I hear. Some men have all the red flags. Like at a circus."

"I…" Catrina floundered. "Is this really happening right now?"

"What? Did you expect us to say we met playing bingo?" Milton deadpanned.

Damien already liked the man.

"He sent me a flirty little heart icon. And I swiped up." She frowned. "Or down. Whatever it was."

"You captured mine the minute I set eyes on you."

The pair made eye contact as if no one else were there. Catrina played with her rolled-up silverware, her face pale.

Recognizing how difficult this was for her, Damien placed a reassuring hand on her knee. She went still for a moment then, hesitantly, she swirled her fingertips across his knuckles.

How long had it been since he'd had this kind of intimate interaction with a woman?

Had it ever happened?

Less than a minute later, the server dropped off drinks and took food orders.

During their meal, Damien took charge of the conversation, keeping it light, away from the things that were upsetting to Catrina.

"What kind of business are you in, Damien?" Milton asked.

It was his and Catrina's turn to exchange glances.

"Mostly investments."

"So, that's how you and my Cat met?" Evelyn guessed.

"We share similar interests," he replied as he squeezed Catrina's thigh.

"Well, Cat, you're welcome to bring a guest to the wedding." Evelyn looked at Damien before taking another drink of beer. "Damien can be your plus one. Say you'll come."

Catrina's eyes were wide, and she quickly replied, "Damien's a busy man, Mother."

"Well, if you're free that day, we'd love to have you," Evelyn said.

Further conversation was interrupted by the arrival of the bill, and he and Milton wrangled for the honor.

As he pulled out his credit card, Damien promised to let Milton pay the next time they all went out.

And he realized he'd enjoy that.

In the restaurant's foyer, they all exchanged goodbyes and promises to get together again soon, and Evelyn repeated her wedding invitation.

Catching Catrina's frown, he gave a noncommittal reply.

Finally, outside, his temporary submissive turned her collar up against a sudden burst of wind.

"You didn't need to pick up the bill. The restaurant could have split it up for us."

"It was my pleasure."

"I'll pay you back," she said as they walked to the car.

"Don't piss me off, Catrina."

She missed a step, and he took her elbow as he bit back his flare of temper.

"It's okay to let people do things for you."

"I… I mean…"

"Let me do things for you."

"That's…"

"Unusual?" he guessed.

"And…"

He really had thrown her for an emotional loop.

"I like paying for myself."

"Keeps things more equitable? You don't owe any man for anything?"

"How do you do that?" She scowled. "Know me so well? Lucky guesses?"

"No." Damien shook his head. "Putting together the complex puzzle that you are."

They arrived at the car, and he touched a button to unlock her door, but when she reached for the handle, he curved his hand around her wrist. "Allow me."

Her shoulders notched up a fraction of an inch.

"I enjoyed myself with your mom and Milton." He captured a stray lock of her hair that the wind had dislodged. "And with you."

Slowly he wound the strands around a finger. "When you're with me, I like taking care of you."

"But—"

"You will owe me nothing. We're always equals." He leaned in a little bit, and her lips were so kissable, temping. "Surely when you're advising clients, you tell them to be generous, but also to be gracious when others do things for you?"

"That's different."

"How so?" When she didn't respond, he added, "Try saying thank you, and allowing me to show you some appreciation."

After blinking a couple of times, she nodded. "Thank you. I'll pay for the next meal."

"Nice try, Catrina." He released her hair. "But hell no." With that, he opened her car door, waited for her to get settled then sealed her inside.

"I'm not used to any of this," she admitted once they were exiting the parking lot.

"Our two weeks together are about learning. Which is why I won't give you a spanking for continuing to challenge me on this."

She shifted in her seat.

At least the argument was over, and they were back in familiar territory.

A few minutes later, he headed west on the interstate.

They were nearing Lookout Mountain before she spoke again. "Do they still do that part in a wedding ceremony where the minister asks if anyone objects when a couple gets married?"

"I'm afraid not."

"What harm is there in them waiting until they know each other better?"

"How long is that?" he asked.

She tugged on her safety belt. "I don't know."

"A year? Five years?"

"Longer than a few weeks."

"If it's right, it's right. Time doesn't make a lot of difference when it comes to matters of the heart. You can know in two weeks if you want to be with someone. And you can still be uncertain after five years."

"After our earlier conversation, I hadn't figured you were a romantic."

"More of a realist," he countered.

She wrinkled her nose. "I'm not sure how you consider that realistic."

"Doesn't it somewhat depend on how they spent their time together? What if they've been talking? Sharing their secrets and dreams." He paused. "Being intimate."

"Eww. If you mention the fact my mother may be having sex, I promise you that I will wash your mouth out with soap."

"If they are living together, it makes sense that they're doing the—"

"No." She put her hands over her ears. "Just...no."

He chuckled.

After a deep breath, she nodded. "I'll talk to her about protecting her financial interests. Maybe I'll suggest a prenuptial agreement. I have a couple of lawyers I can recommend."

"Or consider the possibility she knows what she's doing."

She exhaled. "You don't ask much."

"Look, Catrina. She raised you to be a strong, capable woman. I think she did okay."

"I'm not sure what to say about that. I think it's supposed to be a compliment."

"Do you think you'd be able to change your mother's mind?"

"About *Miltey*?"

"Give him a chance. He's done nothing wrong." He shrugged. "Except, in your opinion, move too fast. But that may be your mom, as well. Maybe she's been lonely?"

Leaning forward, she turned up the heat on her side of car. "He seems nice enough. Which is why I'm suspicious."

"You'd be suspicious no matter what."

"You might be right about that. And there probably is no way to change my mother's mind, no matter what I say."

"Agree. If things do end badly, you can support her."

"True."

"And if you're wrong, doesn't she deserve happiness after everything she'd been through and the sacrifices she's made?"

She folded her hands in her lap. "That's harsh."

"Untrue, though?"

"You know it's not."

Then she stunned him by reaching across the cab to place her fingers lightly on his forearm.

"Thank you," she said. "For going with me without argument. I appreciate it. Having you there helped me. A lot."

"Anything for you, Milady." He was surprised how much he meant it. "I enjoyed myself. I liked Milton's sense of humor, and your mom's a firecracker."

Now, she was more relaxed, seemingly giving the couple a break. "She volunteers for a hundred different things. And she is still a substitute teacher."

Catrina removed her hand. For safety, that was probably a good thing. Her feminine touch was magic, but it was a hell of a distraction.

After a short discussion, they agreed to stop at a grocery store in Evergreen.

He picked up a basket and headed for the produce section as he asked, "How are your feet? You okay to walk through the whole store?"

"Thanks for the reminder." She shook her head. "They were fine until you reminded me of your wickedness."

"More in store for you later, Milady."

Momentarily she closed her eyes.

"Bananas?" he asked, holding up a bunch.

"You're impossible, Damien."

They wandered each aisle, and she compared price per ounce on almost all products.

When she reached for a less expensive version of the cream she liked, he grabbed the quart and added it to the basket.

"Damien! That's not necessary."

"It is. You should enjoy every morning coffee."

"Items are a lot more expensive up here than they are in town."

"Cost of living in paradise."

"In that case…" At the checkout counter, she added three bars of chocolate to their purchase. "This will help keep my energy up."

"And because of that…" He tossed another one on top.

By the time they arrived home, the sun had already set, and the sky resembled inky velvet.

"This is a whole different place when there's no party here. Peaceful."

Though the grounds were brilliantly lit, the house was mostly dark. A light was on in Gregorio's quarters across the way. Other than that, it seemed they were on a hundred acres of deserted land. The way he liked it.

After parking his vehicle in the garage, he grabbed the groceries and her luggage.

"May I help with some of that?"

"Open that door. We'll take the back stairs."

"You can come and go as you please without anyone knowing you're here," she said when they reached the top. "Like a superhero."

He juggled groceries and set down her bag to unlock the door to their suite. "After you."

"Wait, give me a minute. I'm enjoying the image of you in a cape and a sculptured suit. I'm thinking tight pants, too. More like leggings. Really tight."

With a grin, he said, "I'll give you something else to enjoy."

"Will you, Sir?" Her voice purred with sensuality and sass.

How many hours had it been since he fucked her? Not that the answer mattered. It had been too damn long, and his cock was suddenly making him aware of that fact.

He put down the shopping bags, dropped her luggage then took hold of her shoulders and backed her against the wall. "Open your mouth for me." He leaned in. "I'm going to give you something else to do with that tongue of yours."

Eyes wide, she followed his command.

He traced her lips with his thumb, and when her eyes fluttered shut, he took hold of her wrists and pinned them above her head. "That's my girl."

"Damien…"

He kissed her, tasting the first hint of resistance then the sweetness of her response as she opened her mouth wider.

Their tongues mated, and he insinuated his leg between her thighs.

Needing her, Damien plundered her depths, teasing, retreating then advancing again, deeper.

As her body relaxed, she rubbed herself against his thigh.

His Catrina was so responsive, and he loved uncovering her fire.

Softly, she moaned.

He propped his knee higher, granting her silent permission to take what she wanted.

Her movements became faster, and she ended the kiss before burrowing her head into his shoulder.

"Ride me."

She made tiny circular motions against his leg, fucking herself, as she sought to get off.

Enjoying her immensely, he wrapped his arms around her to offer his support. "Come whenever you're ready."

Her breaths came in rapid little bursts. This beautiful woman was as hot for him as he was for her.

In under a minute, she cried out as she convulsed.

Releasing her wrists, he caught her against him.

Now that she was out of her own way, the guarded Catrina was nowhere around.

"How do you keep doing that?" she asked eventually. "An orgasm a week usually keeps me happy. Now I seem to need them every few hours."

Damien stroked his fingers lightly down her spine. "I'll give you as many as you want, Milady."

"You might be creating a monster here, Damien."

He grinned. "That's a chance I'm willing to take."

When she straightened and pulled back a little, he advised her to take as much time as she needed to unpack and settle in while he fetched her backpack and their remaining items from the car.

"I should help put away the groceries."

"No need."

When she opened her mouth to protest, he cocked his head to one side. "Take the opportunity I'm offering. You have a long night ahead of you."

"That sounds ominous."

"It might be."

With a shiver and a small nod, she dragged her suitcase toward the bedroom.

Over the years, he'd kept his suite private. But having Catrina here seemed natural and inevitable. He refused to consider how quiet and empty it might seem when she left.

Once everything was where it belonged, he carried her backpack to her temporary workspace.

In their absence, Gregorio had been in.

The empty brandy snifters were gone, and cables protruded through a hole in her desk. A printer stood on top of a wheeled stand, and office supplies were arranged in a pile next to an inbox.

Satisfied, Damien entered the bedroom to find her stowing her bag on the top shelf.

A few items hung from the hangers, and a drawer stood slightly ajar. He was inordinately pleased. "May I offer you a glass of wine?"

"Not if we're playing."

"We're not."

"Oh?" She blinked rapidly.

"We're listening to music, enjoying the fireplace, and seeing where the conversation leads."

"But I thought you brought me up here to be your submissive?"

"That's only part of a broader relationship."

"I didn't sign up for that."

"Yeah." He nodded. "You did."

"So...would you like me to change?"

"No." It was tempting, though. Since he'd been at her house and decided on the majority of things that had gone into her suitcase, he knew she had a corset that left her breasts bare.

But she was fine as she was. The fact that he could see the swell of her breasts and a faint outline of her nipples was enough for now.

"I'm afraid you're confusing me."

"Good." For her, this had to be unique. Her subs showed up, scened, then likely left.

After removing her boots, she followed him back into the living room.

"Red wine? Or white?"

"Either works for me. Why don't you surprise me, since you seem to be full of them today?"

He uncorked a bottle of his favorite and set it aside for a few minutes while he adjusted the blinds. She perched on the arm of the couch, watching him, with one leg crossed over the other at the ankle.

He flipped the switch to turn on the fireplace then selected a jazz station on the satellite system.

"Frank Sinatra?" she asked.

"Is that okay?"

"Fine. Just..." She paused and linked her hands on one thigh. "I don't know what I thought you'd choose, maybe classic rock. But not that."

"Were you thinking I'd strip you down, or better yet, dress you up?"

"Actually, yes."

"Maybe shackle your naked body while I arouse you to the point you're begging for release?"

She licked her upper lip. "Well..."

Foreplay took many different forms. With a grin, he poured them each a glass of wine.

She was on the couch when he turned back around, but she was pressed against the far side.

"We could watch television," she suggested. "A news show. Or surely there's some sporting event on.

Or maybe a movie. I'm even up for an action adventure, doesn't have to be a chick flick."

"No."

"No? That's pretty domineering."

"It is." He offered no excuse or apology. "Move a little closer to the middle, if you don't mind."

He sat and held her glass just a little out of reach.

"I'm on to your nefarious plan," she said when she'd moved.

"Are you?" He took a drink. "Do tell."

"All this is part of your idea of submission. And it's so different from mine that you're illustrating how complex it is."

"It's part of submission, how?"

She looked at him over the rim of the glass. "I'm guessing you're going to tell me a true sub doesn't get to hide any part of who they are."

"Well done. And yes, you're right. I want to know all about you. What makes your heart flutter? What things sneak up on you when you're trying to go to sleep?"

"I didn't agree to all this," she said.

"You did. You couldn't have imagined that I'd keep you tied up twenty-four hours a day."

"No?"

"Not that the idea is without merits. I love how your nipples harden when you're anticipating the touch of my leather. But I invited you to explore for a couple of weeks. I didn't invite you to my dungeon for a few random scenes."

"It *is* a nice dungeon."

"I'm glad you think so. But when I extended my invitation to you, I intended to share everything, a bed, an office, our time."

The wine sloshed in her glass.

He took the stemware from her and slid both glasses onto the coffee table. "And I'm happy you're here." He took her hand, raised it, and kissed her. Then, still holding her gaze captive, he gently bit her thumb.

She moaned and closed her eyes. "That's —"

"Just the beginning," he said. "Are you curious about what's next?"

Chapter Fifteen

Damien's words, combined with the delicious twinge from his bite, made her pussy tighten. He turned her on in ways no one else ever had.

She opened her eyes to find him staring not just at her, but seemingly inside her. The intensity of the blue chilled her, as if his were made of ice.

He was breathtakingly handsome, and she itched to pull that leather strip from his hair and run her fingers through its thick length.

As he'd planned, he'd turned her idea of submission inside out then he'd dumped it upside down. He made her question everything she'd thought she knew and had assumed.

She used D/s to keep her emotions separate from those of other people. He used it to pry inside. In ways she could never have imagined, he terrified her.

What happened at the end of the two weeks when she went back to her home in Washington Park? If she gave Damien what he wanted, what he demanded, she'd be stripped bare emotionally.

He'd go on with his life as if this had been nothing more than a diversion.

Although she'd hoped to drive home by herself, she'd enjoyed the short trip more than she expected, thanks to his company. Breakfast was wonderful, and so was grabbing a coffee to go. Having him be part of the foursome at lunch had made the time more tolerable. His little touches had helped keep her calm.

His silent strength and support would be normal in a real relationship, but she hadn't expected it from a temporary Dominant.

For the next couple of hours, while she was wondering what truly was next, they discussed mundane things.

She told him more about her business, and he answered questions that she'd had while he was talking to her mother and Milton earlier.

When she yawned, he said, "Let's go to bed."

Finally.

"Since I didn't pack any pajamas for you, you can borrow another of my T-shirts."

While he tidied up, she showered.

He was holding a towel for her when she stepped out.

"Thank you." She lifted her arms, and he wrapped it around her.

Sharing a bathroom was strangely intimate, but she didn't hate it.

He'd taken off his shirt, but his hair was still held back. His enormous biceps rippled tantalizingly as he moved.

The man was a paradox.

Damien possessed both enormous strength and resolve, yet he also displayed infinite tenderness. And with her mom and Milton, he'd been both kind and engaging.

And when they'd played at her home earlier...

It would have been easy for him to have used too much force with the cane, but he hadn't. Instead, every motion had been deliberate. Though his swats had stung a little, he'd aroused her to a fever pitch.

Their time together was changing her.

She just wished she knew whether or not it was for the best.

"Everything okay?"

Catrina shook her head to clear it. Spending too much time in her thoughts was not good for her. "Fine. I'm good."

With a nod, he left for a moment to grab a T-shirt from his closet, and she slipped it over her still damp and warm body.

After combing out her hair, she braided it while she sat cross-legged on the bed waiting for him.

"Don't think I'm not onto you," he said as he entered the room.

"I'm sorry?" She scooted against the headboard.

He stood only feet away, arms folded, naked, cock half-hard, legs spread about shoulder-width apart.

Naked, he was powerfully intimidating.

"Dropping your towel and clothes on the floor and leaving them."

"I apologize." When she'd done it, she'd been hoping to capture his attention, anything to shatter the angsty knot of emotion that crawled through her. "I'm afraid I can be a bit messy."

"No you're not. I visited your house, remember? Lived-in with magazines and all kinds of...stuff, but your dirty clothes were in a hamper and all of your toiletries were put away."

"Ah..."

"Are you hoping for a spanking?"

That, she understood.

"I'll let you think about it for a while," he said.

She exhaled a shaky, frustrated breath.

"We'll talk about it more before we agree on how we handle it."

Talking. His favorite punishment. "About that..."

He raised an eyebrow.

"Why don't we just get it over with?" The physical sensation would have to settle her.

"We will." He let his words hang in the air. "As soon as I say so. Ready for bed?"

Being with him was one of the most confounding experiences of her life.

He folded back the comforter then helped her beneath a blanket before turning off the lamp. "Come to me, Catrina."

Finally.

When he pulled her against him and wrapped his arms around her, she said, "There's no lesson for this evening?"

"You've already had it."

Frowning, wishing it wasn't dark so she could read his features, she said, "I'm not sure what you're talking about."

"The mundaneness of the afternoon and evening. Those are the moments where trust and intimacy are built."

"You frustrate me."

"Milady, I assure you the feeling is mutual. Now, rest."

"I don't snuggle, Damien."

"You do now."

"But—"

"Go to sleep."

His grip was unbreakable.

Less than two minutes later, his breathing pattern changed, indicating he was already asleep. How was that even possible?

Sighing, she started to inch away from him, but his hold tightened.

"Stop, my beautiful Catrina," he murmured against her ear. "This is a battle you can't win." To reinforce his point, he swung a leg over hers, trapping her in place.

Pinned, but oddly comforted, she gave in.

Today had been long, and nothing had gone the way she'd planned, from him dominating her in her house, caning her feet, meeting Milton, and introducing Damien to her mother, to spending the evening chatting in front of the fireplace.

And the next morning, when she opened her eyes, blinking against the bright sunlight pouring into the room, she was alone in the bed.

Placing her elbows beneath her, she lifted her head. "I think I'm seeing things," she said. "A Celtic god, maybe."

Did I say that out loud?

But that's what Damien reminded her of.

Light radiated around him, playing off his raven-dark hair and bright blue eyes.

Then she noticed something even more relevant—he was holding two cups of coffee. "Are you sharing?"

"Potentially."

"I'm willing to sell my soul."

"In that case, yeah." He lifted a cup as he started toward her. "This one has your name on it."

The mattress sank under his weight as he sat near her. "I didn't know whether to let you sleep or wake you up."

"Caffeine is always the right choice. And it's Monday, so I need to get to work." She accepted the handle and allowed the steam to bathe her face before taking the first sip of bliss. "But I guess I think I should be doing that for you."

"If you're up first, you're welcome to. But ensuring your happiness is a priority to me. You matter to me, Catrina."

Despite her wariness, he was systematically demolishing her resistance.

"I have a conference call with London in ten minutes. You're welcome to use your office or relax here. I can keep the call on my earbuds so as to disturb you as little as possible."

"I don't have any calls for a couple of hours," she said. "So don't worry about disturbing me."

"I'll see you in a while." With a wicked grin, he stood. "Even though this area is soundproof, don't think I won't know if you masturbate."

She hadn't even considered it. Now it was the only thing she could think about.

With a nod, he left.

If Catrina hadn't been afraid of spilling her coffee, she would have thrown a pillow at his retreating back.

After draining her cup, she took a quick shower to finish waking up.

Beneath the spray, standing there, soaping her body in the steamy warmth, her thoughts returned to Damien...

The way he touched her, spanked her, used the cane and flogger on her heated body, tormenting, licking her pussy until she grabbed his hair and forgot how to breathe.

She ached to slide her fingers between her folds to relieve her sexual tension...

"Don't do it."

Her knees weakened.

How did he do that?

"Your orgasms are mine to give or deny." To reinforce his point, he reached in to turn down the hot water, cooling the temperature as well as her desire.

The chill made her yelp. "Don't you have a call to take, or a company to acquire, something other than bothering me?"

"Beautiful nipples." He ignored her question completely. "Make sure you get them very clean."

Moments later, she was alone again.

Defiantly, she notched up the hot water again and enjoyed her last few minutes, even though she avoided touching herself.

After rinsing off, she discovered he'd left a fresh cup of coffee on the counter.

How could he be simultaneously annoying and tempting?

Half an hour later, she was dressed, had her hair in a messy bun, and caffeine had sharpened her mind.

Because she'd been denied an orgasm, her pussy seemed to throb.

Why hadn't he made love to her last night or this morning?

On the other hand, because he'd held her so comfortingly, she'd enjoyed one of the best nights' sleep ever.

Changing her mind about her outfit, she went back to her closet. Instead of jeans and a T-shirt, she wore a skirt and heels, stockings, and a garter belt.

Anything for his attention.

She sighed as she checked her reflection in the mirror.

Positive attention, she amended.

Before leaving their suite, she hung up her towel and dumped her discarded clothing into a hamper.

In the kitchen, a full pot of coffee stood on its burner.

Having someone else handle this chore was a blessing.

Maybe being here wasn't *all* bad.

Fresh cup of happiness in hand, she walked confidently to their shared office area.

When she arrived, breath whooshed from her lungs.

Over the years, she'd seen Damien at his sexy best, in leather, in a suit and tie.

Nothing had prepared her for this.

He stood in front of the monitors. One screen showed a glossy conference room table, presumably in England. The other was filled with the face of an aging, attractive gentleman, his tie loosened and askew. His face was drawn in tight lines that radiated his displeasure.

"I do understand, Malcolm, but that's my best, final offer. Look around you. I think the rest of the board will agree you have no choice but to accept."

A pulse ticked in the other man's temple.

Damien was a fucking badass. A hot, fucking badass.

His hair was secured at his nape, and his shoulders were pulled back. He was resolved, unshakable.

Little shivers danced through her.

Now she wished she'd masturbated in the shower, even if she risked his wrath.

She stayed toward the back of the room, out of view as she crossed to her own desk. Obviously having noticed her, he acknowledged her with a tight nod.

While she powered up her computer, she surreptitiously watched Damien in action.

Gregorio, she assumed, had provided everything else she'd need — a printer, paper, notepads, an assortment of pens, even a purple stapler.

A few moments later, his tone clipped, Damien delivered a deadline. "And you won't get a moment longer." With that, he pressed a button to end the call.

As she was checking her email, he joined her.

"Everything in order?"

"Yes, thanks."

"Let Gregorio know if you need anything else."

"Does he live here? Work here?" How little did she really know about the Den's second-in-command?

"He's around, at times."

His vague answer only intrigued her more.

"Join me for breakfast?"

"Sounds great."

In their shared kitchen, he prepared omelets with fresh veggies, and he whipped up a protein smoothie. That terrible-looking green thing with no fruit, she passed on.

Afterward, she offered to clean the kitchen. "To make up for the mess I left last night."

"Apology accepted."

"Really?" she asked over her shoulder as she rinsed a plate. He was at the table, long legs stretched in front of him.

"That doesn't mean I can't or won't deliver a secondary punishment at my discretion."

"I thought the fact you didn't let me masturbate in the shower was your chastisement."

"No. Simply an order because it pleased me. That's my prerogative."

A few minutes later, Gregorio gave a courtesy knock on the doorjamb as he entered. "Got coffee?"

This felt so…normal. It occurred to her she'd had no idea what happened at the Den during the week. She'd always figured the two showed up before an event and threw open the door for the debauchery to begin.

"Am I interrupting, Boss?"

"Come in," Damien invited.

As always, Gregorio radiated sex appeal. Even though it was a Monday, his diamond earring winked in the overhead light. As always, he was in all black.

Evidently his attire wasn't just an image he projected, it was part of who he was. All in all, this wasn't a bad place to work and spend two weeks.

"Morning, Milady," he said. "I like the fact you look like you could run a company but you're up to your elbows in soap suds."

"Damien cooked. So I'm cleaning."

"I think we have a French maid's outfit in the storeroom," Gregorio told Damien.

"Now there's a hell of an idea."

She dropped the silverware into the basket in the dishwasher with a horrific clatter.

"Bring it up," Damien said.

"No." She held up a hand as she turned to face the men. "Absolutely not."

Gregorio grinned, and the motion looked calculatedly diabolical.

"You seem delighted with yourself," she snapped out.

"I'm picturing it right now. My place needs to be dusted."

"Aren't you a switch?" she asked him.

"Oh, yeah."

"Then I'll get even with you for this."

"I'll bare my ass for you, Milady. As long as you don't hit like a girl."

"We can go downstairs anytime you are ready, Gregorio." And she would definitely be meting out a punishment rather than a pleasure beating.

"Boss?"

Damien put his cup on the table with a firm smack. "Fuck off."

"Figured." Shrugging easily, he poured himself a cup of coffee, refilled Damien's, then held up the pot near Catrina, as if it were a peace offering.

"With cream." She dried her hands on a towel. "If you gentlemen will excuse me, I have work to do." She grabbed her cup on the way out of the kitchen.

Settling into her chair didn't help her focus.

The entire space pulsed with Damien's presence, unnerving her.

Setting her jaw, she responded to her emails.

He didn't come into their shared office space until much later, when she was on a phone call with a client.

As he had before, he gave her a silent greeting before taking a seat behind his own desk.

They lunched together, without Gregorio, then returned to work.

Being this close to Damien, hearing the modulated tones of his voice, even if she couldn't make out the exact words, gave her a little thrill.

He looked at her numerous times, not interrupting, but letting her know he was aware of her.

Mid-afternoon, he approached her desk. "You dressed that way on purpose. After I told you not to play with yourself in the shower."

No sense in denying the truth. "Yes."

"Provocatively."

In silent agreement, she inclined her head to one side.

"What were you hoping I'd do to you?" When she sat back, once again without replying, he continued, "Hike up your skirt?"

Her breath caught.

He placed his palms on her desktop and leaned in, close, so close, marking her space as his.

No matter how hard she tried, she couldn't look away from his intense eyes.

"Maybe run my hand between your legs?"

She blinked, unable to answer.

"Finger your pussy?"

Her mouth dried.

"Spank your ass?"

Catrina inhaled his scent, that of leather and power.

"Maybe fuck you?"

"Damien..."

"Answer me."

He was so forceful, he compelled an answer. "All of those," she confessed breathlessly.

His power play did a number on her brain. Never knowing what he'd say, how he'd react or when he'd approach her kept her on edge. She hated the uncertainty.

The more he denied her, the more she craved his touch.

"Can you take a break from your work?"

When she nodded, he said, "Please stand."

No matter what he had in store, she wanted it.

Each moment with him brought her closer and closer to total submission.

Slowly, she rolled back her chair then followed his instruction as she waited for him to speak again.

He crooked his finger then pointed at a spot on the floor right in front of him.

Captivated, she went to him.

"I may ban jeans from our workspace." He lifted the hem of her skirt. "Though I'd be stupid to if I want to get any business accomplished."

At the barest brush of skin on skin, she became wet.

"Love the stockings," he said. He traced one of the garters upward, bypassing her pussy to skim her belly.

She could barely breathe.

"You've been seducing me all day, Milady."

"I've seduced you, Damien?"

"Is it mutual?"

You know it is.

His motions deliberate, he unbuttoned her shirt and caressed her breasts through her bra. If this was part of submission, she liked it.

Her body zinged with anticipation.

Though he didn't linger anywhere, he studied her intently as he moved between her legs. "You can come anytime, Milady."

"I need it," she said.

"I know. *I know.*"

She suspected he really did.

Catrina allowed her head to fall forward to rest on his broad chest. He brought her off slowly.

She cried out as the orgasm snuck up, knocking her off balance.

He was there to catch her.

Before she knew what was happening, he had her folded across the desk.

"Grab the other side."

Breath knocked out of her, she complied. *Yes.* She wanted, needed him.

A rustling reached her, but when she turned her head, Catrina couldn't see what he was doing.

Then before she was ready, he rubbed her ass hard then scorched it with what had to be his belt.

She yelped.

"There's a price to be had for your misbehavior."

"I'll gladly pay it, Damien." *Again and again.*

This was better than being ignored and having orgasms denied.

He spanked her once more.

Her Dominant wasn't landing hard strokes, just ones with enough force to get her attention. But on top of yesterday's caning, it didn't take much to ignite her senses.

"Don't let go," he instructed.

The orgasm he'd given her minutes ago didn't make this any easier. She was aroused and hungry again.

"Your ass is so red, Milady. Made for my belt."

She loved this.

Now she understood why her boys asked for certain implements rather than others. Each—his hand, belt, cane, flogger—created a different sting or sear... satisfying emotional as well as physical needs.

His leather, with the way it covered so much of her skin, suited her.

Swimming through a minefield of sensation, she lost count of the strokes.

Nothing existed but her and Damien, the numbness of her fingers where she gripped the desk, and the dampness of the wood where her tears marred the surface.

She barely registered that it had ended, but she felt his cock at her entrance.

"Say it, Catrina."

"Damien..."

"Tell me what you want. Beg me to give it to you, like the perfect little submissive you are."

He demanded a lot. Maybe too much.

One more, he striped her, leaving her panting.

"Say it, Catrina. Or shall we end this here and now?"

Chapter Sixteen

Relentlessly, he continued with his belt, leaving her swimming in a sea of deep, deep hunger. "Fuck me, Damien. Fuck my pussy."

But he didn't.

Voice broken, she pleaded. *"Please."*

Her capitulation finally complete, he did, slamming into her with the same ferocity with which he'd belted her, satisfying the craving he'd created.

Crying out his name, she came.

Then she climaxed a second time as he pulled her hips backward, held her imprisoned and kicked apart her legs a little more.

In that moment, she was his.

She wanted no one else.

Didn't want this to ever end.

Time merged then ceased to exist.

He relentlessly played with her clit as he issued a guttural order, "Squeeze my cock, Catrina, and come for me."

She would have insisted she couldn't climax on command, but he surged in her so deeply, she was helpless.

With a deep whimper, she came.

"That's my girl." His cock grew even thicker, pulsing inside her, signaling his impending orgasm.

Stunningly, that was enough for her to tip into the abyss once again.

Damien pistoned his hips before groaning.

Then, hands clamped around her waist, he came deep inside her.

Spent, utterly destroyed by his lovemaking and sensual demands, her body went limp.

What was happening to her?

Leaning forward, Damien moved aside her hair to stroke her nape. "You... Milady. Thank you."

She said nothing.

A dozen thoughts tumbled through her mind, but she was incapable of articulating them.

Finally, after holding on to her for at least a full minute, he helped her to stand and straighten her skirt.

Then he turned her to face him, and he watched as she tucked her shirt back into her waistband.

"Back to work."

"Are you serious?" She blinked furiously.

"I have a meeting with Gregorio then I'll take you to dinner." He checked his very expensive Bonds watch. "Can you be ready in about an hour and a half?"

Damien made her mind spin. "Yes."

"Wear the clothing that I leave on the bed for you."

With that, he stroked her chin before walking off, presumably to dispose of the condom.

Her legs nerveless, she sank into her chair.

Nothing could have prepared her for this time with Damien.

From kind to demanding, from protective to steely Dominant.

She never knew which version of him she would be dealing with.

Had she ever been more emotionally uncertain in her life?

A few minutes later, she once more noticed the streaks her tears had made on the desktop. So that she wouldn't have a constant reminder of what he'd done to her while she worked, she needed to find some furniture polish.

First, to give her some time to put her world back together, she took a long drink of her water.

Telling herself she would survive this, she tried to get back to work.

Twenty minutes later, she gave up the pretense. Between the spanking and sizzling sex, she was unable to concentrate.

Needing something else to think about, she picked up her phone and called her mother.

"How's your young man?" Evelyn asked.

Stalling, she took her time responding. "You mean Damien?"

"Yes, Damien. How many do you have?"

Quickly she protested, "He's an acquaintance."

"Hmm. Sure he is."

"What do you mean by that?"

"I wasn't born yesterday, my Cat. Business meetings aren't typically held on Sundays. And associates don't touch each other the way he touched you."

She sank a little lower into her chair.

"Furthermore," Evelyn pronounced with the same flourish as a television lawyer, "you wouldn't have brought him along unless you were in one car, which you wouldn't have been in unless he'd picked you up somewhere."

You're giving me a headache.

"So...how is he?" Evelyn persisted.

Not knowing how else to answer, she exhaled. "Fine."

"He must be special to you."

Catrina paused. There was no way she could tell her mother the truth...that he was fucking her and dominating her, for almost another two weeks.

After that, they'd go their separate ways. "What we share is nothing serious." Then, more forcefully, she tried to end her mother's questioning. "I mean that."

"Mmm." Finally, Evelyn went pressed forward. "You're the one who tells clients it's okay to fall in love again. You even told me that."

"I'm not..." Catrina sighed. "Love has nothing to do with this."

Why did the words sound hollow, even to herself?

To clear her mind, she shook her head. "I didn't call to talk about my life."

"Of course not. You called to stick your nose in mine."

She opened her mouth before snapping it closed again. "That's not true."

"Look, sweetheart, I realize you think you know best." Evelyn's voice was soothing. "You want to reassure yourself that I'm aware of what I'm doing, but you're positive I don't."

"A prenuptial—"

"Stop it." Her mother snapped in a way that instantly silenced Catrina. But when Evelyn went on, her tone softened. "I appreciate that you don't want me to get hurt and lose everything again, but honey, that was over twenty-five years ago."

"I know, but…"

"You took on my burdens in ways you never should have. And then when that jackass fiancé of yours did the same things your father did, it reinforced your worldview." Evelyn sighed. "It was a struggle back then, I grant you. I wish I'd never allowed you to see how hard it was."

"Mother, you couldn't have hidden it."

"I tried to protect you," Evelyn said. "But I could have done better for you."

She recalled Damien's words. "You did a great job."

"I wish I could be as sure. But I do know this. Milton makes me laugh. I feel alive more than I ever have. He has plenty of his own money."

Does he? "So why do you need to get married?"

"We don't need to. I want to be a bride and have flowers and a cake." She paused. "I never had them."

Catrina's shoulders slumped forward. "I didn't realize."

Like a schoolgirl, Evelyn giggled. "And I want a honeymoon. One of my friends already bought me crotchless panties."

What? "Moving on." She couldn't listen to another minute of this. "If I promise not to mention a prenuptial again after this, do you promise not to tell me stuff like that?"

"Oh dear. I'm sorry. I was hoping you had a recommendation for a vibrator."

"*Mother.*" She broke the word into two distinct syllables. "Ask Aunt Peggy. I'm sure she knows."

"She recommended two different models. One of them plugs in and she says that kind is actually used in a lot of adult movies and—"

No. "I recommend you exchange financial plans. Make sure your goals align and that you have adequately saved for retirement. Social security will not be enough to keep up with cost-of-living increases—"

Evelyn's infectious laughter rippled around her.

Finally, Catrina relented.

"Life is short, my Cat. Miltey lost his wife a couple of years ago. Don't let fear rob you of possible joy. Be smart but be happy."

With that, Evelyn said she had to go. Miltey had bought her a gift certificate for a massage, and she had an appointment to use it.

Shaking her head in wonderment at the transformation that her mother was undergoing, Catrina ended the call.

After placing her phone down, she glanced up to see Damien on one of the monitors.

Standing in the kitchen, filling an entire screen, he looked directly into the camera, as if aware of her scrutiny.

Even though they were nowhere near each other, she felt his presence as keenly as if he were standing in front of her.

Then, he pointedly checked his watch.

She was almost out of time. And if there was one thing she'd learned, it was to take Damien's dictates very, very seriously.

* * * *

Over the next few days, they fell into a routine. He brought her coffee in the mornings. They'd work. At some point, when they had privacy, he'd torment her.

At night, he'd teach her something new.

Thursday, she drove to Denver for an in-person meeting, and he called to make sure she had made it safely. Rather than chafing at the intrusion, she appreciated it. It was nice to have someone know her comings and goings, even though it meant she was more connected to him.

She met with her client, Jenny, and they spent most of the time talking about her soon-to-be ex and her grief.

Catrina helped Jenny draw up a realistic plan for saving, paying down credit card debt, and investing, giving her real tools to use.

"This feels better," Jenny said. "It's something I can do other than wring my hands."

In the doorway, Jenny hugged Catrina. "Thank you, again."

As Jenny drove away, Catrina grinned with satisfaction.

Helping others filled her up in ways she wouldn't have known possible.

Her first reaction was to call Damien to tell him about her day.

Stunned, she closed the door and leaned her shoulders against the wood. *Tell Damien?*

In such a short time, he'd become important to her.

Since Todd exited her life, she'd chosen freedom over intimacy.

For the first time, she questioned that decision.

A shudder of discomfort tracing down her spine, she tipped back her chin and pushed away from the door.

After straightening her office, she texted him, letting him know she was on her way back.

Sliding behind the steering wheel, she realized how much she was looking forward to seeing him, and that bothered her more than anything.

Friday afternoon, he dropped into a chair across from her desk.

"Would you like to attend this evening's event?"

Because they'd been in their own little world, it hadn't occurred to her that others would be arriving soon.

"We could stay in our quarters, go out for dinner? Or we could go to my house for the weekend."

She appreciated his thoughtfulness. "How about dinner out?" she asked. "Then we can sneak in the back way? I'm not ready to step out in public as your sub."

"Even though you wore a white wristband and scened with me last week?"

"That was different."

He steepled his index fingers.

"I can't explain it. It just is." When he just looked at her, waiting for her to expand, she thought it through. "Maybe the same reason you didn't want me to play with Gregorio. It's just not..." She lifted a shoulder. "A week ago, things were different." *I was different. I didn't know how much I would like this.*

When he remained silent, she continued. "I didn't know how you'd react to seeing me, if the invitation was still open. But now..."

She couldn't say what was on her mind.

That she was possessive of him.

That he mattered to her.

"In that case, let's go to Winter Park? Unless you'd like to go the opposite way? Granby? Grand Lake?"

"Any is fine with me." After lowering her gaze for a moment, she added, "Thank you."

"Keeping you happy is my number one priority."

The sincerity in his tone almost made her believe it.

"I'll leave your outfit on the bed."

"Oh?"

"No bra," he cautioned.

At this point, she wouldn't even think of it.

"A gift arrived for you."

"For me?"

"Get ready to go and meet me in the living room."

Half an hour later, she joined him. He was staring at the fire, an ankle propped on his knee.

The moment she entered, he stood.

No matter where or when, he treated her as if he was glad to see her. She appreciated that more and more.

"You look beautiful, as always, Milady."

"Thank you, Damien."

"Come here, please."

She recognized that tone. He had something planned, but it wouldn't do her any good to ask what it was. Rather than raw nervousness assailing her, curiosity tripped through her.

When she stopped in front of him, he said, "Lift your shirt and show me your beautiful tits."

Fingers shaking though they shouldn't be, she followed his instructions.

When she had, he pulled out a pair of unusual-looking clamps.

"Your gift," he said.

"Nipple jewelry?" The small hearts were pretty, and she suspected they'd stay in place just fine. They weren't meant to inflict discomfort like some clamps, but rather, she suspected, they were intended to create constant pressure.

"Present your breasts to me, Milady."

Obediently, she cupped them in her palms and lifted them toward him.

"So beautiful. We may be returning as soon as dinner is over."

His hoarse admission delighted her. The knowledge that she affected him as powerfully as he affected her thrilled her.

Leaning down, he sucked on each nipple to distend them before attaching each heart.

"How is the pressure?"

"I know the jewelry is in place," she said. "But it's not unbearable."

"Let's go before I end up taking you to bed without feeding you."

"Oh?"

"Don't tempt me," he all-but growled as she grabbed her coat.

At the restaurant located at the golf club near Granby, he asked for a window table next to the fireplace, and he ordered them each a glass of champagne.

"Are we celebrating something?" she asked once the server moved off.

"Indeed we are. I closed the deal with the firm in England."

"Congratulations."

The bubbly arrived, and she toasted his success.

"A banner week for both of us," he agreed, clinking the rim of his glass against hers. "With your new client and the way you helped her."

She appreciated him acknowledging her, as well.

Sharing successes wasn't something she'd really done before. The feeling was novel. And a little frightening.

Once more, the ending of this arrangement loomed in front of her, closer every moment.

After dinner, she was debating whether or not to order dessert when he said, "Get the chocolate cake. You'll need your energy."

"Really?"

The combination of his words and the nipple jewelry put her on the edge of her seat.

When the server returned, he ordered the chocolate cake and coffee.

"Just the cake," Catrina amended. "If it's okay, I'd rather not linger."

"Ready to go home?"

"More than."

"So you don't want to go to a movie?" he teased. "Maybe dancing? Ice skating?"

"No."

He smiled. "Ah. This must be about your nipples and state of arousal? How does the jewelry feel?"

"Even though the pressure isn't terrible, they're starting to drive me crazy." *As if you don't know.*

"I like looking at the outline, and I like you putting up with them because I requested it."

"Requested?" She lifted an eyebrow.

"You're always free to refuse."

Of course. But she liked pleasing him. In return, he went out of his way to ensure her happiness.

He took care of the bill then escorted her outside to the car where he opened the door for her. "Wait." He slid his hands inside her coat and across her breasts to flick at the hearts.

She hissed.

With a wicked grin, he indicated she should enter the vehicle. "Milady."

Catrina wasn't sure if he had been trying to teach her the importance of reaching out to her subs before the scene. But now she understood it on a whole new level.

All afternoon, with his words, his actions, the way he mixed in serious conversation with smoldering, blunt sex talk banked the embers of desire. He stoked it along the way so that when he finally touched her, need threatened to consume her.

"I've been thinking about having you naked all day."

"Me, too," she replied, looking at him.

Everything he did—from driving, to running a corporation, to dominating her—exuded his controlled power. Experiencing it was something she'd never forget.

They returned to the Den with only the valet noting their arrival. The man gave a quick salute, acknowledging Damien as he pulled into the garage.

After exiting the vehicle, he came around to her side, then put a hand on her shoulder to stop her from getting out of the car. "Show me your breasts."

The unexpected way he issued commands always startled her. She was certain he did it on purpose to keep her guessing. Knowing there was a houseful of people only feet away increased her tension.

Her hand trembled as she pulled apart the knot in her coat belt.

Damien stood close, not helping, just watching as she followed his order.

She lifted her shirt, and the cool air chased goose bumps up her body.

"Even better than I imagined," he said. He squeezed her nipples.

She winced. "Oww."

"How do they feel now?"

"Achy." It would have been impossible for her to have worn actual clamps the entire evening. As it was, the dull ache became discomfort.

"Do you want me to take them off?"

Her shirt still raised, she looked up at him and knew this was another lesson. "If that's your pleasure."

"Well done, Milady." He released his grip on her nipples.

Pain ricocheted through her, leaving her pussy wet and anxious.

"Leave the hearts in place." Then he added, "Put your top back down."

She exhaled but didn't protest. While she would have liked to remove the jewelry, submitting to his will gave her pleasure.

When he offered his hand, she accepted his gentlemanly assistance, following him to the door, then preceding him up the back stairs.

"Have you ever been fucked in the ass, Milady?"

She gripped the banister tight to avoid tripping.

"I mean before tonight?"

Tonight? Looking over her shoulder, she said, "Uhm... No."

"Then I look forward to being your first."

Her body shook as she entered their rooms.

"You know where I keep the lube and condoms," he said after he flipped the switch to turn on the fireplace. "There's also a butt plug on a shelf in the bedroom closet. Put it in. That will be the only thing you'll be wearing when you return to me."

Shock immobilized her.

When she didn't reply, he asked, "Are my instructions clear?"

Catrina gave herself a mental shake. "Yes," she whispered. She cleared her throat and said again, "They are."

"First, your nipples."

She removed her coat and draped it over the back of the couch. Then she took off her shirt.

"Maybe I'll make you keep them on. I love the way they look."

"Of course, Damien."

"Come here."

When she stood in front of him, he closed his fingers around them.

"I wouldn't do this with actual clamps..."

Curious, fearful, she met his gaze.

Rather than releasing each like he normally did, he pulled them both off at the same time.

She cried out, reaching to soothe the ache.

But he brushed her hands aside. "Just as gorgeous." He curled his palms around her breasts then sucked on the peaks to ease the sting himself.

Instantly, the pain morphed into arousal.

"Now, go." He nodded, and she hurried away.

Near the bedroom doorway, the sound of his voice froze her in place.

"I like that view of you shirtless, with jeans, and the way your hair hangs down your back." He sucked in a breath. "Everything about you does it for me, Catrina."

No man had ever shown her this kind of approval.

Maybe because she wasn't looking at him, she found courage to return the compliment. "And everything about you does it for me, Damien."

For a moment, he didn't speak.

Then, very softly, he said, "Now get on with it, Milady. The clock is ticking. And I promise, you don't want to keep me waiting…"

Chapter Seventeen

Shaking from his implied threat, she hurried away, his diabolical laugh following her.

Images and thoughts crowded her mind as she went into the closet. At her house, he'd had no qualms about going through her clothing, but entering his closet and rifling through his drawers seemed overly personal.

It wasn't just a drawer. It was a treasure trove. Clamps, floggers, even a vibrator. Toward the back, she found the small plug, and her breaths came closer and closer together.

While there, she finished undressing before going into the bathroom with the glass piece. It took her several tries to insert the slippery thing, and she was ultra-aware of its presence, shifting in her as she moved.

Carrying the lube and a condom, she returned to him.

Damien was seated on the couch, one arm across the back.

He left her emotions devastated.

As always, being nude while he was fully clothed reminded her of her submission, as she was sure he'd intended.

"Ah. There you are." Studying her, he rose.

His cock pressed against the front of his slacks, and the evidence of his arousal made her heart flutter.

"As beautiful as I expected."

She'd never known a lover as generous with praise as he was.

Damien gestured with his index finger, silently ordering her to face the opposite direction. "I'd like you to show me your plug."

Embarrassed, grateful for his order, she placed his requested items on an end table before showing him her backside. Then, taking her time, she spread her legs and grabbed her ankles.

Her hair fell around her, giving her some much-needed privacy.

But she was hyper aware of him watching her, studying...

As she waited for another command, she schooled herself to breathe.

As the seconds dragged past, self-consciousness receded, leaving empowerment in its place, something she'd never expected to feel as a submissive.

He'd been right that there was much more to this experience than she'd ever considered.

"Even more tantalizing than I could have imagined." His tone was soft, the words thrilling. "And what I imagined was pretty damned good. Now, reach back and spread your buttocks so I can see it better."

Struggling to keep her balance, and glad she'd kept up her morning routine of yoga stretches, she did as he requested.

"Oh, yes. Your obedience is the stuff of dreams."

For a long time, silence pulsed.

"Good. Now please get on the coffee table. On all fours."

Are you serious?

When she faced him once more, his arms were folded, all Domlike, across his chest.

Then, like the gentleman he also was, he offered his hand for assistance.

Suddenly more nervous than she'd ever been, she did as he'd said, struggling to remain in place as he circled her.

"Your nipple jewelry would add to your experience." He crouched in front of her. "What do you say?"

Another way to drive me out of my mind? But she couldn't say that. "Your choice, Damien."

Without her knowledge, he'd had them in hand the whole time. She sucked in tiny gasps of air when he closed the hearts on her already-swollen nipples.

"I may buy you a dozen different sets."

Lightly, he squeezed her breasts, but even that much was enough to make her sway from side to side, and she tightened her ass cheeks.

"You're thinking too much." He skimmed his fingertips down her spine, soothing her with both his words and his touch.

He continued lower to massage one of her buttocks, and the motion shifted the plug, making her moan.

Then his unrelenting touch was everywhere.

He played with her pussy, spanked her ass lightly, then reached beneath her to toy with the hearts.

"Give yourself over to me."

Not long ago, she would have insisted that wasn't possible, but as she concentrated on pleasing him, nerves receded, and she became more and more aroused.

"Do you enjoy this, Milady? Being the center of my attention, knowing that what I'm doing is for you?"

For me?

Is it?

Because she knew manners were expected, she murmured, "Thank you."

Damien left her, and soft sounds reached her, the clank of his belt, the rasp of his zipper, the thud of his shoes being tossed on the hardwood.

As she waited, a tiny knot of fear deep inside, the condom package rustled.

"Are you ready for me, Catrina?"

She wasn't sure she ever would be. "Yes, Damien." No matter how hard she tried, she couldn't make herself believe the lie.

Even as he took the time to ensure she was aroused, he chuckled, the sound deep and rich.

Then he pressed against the entrance to her pussy. "Damien?" He wasn't taking her rear, as he said?

He slid his thick cock into her, and the combination of his penetration and the pressure from the plug threatened to overwhelm her.

"Oh, hell..." His actions stole her breath.

Pushing her even further into sensation overload, he played with her plug.

Helpless, needing relief, she dropped her head to the table, hoping the change of angle would alleviate some of the fullness.

"Back into position, Milady."

"But..." She wasn't sure her arms would support her.

He placed his forearm beneath her chest, helping her. "This is how I want you. Understand?"

How could he be so awful?

He thrust his hips, filling her pussy over and over, leaving her dazed. "Damien!" This was too much... "I'm going to come." That shouldn't even be possible.

"Are you?"

Miserably, she whimpered.

"Not yet."

"I can't wait..." Squeezing her eyes shut, she concentrated on behaving while ignoring the tension in her lower body. "It's too much. *Please?*"

His fingers were dug into her hip bones, but he stroked her with his thumbs. "You're doing fine, Milady."

As he intended, she drank strength from his words.

"Transcend your needs to think about your Dom's commands."

My Dom's commands.

Not only did he continue, he increased the speed of his thrusts.

Frantically, she thrashed her head.

She was dazed, lost when he pulled back. "What?"

"Relax for a moment."

He tugged on the plug, and she gasped.

"It's coming out, Milady."

No. Surely the thing was stuck in there.

"If you stop the struggle, it won't be as uncomfortable."

Intellectually she understood what he said, but she still tightened her buttocks.

"Arch your back."

Which raised her rear higher.

He slapped both her butt cheeks hard, pitching her forward, and he plucked out the plug while she was distracted.

"That wasn't so bad, was it?"

"Terrible." Then before she even had a chance to register the fact that both her rear and pussy were empty, his lube-coated cockhead was pushing into her ass. "Good God!"

"You're allowed to move around if you need to."

Desperately panting, she tried to escape.

But he was stronger, and he pressed on, entering her deeper, stretching her impossibly wide.

"Almost there," he promised, soothed.

Lied.

The possession seemed to take forever, and she gulped oxygen. The razor-edge of pain and pleasure blurred.

Finally, he had her imprisoned, balls-deep in her tightest hole.

"Very well done, Milady."

"I..."

Now that he'd claimed her completely, she was better.

"So, so tight, Milady. Now, I want you to kneel up."

"You can't be serious."

Even without his affirmation, she knew he meant every word. "I am."

Because he was so much bigger than her, he was able to reach around her. His arm was like a band as he lifted her upper body.

As he moved her, his cock went deeper and deeper, threatening to rip her apart. "I can't do this!" she cried out.

"You already did," he reassured her, kissing the side of her neck.

"Damien, it's…" She shook her head frantically. "Too—too much."

"Either safe word, or work through it. Either way is fine with me, Milady."

He whispered the promise against her ear.

"You could never disappoint me."

If he believed in her and offered a lifeline, she could endure a few more seconds.

"Want to try?"

Pursing her lips in determination, she nodded.

"Say it. I want your consent."

Halt lingering on the tip of her tongue, just in case, she said, "Yes, Damien."

"Good girl. Now put your hand behind my neck."

"I'm not a contortionist," she protested.

"No need. I've got you."

Since there was no way she could comply without his help, she reached back to curl her arms around his neck.

Using all of her ab strength as well as the leverage, she tried to draw herself upright.

As usual, he was there, using his strength to get her into the position he wanted.

Her motions agonizingly slow as she adjusted to his depth and the unusual angle, she arched her back.

"That's it, Milady."

She squeezed her eyes shut. "I've never experienced anything like this." It was as if he'd engulfed her.

"Good. I don't want you to ever forget our time together."

How could she?

Damien kept one arm in front of her, offering support while he tweaked her nipples with the other.

Breathlessly, she moaned.

"Hang in there for me."

"You're killing me, Damien!"

"It just feels that way."

Now that he was as deep inside her, he bent his knees, giving him a little more leverage.

As he drove into her again and again, she cried out.

Perspiration dotted her entire being as he possessed her. But shockingly, even though it didn't seem possible, arousal unfurled. "Do me," she pleaded.

"Fuck, Milady. It's my absolute pleasure."

He pulled back until the only part inside her was his cockhead then he surged forward again.

Needing more, she urged him on. "Yes, *yes.*"

He moved both hands to her waist, holding her firmly, and drove into her with the force she wanted.

"Amazing," she breathed.

"I want you to come."

His touch skillful, he fingered her clit.

Shattering completely, she pitched forward.

"That's it." Damien pulled her upright again.

Jerking his hips, he groaned. Finally, he came, ejaculating in powerful spurts.

The change in pace, the way he touched her, and the swelling of his cock were a lethal combination. She muttered things that were incomprehensible as she came a second time.

Damien continued to support her as their breathing returned to normal.

Even then, he muttered approving, nonsensical words that sounded magical, leaving her happier, and more connected to him than she ever remembered being with anyone else. "I had no idea…"

"That…?"

"Anything like this was possible." Orgasming from anal penetration, a momentary belief that they were the only two people in the world.

Slowly, he lowered her to the table's surface.

He withdrew his cock then picked her up and carried her toward the master en suite. As he strode, she rested her cheek against his chest.

Lesson learned.

After their time together, she'd never again be the same.

When he placed her on the bed, he grinned wickedly. "I'll give you a moment to recover."

She blinked.

He wasn't finished with her yet?

Before she could formulate the question, he disappeared into the bathroom, only to return with a washcloth.

He'd discarded the condom. Stunning her, though, his cock was already more than half hard.

"Lift your legs."

Was there no limit to her humiliation?

"Now part them."

Exposing every little bit of herself to him.

She turned her head away from him, not that she'd be able to hide from him.

"Not too swollen."

"My body disagrees with you."

"I'm sure it does." Though he agreed, he didn't offer an apology. In fact, he sounded quite pleased with himself. "Before we get started, I'd like you to change."

"I'm sure you have something in mind?"

"There's an outfit waiting for you in my top dresser drawer."

"Really?"

"Go see."

Her eyebrows knitted in a serious frown, she slowly rose.

Thirty seconds later, she picked up a garter belt, stockings, and a shelf bra.

"Please put them on," he called out. "And then be prepared for the spanking of your life. Every bit of your ass belongs to me tonight..."

Chapter Eighteen

"Something on your mind?"

Jolted back to the moment, the fact they'd just finished eating dinner at the kitchen island, Damien shook his head and met Catrina's gaze.

"You appear to be somewhere else."

He was.

Their time together was almost up.

When he'd challenged her to spend two weeks with him, he'd promised that she would learn a few things about submission. But he hadn't expected he'd be changed by the experience.

In the time they'd spent together so far, he and Catrina had fallen into a familiar and appealing routine.

When they ate at home, he cooked. Unless she was still working, she'd pull up a barstool and keep him company.

Afterward, she'd load the dishwasher and wipe the counter and table while he put away the leftovers. They made a small, but very effective team.

And he didn't know what the hell he'd do when she vanished from his life, never to kneel for him again.

Forcing himself to focus, Damien refilled their goblets with sparkling water. "When you're ready, there's an outfit for you in the closet."

She frowned. "Now?"

To keep her guessing, he'd left her something to wear every day for over a week.

"Or do you mean later this evening?"

"This moment, Catrina."

That she didn't argue further showed they were making progress.

With a curious nod, she slipped from her seat and walked away, her heels forcefully striking the hardwood floors.

Less than two minutes later, she returned, carrying a black, frothy dress with plenty of white lace around the hem of the skirt and the neckline. "Are you freaking kidding me?"

"Not at all," he swore.

"But... This is a French maid's outfit."

"It is indeed." Complete with a garter to go around her thigh.

Indignant, with one hand on her hip, she scowled at him. "You want me to wash the dishes wearing..." She raised a hand. "This?"

"I can't think of anything I'd enjoy more." Except, maybe having her naked.

"But there's nothing wrong with what I'm wearing."

"You're right. In fact, it's lovely." He enjoyed seeing her in skirts and stilettos. "But this is my choice for tonight. And I suggest you put it on in the next two minutes unless you want to wear it all day, every day for the remainder of your time here."

"I don't understand what you're trying to get at."

"Service can be integral to a BDSM relationship, just as much as impact play. Some subs get off on the opportunity."

"Others do not."

"Agreed." He nodded. "But it's part of what you're learning."

She rolled her eyes, which was something he'd deal with later. "Change into the outfit, Catrina."

"Be reasonable."

"A reddened ass would go nicely with it, don't you think?"

She glared.

But she didn't use her safe word.

"You're a beast, Damien."

"Diabolical," he agreed. "I'll give you one minute."

This time her shoes pounded an angry tattoo as she strode away.

With a grin that he was glad she couldn't see, he sipped from his glass. This was going to be a hell of a show.

Five full minutes had passed by the time she returned.

With a soft, sultry walk, she headed toward him.

Instantly, his cock hardened.

Damn. She was worth every moment of the wait.

While she was gone, she'd fluffed her hair, tied the apron way too tight, and cinched the satin laces on the corsetlike top until her cleavage appeared to be twice its normal size.

In addition, she'd tied a black fabric collar around her throat.

What the hell…?

"Hello, Sir," she purred. "How may I serve you?"

He rolled the globe of his glass between his palms.

This was clearly not one of his better ideas.

Her motions exaggerated, Catrina moved behind him. The hairs on his nape rose in response to the stir of her breath. Leaning forward, she nipped the tender flesh of his earlobe before instantly laving away the hurt.

If she kept this up, the kitchen would never get clean.

She brushed her breasts against his upper arm as she took away his plate.

Christ.

His cock throbbed painfully, and she'd barely started cleaning up the kitchen.

Then she lifted onto her toes and reached across him to pick up her dishes, exposing her bare bottom.

"Think carefully about what you're doing, Milady," he warned. She was supposed to be wearing the thong that he'd placed on a shelf next to the costume.

"Oh, yes, Sir. Thank you for the advice, Sir."

God, he loved how that rolled off her tongue. Now, if only she'd say it so easily when she wasn't teasing.

She took her time doing the dishes, bending over to pick up some unseen item from the floor, making sure she wiggled her hips as she moved each plate from the sink to the dishwasher.

Watching her was delicious torture.

After she'd finished that, she returned with a damp towel.

"Pardon my reach, Sir." She leaned across him and wiped the table. Twice.

Finally, unable to take it, he pulled her off her feet and settled her in his lap, facing him.

"Oh, no, Sir!" She wiggled as she straddled him. "Are you going to have your wicked way with me?"

"I'm afraid so, Milady." He maneuvered them so that she was sitting and he was standing. He kicked off his shoes, socks and pants then grabbed a condom from his wallet.

He sheathed his already-hard dick.

She licked her upper lip.

He throbbed.

"But what of my virtue?" she asked. "An employer isn't supposed to have his wicked way with the help."

"Milady, when I'm done with you, your lack of virtue will be the least of your worries."

He picked her up, sat and pulled her down on his cock. She was already wet, and her pussy welcomed him with a tight squeeze.

"Oh, sweet God," she whispered.

"Ride me."

She moved on him, raising and lowering herself. He groaned. His little vixen had clearly won this round.

He yanked open her front laces and palmed her breasts, lifting them so he could suck her distended nipples.

Catrina pulled the leather strip from his hair and dug her fingers in, holding him tight as she fucked him.

Wanting to drive her even madder, he pressed a finger against her anal whorl and slowly worked his way inside.

With a groan, she leaned forward, giving him greater access.

Apparently lost, she murmured his name over and over.

He made sure he gave her an orgasm before he reached his climax, but damn, it took everything he had to hold back as long as he did. He could have come the first time she lowered herself on him.

"Well, Sir, that was unexpected."

"Let that be a lesson to you," he cautioned sternly.

She pulled back his head so she could look at him. "Why, yes, Sir. Of course, Sir." Then she kissed his forehead before scampering off his lap and dashing toward their suite.

It was then that he realized she'd left him with the remainder of the clean-up.

Yep.

He'd definitely proved who mastered who in this relationship.

* * * *

A couple of mornings later, two cups of coffee in hand, Catrina stopped in the doorway of the office space she shared with Damien. Intrigued, as always, she watched him. He was on his headset, pacing. His hair was loose, long, rakish.

She didn't get tired of seeing him like this, in charge with his take-control power radiating, affecting everything and everyone in his orbit.

Including me?

His T-shirt showed his biceps, and damn, had he poured himself into those jeans?

Seeming to sense her, like he always did, he pivoted.

Even though he was in the middle of a conversation, he beckoned her in, indicating she should sit on his desk.

He walked over to accept the coffee she offered, and he pulled out his earpiece long enough to place a gentle kiss on the top of her head.

Since her first meeting wasn't for another thirty minutes and they'd both worked late the evening before, she decided to wait while he finished his call.

She wasn't sure what was being discussed, but the financial planner in her was intrigued by the word *millions*, particularly when it was followed by *dollars*.

He was nodding in response to something being said, and she took a drink that she'd added extra creamer to. With the number of calories she burned every day, she could afford the treat.

Through the open blinds, dappled sunlight filtered in. The screens behind him showed only the outdoor cameras, a blanket of snow on the trees and grounds. Steam rose from the hot tub, and a deer wandered just outside a fence.

Such a peaceful, wonderful place.

Not only did she love the setting, but she enjoyed his company every evening as they sat on the couch, music in the background, a fireplace glowing. Sharing the day's events with another person was something she'd never experienced before. Even when he pried more information out of her than she liked, it was nice talking to someone who was supportive and non-judgmental.

A couple of times, they'd taken their morning beverage onto the front patio, though she'd needed to wrap up in a blanket to stay warm.

Now, the idea of leaving here — and him — ached like a physical pain.

Catrina breathed in and reminded herself to keep her emotional distance. She'd known from the start this was a temporary arrangement, orchestrated to teach her some things about submission.

She shoved away the nagging whisper that it might already be too late.

After ending his call, he strode over to her and set his cup on a coaster. Then he plucked hers from her hand to slide it next to his.

"Time to say good morning to my lovely sub." He linked his arms around her and pulled her up until she stood barely inches from him.

Her pulse fluttering, she tipped back her head to look at him. "I don't know what you're thinking," she said. "But I don't think I'm going to like it."

"Why not?"

"Because you are looking down your nose and you appear very serious. So your head is either still thinking about business or you're considering doing something wicked to me."

"You're on to me."

"Yep."

"Hold out your tongue."

She blinked.

"Don't make me repeat myself." The teasing was gone from his voice, replaced by a stern, wouldn't-tolerate-disagreement tone.

"Pretty sure I don't want to."

"No?" He pulled her a little closer, until his cock pressed against her.

Her resolve wavered. "It will hurt."

"Are you certain?"

The question piqued her interest, just as he'd intended. If she'd had any doubts before about Damien Lowell's ability to own her, it was gone now. He knew exactly how to get her to do what he wanted.

Butterflies doing a backstroke in her bloodstream, she stuck out her tongue. Before he could touch her, she chickened out.

"Catrina," he snapped.

"Sorry." She obeyed his command but closed her eyes.

He gently held the tip of her tongue.

It was everything she could do not to dance away.

When he increased the pressure, she whimpered, not from pain but from the raw pulse of desire.

Damien took one of her hands and placed it on the front of his trousers.

"Think about how much this is turning me on."

Yes. She squeezed his cock as she surrendered, leaning into him.

Time was swallowed by sensation.

She barely registered the way he decreased the pressure until he sucked her tongue into his mouth. Then it became a kiss that left her raw, ragged and breathless.

When he finally ended it, setting her away from him, she couldn't hold up her head.

"Thanks for the coffee, Milady. Now get to work."

She shook her head and looked at him. "Seriously? That's it?"

"It's a workday. What else did you expect?"

"You to finish what you started." Certain he was teasing her, she continued to stroke him. "We only need a few minutes for both of us to be completely satisfied."

Forcefully, he clamped her wrist, stilling her movements. "You'll have to wait until tonight."

"You're the most frustrating man I've ever met."

"It's my decision."

She tried one more angle. "I'd focus better if I had an orgasm."

"This way you'll also be thinking about tonight. I'd like you to meet me downstairs after dinner."

"Oh?"

"That was foreplay, Milady, not a tease."

He moved her hand to her side before letting it go.

"Yes…Damien." It would have been easy to call him Sir. In fact, not using the title was becoming more difficult. She was thinking of him in those terms, but actually saying it would mean she'd accepted his domination.

"Don't even think of using a vibrator," he said as he let her go.

"But…"

"Please honor my request."

The morning dragged. "I'm not sure I like your idea of foreplay," she said over lunch.

"That's good to know."

He gave her a quick kiss before excusing himself to return to work. She sank against her chairback and blew out a breath, ruffling her hair.

Since she couldn't settle and, needing a jolt of caffeine, she went downstairs to the main kitchen where extra sodas were stored. After digging around on the bottom shelf of the refrigerator, she found her favorite diet flavor.

Moments later, Gregorio entered. "Milady." He brushed snow from his sleeves before hanging up his black leather jacket.

What was it with the men and leather around here?

"Where's the boss?"

"Back at work."

"Everything okay?" He helped himself to a cup of coffee. "Yuck."

"Been there a while, I imagine. You probably brewed it this morning?"

"Maybe yesterday." He put it in the microwave and pulled out a carton of cream. "So, dish, Milady. What's up? It's not like you to sulk."

She thought about denying it but figured that would do no good. "Damien can be confounding."

"Submission challenges?"

"I think I'll stick with being a Domme."

"Really?" The microwave dinged and he took out the cup. He added a dollop of cream, tasted it again, then added another drop.

"Is that a coffee or a latte at this point?"

"Neither. Putting this tar in the java family is an insult."

"Want me to brew you another pot?"

"Thought you were done being a sub?"

"Damien is clear about common courtesy and D/s."

He dragged back a chair and sat across from her. "You're a quick study. Has this been a challenge for you? Confusing?"

"Yeah." She paused. Even to herself, this didn't make a lot of sense. "The time together has been instructive."

"But?"

"I like Damien." Trying not to fidget, she folded her hands around her aluminum can.

"And that's a problem because…?"

"As you said, challenging. That's a good word."

"It's a hell of a journey," he agreed.

"The submission part, I get. Or at least I think I do. He was right that I'll be a better Domme when this is over."

"Is that what you want?"

Catrina stilled.

Is it?

She'd become a Domme after that handsome man had vowed to worship at her feet. She knew she wanted to make the experience wonderful for her boy, so she'd done her research and plenty of experimenting to make sure her subs were satisfied.

Before that, there'd never been a time when she'd dreamed of dominating anyone. In fact, she'd wanted to be protected and nurtured…then ended up with men who didn't provide that.

Still, she enjoyed sceneing.

And mostly, she kept her heart safe, and that was the main thing.

Realizing Gregorio was quietly watching her, she shook her head to clear it. "That's why I'm here." Her words were a half answer. And maybe not completely truthful.

"What about the rest?"

She tried to remember where they'd been in the conversation…and now she was getting dangerously close to admitting things to him that she was trying to hide from herself. "Sitting with him on the couch." She paused. "At night. The talking. Maybe watching a movie. It's…intimate. Not sex, but sharing things, even seemingly insignificant details. I've never had anything like it. I'm going to miss it, even though I have convinced myself that I don't want it."

Very carefully, he asked, "Who says you have to give it up?"

"Do you see Damien keeping me around when this is done? If I want to meet him as an equal?"

"You're still seeing a submissive as someone less important or inferior to a Dom?"

"I didn't say that."

"Didn't you?" he challenged right back.

She tucked a stray lock hair behind her ear.

"Discuss this with Damien. I'd give you my opinion, but you need to hear it from him." When she didn't respond, he added, "If that intimacy thing you're talking about is real, then you'll trust him enough to go to him. Tell him what's on your mind. Listen to what he has to say. He could want the same things as you. Maybe you can work out a compromise."

"How do two Dominants have a relationship?"

"Unless they have that conversation, they don't." He took a big drink from his cup. "Tastes like shit."

"Dump it out."

"It's caffeine, and I had a long night."

She tilted her head to one side, studying him, noting the bruises beneath his eyes and the lines etched next to him. She'd been so wrapped up in her own problems that she hadn't noticed how exhausted he looked. "Doing what?"

"That, Milady, is none of your business."

Rude. "I should give you a flogging for that."

"Not on my fucking watch," Damien said.

The arctic chill in his voice froze her.

"Something you'd like to tell me, Catrina?"

Chapter Nineteen

Gregorio shrugged. "Security cameras, Milady."

Her heart thundering at double time, she swung around to look at Damien. "It was a joke," she swore, silently imploring him to understand. "Since Gregorio is a switch... I'm babbling."

"Go on."

"I was telling him about my frustrations over the last few days." She dropped her gaze. "Sorry if I was out of line."

"You're an adult, Milady. You can discuss anything you want with anyone you wish. I'd like it if you would come to me."

"After lunch, I tried."

"So you're complaining to Gregorio you're sexually frustrated because I wouldn't get you off upstairs?"

"*God.* No." Exasperated, she stood and took a step toward him. "It's about me. My confusion."

"Fears?"

"Yes."

"I'm glad you talked to Gregorio. And I want you to know that I'm available to listen, too. I may be a caveman, but if you whack me up the side of the head, you can get my attention." He took the final step that would bring them within inches of each other then he took hold of her upper arms with the reassuring gentleness that could only come from such strength. "I have broad shoulders, Milady. To help carry whatever troubles you have."

"That's what I told her."

"You…" He addressed Gregorio over his shoulder. "I thought we had a one o'clock meeting?"

"I'm here, Boss."

Damien jerked his head toward the back stairs.

"Oh. Right. I'll be waiting in your office." He picked up his coffee cup then headed up.

"To be fair," she said when they were alone, "Gregorio did tell me to talk to you."

"I believe him. And you. As long as you're here as my sub, you scene with no man but me. I was clear about that."

"You were."

"If that's not acceptable, we can discuss it. But you're not free to scene with others without first seeking permission."

"Were you listening, Damien? It was a joke." Her voice was higher pitched than normal, and she closed her eyes to get hold of her fraying temper. When she did, she hit them both with the raw truth. "I don't want to be with anyone but you."

"Good." He loosened his grip and made tiny circles with his fingers. "I appreciate you saying so." He dragged her onto her toes. "We have a lot to talk about tonight."

"Yes," she agreed. "We do."

He eased her toward him, and his thick cock pressed against her.

"What about the security cameras?" she reminded him.

"There's no volume unless I turn it up."

"But we are providing a peep show for Gregorio."

"If he knows what's fucking good for him, he won't be watching."

"Still…"

"Come here."

He led her into the powder room.

"A clandestine meeting, Damien?"

He spun her around so fast her breath whooshed out. She desperately pushed her hands flat against the wall as he lifted her skirt and blasted her with five hot slaps on her rear. Then he yanked aside her thong and masturbated her until she screamed out an orgasm and collapsed in a sobbing heap.

It hadn't taken him thirty seconds to give her the relief she'd all-but begged for.

His motions now tender, he turned her back to him and held her tight against his chest. In his arms, she shook. Damien didn't let her go until she found the wherewithal to push him away.

"I needed that," she admitted.

"I know." He took a washcloth from a drawer and daubed her face. "Better, Milady?"

"Much." She offered a half smile. "Thank you." But she was lying. And she wondered if he knew it.

"This isn't finished."

She nodded.

Then, more conflicted than ever, she followed him from the room.

The restless energy that had been churning all day worsened during the afternoon. The scene with Damien should have soothed her, but it didn't. In fact, it contributed to her cauldron of angst.

She craved his touch, didn't want their temporary relationship to end, couldn't figure out a way for it to last. The more often they scened, the deeper she cared for him. The more they shared, the more she ached to share.

Trying to work was impossible, and being separated from him and Gregorio by only a glass partition was torture.

Unable to concentrate, restless, she went into the suite and grabbed her coat from the closet. "I'm going for a walk," she told Damien.

"Would you like me to go with you?"

"No problem," Gregorio said, pushing back his chair. "We can finish up at a more convenient time."

"Thanks, but I'd rather be alone."

"I don't like this." Damien folded his arms across his chest.

"I'll stay close."

"Take your phone."

Since arguing might get her confined to the house, she nodded.

Even though she walked for less than an hour, her toes had turned numb in her boots, and her fingers were frozen even though she'd kept them in her pockets.

She was grateful her hair covered her ears. As it was, the wind had seemed to gnaw on the lobes.

Frustratingly, the physical exercise had done little to relieve her tension.

When she entered the main kitchen, Damien was standing in front of the stove, whisking something in a pan. "Right on time," he said.

"Security cameras?" she guessed. "That's how you knew I was on my way back. You were watching me?"

"You were always in my sight."

"I don't know whether to be relieved or freaked out."

"Grateful," he suggested. "If you'd had any troubles, I'd have found you. And I knew when to have the hot chocolate ready."

"Hot chocolate?" She stamped the snow off her feet, hung up her coat then wandered across the room. "With milk?"

"Of course."

She glanced around. "Where's the little packages?"

"I'm insulted," he said.

"Why?"

"It's homemade. Milk, cocoa powder, sugar, a pinch of salt."

"No packages?" she asked again.

"No packages," he confirmed.

"Homemade?" she repeated.

"With whole milk."

Little things like this were why she was falling for him. "I'm salivating."

"Have a seat at the table. I'll bring you a mug."

"Is Gregorio gone?"

"Yes. You're alone with me." He filled two mugs.

Catrina took a chair. "You didn't have to do this," she said as he slid a yellow ceramic mug in front of her. Gratefully, she wrapped her cold hands around it and lifted it close to her face. "But I'm glad you did. It smells divine." She breathed in the rich, chocolate scent. "Thank you."

"A Dom takes care of his sub, always."

She looked up at him. He'd remained standing.

"It's a responsibility I take seriously."

When she didn't respond, he added, "One I'm honored to have."

Again, he'd taught her a lesson. Being a Dominant was about more than meeting someone's physical needs. Emotions and feelings could create a ball of complication that took time and energy to work through. And he not only seemed to feel obligated, but also compelled to untangle the mess. No relationship with a man, ever, had coaxed her to commit to that type of energy.

"More than that, it's how a man takes care of his woman."

Breath left her lungs. Until now, *until him,* that hadn't been her experience with any man in her life, even her own father.

Because she was flustered, she settled and changed the subject. "I didn't mean to interrupt your afternoon's work," she said.

He took a chair, turned it backward and straddled it as he faced her. "The schedule can be rearranged. Whatever is bothering you needs to be discussed."

She took a drink of her chocolate. "It's amazing." Rich and creamy, warming her from the inside.

"Talk to me," he encouraged her.

"I'm sure Gregorio filled you in."

"Not at all. This is between us, Milady. Gregorio is loyal to a fault. To you, as well as me."

"I don't know what to say," she admitted, repeatedly tracing the handle, stalling. "This..." She waved a hand. "Our time together has been so much more than I could have imagined. Thank you for it. You're right. I'll be a much better Domme. I guess part of me isn't ready for it to be over."

"We're not done yet."

"I know." That frightened her the most. It was already becoming difficult to imagine life without him. And she was determined to be self-sufficient.

"I intend to have you in the dungeon tonight."

"And we'll have tomorrow night."

When the Den was hosting an event.

And Saturday, she was leaving.

With a vice squeezing her heart, she told herself to enjoy the moment rather than living in the future.

"Would you like to go for an early dinner?"

"Do we have any leftovers? I think the hot chocolate has spoiled my appetite." Either that, or her emotions had her stomach in knots.

"We can start our play earlier that way," he said. "If you're hungry afterward, we can go out to dinner then."

The way he lowered his eyelids slightly as he looked at her and reached across to tuck the hair behind her ears made her thought process scramble.

Common sense urged her to run away, but a stronger compulsion forced her to stay.

Upstairs, in their private space, he warmed up food while she set the table.

They worked in tandem, already having learned to anticipate the other's needs.

Generally the conversation flowed, but not now. He seemed to be giving her long spaces in case she wanted to fill the silence. Since she really didn't know how to say what was on her mind, she remained silent and picked at her food, using the hot chocolate as an excuse to not eat.

When the kitchen was clean, he said, "Would you still like to meet downstairs? I'm happy to take you out, maybe to a movie? A nightclub? Bowling?"

She blinked. "Bowling?"

"Seeing if you were paying attention."

"My average is ninety-nine," she said with a laugh. "So I only go with girlfriends and mainly for the beer."

"We could stay up here if you prefer, talk."

Suddenly that was the last thing she wanted to do "No." She shook her head. "I'd prefer to play, if you would."

"Ten minutes? Be naked, waiting on your knees in the third room on the left."

She frowned. "That's the one with the St. Andrew's cross."

"It is. You ever been on one?"

"Of course not."

"Sublime experience. You'll enjoy it."

The idea of being spread wide and attached to the wooden structure shaped like an X sent a jolt through her. And if it hadn't, the look on his face would have.

"Ticktock, Milady."

She didn't need to be told a second time.

Walking through the Den all by herself seemed strange. Without dozens of people around, the rooms appeared extra-large, and her footsteps echoed hollowly.

She descended the stairs and made her way to the room he'd indicated.

As she stood in front of the apparatus, anxiousness drifted away, leaving her oddly content.

When she'd arrived almost two weeks ago, his orders had made her nerves taut. Now they comforted her.

After taking off her clothes and folding them she knelt.

Then she listened for sounds of Damien's approach.

Moments later, probably because of the home's emptiness, the sound of his solid footfall reached her.

Drawing a breath, Catrina spread her knees apart and put her hands behind her neck. As he entered, she lowered her gaze to the floor.

"Damn it, Milady." He balled his fist and cleared his throat. "You've pleased me."

"Thank you, Damien."

"At times like these, playing is difficult. I'd rather fuck you."

Blinking at his honesty, she looked up. "That would be okay with me."

"I want this for you. But I promise you, I'll take you completely."

Yes.

"Onto the cross."

The structure seemed more imposing than it did when she affixed subs to it. "Which direction?" With her question, nerves unexpectedly skittered through her as she wondered what he had planned. So much for feeling settled.

"Facing me."

She'd been afraid of that.

He made quick work of securing her wrists and ankles.

"I'm going to introduce you to the crop."

"Good thing you tied me up before you said that."

"Scared?" he asked, his voice terrifyingly soft.

"Should I be?"

"Yes."

Her stomach dropped.

"You always have your safe word."

Along with trust in him. Since they'd been together, he'd asked for a lot, but never too much.

Damien made a show of rolling back his cuffs.

Though she wanted to look away, she was transfixed, and she tracked his every motion as he crossed to the wall and selected a crop with a large flapper. "Looks painful."

"Potentially, yes."

"Could we trade it in for a flogger?"

"Have you ever used one of these on a sub's testicles?"

"At his request. One time."

"Then you should know what it feels like. How it can feel like a feather and how it can sear and how to mix it up for maximum effect."

His words meant he planned to use the crop on her most delicate places.

Still across the room from her, he tested the length, sending it whistling through the air.

She gasped.

"I'll start very softly. Then I'll increase the intensity a slight bit, but on sensitive areas, I'll be exceedingly controlled."

Instinctively, she tightened her entire body.

"You'll be able to take more than you might think."

She scowled at the implement. "I'm not so sure about that."

"Part of you is curious. Which is why you haven't safe worded."

"Doesn't mean I won't."

"Fair statement." He nodded in acknowledgment. "Shall we start with your pussy?"

Catrina licked her lower lip.

"Milady?" He laid the crop's length against his calf. "Look at me. Not it. At me."

His request was surprisingly difficult.

"When you're ready, tell me to proceed."

Being honest with him — with herself — instead of hiding behind a shield of bravado was one of the gutsiest things she'd ever done. "I'm nervous."

"How can I help?"

"Kiss me?" Her words stunned her. She'd never made this kind of request for intimacy during a scene before.

His smile and murmur of pleasure came instantaneously.

Closing the distance between them, he wrapped his hand in her hair, then he tugged to angle her head back.

Damien gifted her with the gentlest of kisses. Then he pulled away, allowed her to catch her breath, then leaned in again. Over the course of a minute or more, he played with her, teasing, taking more, offering everything she could possibly want.

Forgetting her fear, she kissed him back, meeting the thrust of his tongue.

"Now open your mouth."

When she did, he plundered the depths.

His kiss lasted forever, and with her surrender, she said the things she couldn't out loud.

Eventually, when she was breathless, her thoughts scattered, he pulled back.

"Will you..." She couldn't bear to be apart. "Will you fuck me after we're done?"

"You can count on it, Milady. I've desired you all day."

After pressing her lips together bravely, she nodded. "I'm ready."

He ran his palm over the crown of her head. "You thrill me. Again and again."

For his words of approval, she'd do anything.

After trailing his finger between her breasts, he moved away.

She arched her back.

His kiss had given her confidence, so much so that she was no longer shrinking in her bondage. Rather, she was anticipating the scene.

Very slowly, Damien approached. "Eyes on me."

He trailed the leather flapper down her chest, between her breasts, then lower, over the slight swell of her stomach.

She tensed right before he landed the first tap.

When it was over, she exhaled. "That wasn't what I expected."

"Milady, perhaps one of these days, you'll trust me."

"I…" Exhaling, she admitted, "I kind of liked it."

"That was my intention." He grinned. "This little demonstration is meant to arouse you."

"Do it again?"

Again and again, he did so, leaving her turned on, her entire body relaxed.

"Still doing okay?"

"Amazing."

He brushed her nipples with the flapper until they each hardened. As he continued, he used more pressure.

She gasped. "Oh, Sir!"

"You like that, too?"

"Very much." If she'd had any idea that having a crop used on her body could be like this…

"Ready for more?"

"I don't know. Am I?"

He eased his fingers across her chest, tightening her nipples, and igniting a response. "Tell me if you're not."

But she was.

The strikes came faster, and he mixed it up, cropping her breasts, her belly, her pussy, her inner thighs.

She understood how it could be used differently to cause anguish, even damage, but in the hand of a master — like him — the toy was the ultimate seduction.

"Let go," he instructed.

"I'm totally relaxed."

"Almost," he allowed. "But not quite."

His crop seemed to be everywhere at once, licking, biting, caressing.

Surrendering, she closed her eyes and allowed her head to tip back.

From far away, his voice reached her, but she couldn't make out the words.

Catrina's body burned with the fire he stoked.

"That's it, Milady."

He blazed her pussy, and in response, she became damper.

"You're getting closer. I smell your heat. If you can, give me your climax."

That couldn't be possible, yet she didn't have the energy to argue with him.

Relentlessly, he used the flapper on her swollen breasts and nipples.

Her body jerked, and she screamed.

Her Dominant was ceaseless, dragging sensation from deeper than it had ever been before. "Damien? Damien!"

"Take it." He continued to crop her inner thighs and pussy.

"I…" She couldn't get there.

"What do you want?"

An orgasm. You.

She arched forward when he blazed a path up her inner thighs, the squared-off end of the flapper nipping at her swollen clit. "Damn it."

"Tell me," he encouraged.

His voice came from a long way off.

The whole time, he continued to work her body. There wasn't an inch of her skin that didn't zing with fever.

He went back to the gentle tapping on her pussy. After the recent blazes, this was maddeningly soft.

When she didn't respond, he used the leather to brutally lick her labia.

Coming apart, she writhed.

The louder her cries, the harder his spanks. She yelled, tugged at her bonds, twisted her body. "I want to come! For the love of God… *Damien!*"

The crop crashed to the floor.

Thankfully, he slid his fingers inside her to press against her G-spot. "That's it." He forced the orgasm from her, and she sobbed, desperate, frantic, grateful.

"Now, Milady, the fucking."

After undressing, he rolled a condom down his shaft. "On your tiptoes."

With her fully secured to the cross, helpless to him, he drove his cock up inside her.

If she'd had any doubt before now, it was erased.

Damien had dominated her.

Thoroughly.

Completely.

Leaving her shattered.

And he still wasn't finished with her…

Chapter Twenty

"I've got you." Damien wrapped one of his arms around her back, and he placed the other on her rear.

Then, bending his knees, he surged up inside her, filling her desperate pussy with his magnificent cock.

"I... Yes."

"I want everything from you, Catrina. Your respect, your trust, your total submission."

He fucked her so hard, so deep, she couldn't deny him. "Yes. Sir! Sir, sir, *sir.*" Desperate to touch him, she fought against her bonds, trying to escape.

Seeming to know her needs as well as she did, he leaned in closer.

That drove her madder.

Since her body was still sensitized from his crop, their skin-to-skin abrasion made her wild.

He continued his loving assault, giving her more and more, until he shoved her into the abyss.

With a cry, she curled her toes as she dropped her head onto his shoulder. "Take me, Master."

For a moment, he stilled, and silence echoed around them, thundering in her ears.

"God. Catrina. What you do to me." With a deep groan, Damien tightened his grip, and his movements became shorter, even more powerful.

With one final thrust and a deep, masculine, guttural sound, he shouted her name.

Together they spiraled, and he pulsed inside her.

Forever, he held her, her head on his shoulder, his arms looped around her. "Jesus, Catrina."

She had no words.

He'd taken her to a place she hadn't known existed, wouldn't have believed possible.

"Thank you, Milady."

The way he held her combined with the way they breathed together created a pulsing intimacy.

For long minutes, while they recovered, he remained in place, tenderly placing a hand at her nape to cradle her as if she were the most precious thing he could imagine.

When she eventually blinked the world back into focus, he eased back, sliding out of her.

Instead of walking away, he placed a thumb beneath her chin. "Let me untie you."

He took his time, caressing her skin and rubbing circulation back into her body as he released each limb.

Gently, he traced a tiny red mark he'd left on her breast. "I'll put some cream on that."

"It'll be fine," she said.

"I said I'll put some cream on it."

Was there any arguing with him once his mind was made up?

Only then did he leave her to dispose of the condom.

Now alone, reality returned, and with it, the realization that she'd called him Master.

As confused as she was upset, she wrapped her arms around her middle.

Moments later, he was back with a white tube of arnica.

His ministrations were heart-meltingly gentle.

Once he was satisfied, he nodded and captured her gaze. "How are you doing?"

"I'm fine." To cover her confused emotions, she forced a smile. "Thank you." She didn't add Sir as an honorific, though a deep yearning urged her to.

Slowly, he swept his gaze over her body, as if making sure for himself.

"That was even more than I could have hoped."

"Let's sit for a minute."

"I'm—"

"Shaking," he interjected, his tone no-nonsense. "You just endured something unique."

Had he noticed the slip of her tongue?

And that was what it was. Something accidental, not something she meant.

Without waiting for an argument, he drew her toward a chair. "Give me a second." Once he had pulled a blanket out from a cupboard, he took a seat then pulled her onto his lap.

Moments later, the blanket was tucked into place, and she was enfolded in the warmth and security of his strong arms.

"How are you doing?"

Part of her couldn't believe how deep she'd gone, how vulnerable she'd been.

"Catrina?"

"You're really good at that." It was a half-answer, as well as the total truth. And she prayed he wouldn't push for more information than that.

"I appreciate your trust."

During their time together, everything he'd done had made her respect him more.

Which was only going to make it more difficult to leave.

Her body finally stopped trembling as her temperature returned to normal. Only then did he help her to dress.

"You can go ahead and go upstairs if you want. I'll clean up here."

"I can help." It would give her something to do, besides ruminate and pray he'd put his own clothes back on. As it was, she could hardly keep her gaze off his rippling muscles, and she forced away memories of the way he'd possessed her.

"I'll handle it." Damien shook his head. "You need some time to recover."

Which was the absolute truth. "You're sure?"

"I'll join you in a few minutes."

Grateful for the respite, she escaped, walking back up the stairs to their private space.

When she was there, the word Master seemed to reverberate from the ceiling.

Determinedly, she shook her head.

Of course she hadn't meant it. She was a Domme in her own right. And by this time next week, one of her boys would be kneeling at her feet.

Needing to banish her thoughts, she turned on the shower, set the temperature to scalding, then stood beneath the spray.

Even when steam billowed around her, she couldn't chase away thoughts of the scene they'd shared or the way he'd so thoroughly taken her.

While she was soaping her body, imagining his touch on her skin, Damien entered the bathroom.

Considering her, he stripped off then joined her.

"May I?"

She should make an excuse to leave, put some desperately needed distance between them, but his soothing tone and take-charge manner did her in.

He took down the showerhead.

"Spread your legs."

Despite her resolve, he had her aroused again.

"Can't get enough, Milady?" he asked as he spread her labia and turned the dial to the pulse setting.

Instinctively, she jerked, seeking satisfaction.

"You've earned this."

Needing stability, she braced one hand on the tiles, and she wrapped the other around his shoulder.

"Beautiful!"

Eyes closed, whimpering, she came.

The man knew exactly what to do to give or offer pleasure.

When she'd ridden it out, he shucked stray droplets of water from her face before turning off the faucet.

"Thank you for that." At this point, manners were reflexive instead of something she needed to be reminded to use.

And right now, that bothered her.

He exited the shower, grabbed a towel for her and wrapped it around her.

Always, he cared for her before satisfying his needs.

Catrina shrugged into a robe while he dressed in a pair of lightweight workout pants and a soft T-shirt.

"May I offer you a glass of wine?"

Grateful they were done playing, she nodded. "That would be nice." Hopefully, the alcohol would help dissipate the dull agitation that was now working its way through her.

"I'll meet you in the living room."

After drying her hair and clipping it back, she donned a pair of yoga pants and a sweater. Barefoot, she joined him on the couch. In front of them was a charcuterie board. "You think of everything. Thank you."

Once she'd accepted the glass he offered, she rested her back against the arm, facing him, sitting cross-legged.

"Do you want to talk about whatever you were discussing with Gregorio earlier?"

She shouldn't have been surprised that he'd circled back to this.

But at least for now, he hadn't mentioned the fact she'd called him Master.

"I'd rather keep it private."

Saying nothing, he contemplated her.

Maybe because he allowed silence to grow, she shifted.

The emotions that had been swimming through her now threatened to swamp her.

Until earlier today, when she'd been totally honest with Gregorio—and herself—she hadn't truly realized that she was starting to care about Damien.

And maybe that had partially led her to say what she did in the dungeon.

Still, falling for him was the last thing she should do.

She'd spent the last couple of years carving out a life she loved, playing with her boys, building her business, taking care of others.

Never again would she be as vulnerable as she had been in her previous relationships.

Even if that meant spending the rest of her life alone. And yet...

The time with Damien had meant so much to her.

Their scenes rocked her world, the sex, the orgasms, working in the same office, brainstorming, talking, sharing an occasional smoldering kiss, or even heading to the bedroom during the day to make love.

Then there were the evenings in front of the fire, always followed by falling asleep in the comfort of his embrace.

Maybe she shouldn't have agreed to his ridiculous challenge.

Saying goodbye was going to tear her apart.

He propped an ankle on his opposite knee and drummed his fingers on his thighs. By staying where he was, he gave her room to breathe.

As always, he seemed to know what she needed.

"Is something about the way we interact bothering you?"

"No." *My own emotions are the problem.*

But how did she satisfy him, without revealing too much?

"I appreciate your lessons. You were correct that I understand the BDSM dynamic better, in ways I never did before." And she'd learned the benefits of spending more time talking to her boys beforehand to build their anticipation for the scene, letting details fill their minds to the point of obsession, making the culmination even more powerful. "You've made me a better Domme." Which was the entire point.

So why was she feeling mentally unmoored?

Her hand shaking, she put down her untouched glass of wine.

Swallowing back her sudden tears, she inhaled. "This has been really instructive." Then, before she could change her mind and give him an even bigger part of her heart, she added, "I need to go home."

He didn't protest, didn't touch her. But leaning forward, he quietly asked, "What are you scared of, Catrina?"

"Nothing." *Everything. That I'm in so deep I'll never find my way back.* And how stupid was that? He'd been up front in saying he didn't believe in love. Not that it mattered since she'd sworn off the fickle emotion. "The two weeks are almost up, anyway. If I leave now, I'll have the weekend to get settled and be ready for work on Monday morning. And you can be the host of your party rather than hiding up here with me."

"We could always attend."

With me on the end of your leash.

To save herself, she needed to get her life back to normal as soon as possible.

"Your decision is made?"

"It is."

"Is this open for discussion?" he asked.

"*No.*" She made her response emphatic because if it wasn't, she'd relent. Her clothes would be off, and his hands would be all over her. In less than a couple of minutes, she'd be begging for his lash. And she'd be falling for him even harder.

Bringing up her chin, she added, "My mind is made up." *Don't make me use my safe word.* "I insist you respect my decision."

"*Fuck.* Catrina —"

"I mean it, Damien." Her voice wavering, damnably betraying her emotions, she stood.

"Of course." He inhaled sharply. "As you wish."

Even though her knees threatened to buckle, she forced herself to walk to the closet. Fighting back a deep desire to stay — and knowing it would only be harder to leave on Saturday if she did — Catrina started throwing her clothing back into her bag.

Every drawer she opened, every shelf she scanned, held memories.

Coming here was a terrible mistake.

With her shoulders pulled back, she double checked that she had everything then returned to the living room.

Their drinks were where they'd left them, but Damien was nowhere in sight.

Though she should be relieved, she fought off her disappointment.

He wasn't in his office, and she checked the security monitors. She didn't see him on any of them.

On automatic pilot, she disconnected her computer from the printer and started to clear out her desk.

She heard the firm sound of his footfall on the stairs and the file she'd been holding slipped from her nerveless fingers.

"I started your car."

"Thank you." She wanted her words to be strong, but they were nothing more than a whisper.

"For safety reasons, if nothing else, it would be smarter for you to stay here overnight. Or I could ask

Jeff or Gregorio to drive you into Winter Park so you can stay at a hotel."

Always looking out for her. *Like a good Dom.* "I'll be fine." When had she become so adept at lying?

"You're determined, then?"

Not trusting that her voice wouldn't tremble, betraying her feelings, she pressed her lips together and nodded.

"In that case, I'll help you with this."

An argument would cost her precious time, so she kept her mouth closed.

After she tucked all of her files into her computer backpack, he slung a strap over one shoulder then headed down the stairs, leaving her to grab her bag and purse.

He'd moved her car to the driveway, the hood pointed toward the street, which meant he'd backed it out then turned it around so she could drive straight out. It was running and the wipers made lazy swipes across the windshield, batting away the occasional snowflakes.

He opened her door, and she slid past his body, making sure they didn't touch, and into the warmed cab.

While he stowed her belongings in the trunk, she lowered the window.

"I've enjoyed your company."

"You were an excellent…" *Dom. Lover.* "Host."

"Come back anytime."

Not ever. And she suspected he knew that.

"Call if you need anything," he said, hands propped on the top of the car. "*Anything.* Remember that I'm always available to talk about things, discuss your fears."

"I appreciate the offer." Impatience gnawed at her. She had to escape...*now.*

"Send me a text when you get home."

"No."

"That wasn't a request." He leaned into the window, heating the air, filling her with his spicy, masculine scent. "It's just common fucking courtesy, Catrina," he snapped. "It's late. It's dark. There's not one single part of me that wants to let you go. Show some decency and let me know you're safe."

"I—"

"Either that or I follow you home. Your choice."

The implacable note in his voice made her blink. "You're serious."

"Fucking serious," he confirmed.

"Fine. I'll send you a message."

The moment he leaned back a little, she hit the button to close the window. Then she slipped into drive and hit the gas harder than she should have.

As the lights of the Den faded in her rearview mirror, she started to shake.

Beneath the inky sky, she was alone and lonely in ways she'd never experienced before.

Hot tears streamed down her face.

What the hell have I done?

* * * *

What the fuck just happened?

"You look like you could use a drink."

Damien glanced at Gregorio as he entered his office uninvited. "Any excuse?"

"I'm doing you a favor. It's what friends are for," Gregorio said, zeroing in on the sideboard with its secret panel.

"Friends are for drinking your most expensive alcohol?"

"Who else is going to suffer like that for you, Boss?"

Damien reached forward and clicked a couple of keys on his keyboard. Obviously, Catrina wasn't turning her car around and coming back, so staring at the feed from the outdoor cameras was pointless.

Instead, he brought up images of a tranquil beach scene. Palm trees and hammocks were on the left-hand side, with crystal blue waters and white sand on the other. It looked sun-drenched, and as far away from here as he was from Catrina.

"Maybe I should have made us something with rum instead," Gregorio suggested when he looked at Damien's computer screens.

"This will work." Damien accepted the snifter then leaned back. Lost in thought, he warmed the glass in his palms.

"I take it Milady left us."

"The two weeks were almost up."

"I'm not surprised."

Obviously, Gregorio, too, had seen the way her car fishtailed as she'd accelerated away from the property.

"Something to say, Gregorio?"

"Not at all, Boss." He lazed back, legs stretched in front of him, crossed at the ankles.

Damien sat up straight. "What did she say to you in the kitchen?"

"You know damn well I'm not going to break her confidence."

"If there's something I need to know..."

Gregorio shook his head. "You scare the hell out of her. It's one thing to scene with a Dom, even to be a trainee. It's another to offer total submission."

"Spoken like the voice of experience."

"Yeah. It's demanding," Gregorio said. "Think about what you wanted from her. Were you satisfied with teaching her how to be a better Domme?"

Damien glanced up and stared at the beach screenshot without actually seeing it. That was a question he didn't want to answer.

When he'd goaded her into accepting his challenge, he'd wanted to crack her toughness to see the woman beneath. He'd wanted to master her. But at what cost to her?

And at what cost to him?

He'd caught glimpses of her vulnerability, and he'd relentlessly pushed, forcing her to expose them while offering little to nothing back in return. He hadn't mentioned what he was feeling or experiencing, even when she'd talked with Gregorio. He'd had a second chance when she'd come back after her walk.

And then...

Christ.

She'd called him Master when she'd submitted to his crop earlier.

Catrina had transcended a barrier she'd been keeping between them, given him a gift, and instead of immediately acknowledging it, sweeping her into his arms after rewarding her with a powerful orgasm, he'd... Stayed in the scene. Kept his emotional distance.

Even when she'd announced her intention of leaving, he'd invited her to attend Friday night's festivities at the Den.

For someone reputed to be an excellent Dom, he'd screwed up. Bad. Who the hell had he been to think he could teach her anything?

"You're not the biggest fuckwad on the planet, Boss. You just look like it at this moment."

"Was that supposed to help?"

Gregorio shrugged.

Damien cared about her more than he would have believed possible. And he'd figured they had two days remaining to discuss their relationship.

Gregorio took a sip of the brandy. "Damn, I forget how good this stuff is. Not sorry to be drinking it, even at your expense."

"What are friends for?" Damien said dryly, repeating Gregorio's earlier words. With that, he motioned for Gregorio to refill his glass.

"Got a plan, Boss?" Gregorio asked.

No fucking clue.

For the first time in his life.

Damien knew only one thing for certain. *I'm not letting you go, Catrina. You're mine…*

Chapter Twenty-One

"Oh, my Cat, it's one thing to lie to us," Evelyn said softly, "but you need to ask if you're lying to yourself."

Caught.

Catrina looked at her mother over a beer. They were having lunch at the same brew pub where she'd met them three weeks ago. Three weeks that could have been a lifetime. "How do you do that?"

Evelyn nodded. "Mothers know these things."

"Your eyes give you away," Milton added. "The way you look away, down and to the left."

Just like Damien had said.

"Miltey!" Playfully, Evelyn smacked his arm. "Hush! Don't give away my secrets."

With a grin, Catrina reached for a roll and tore a chunk off it. "Next you'll be telling me she doesn't have eyes in the back of her head."

"Actually..." Milton nodded. "Those she does have."

Catrina laughed for the first time since leaving the Den and its enigmatic owner.

She hadn't left the house in over a week.

And she'd yet to set up a meeting with any of her boys.

Seeing her mother today, even if her appendage was with her, was something Catrina had desperately needed.

"So not hearing from your gentleman friend *does* bother you?" Evelyn asked.

That was an understatement.

Even the reminder of Damien was a metal band wrapped around her chest, constricting her breathing. "Yes." She sighed. It relieved her not to pretend otherwise.

"You two were closer than you let on."

"I was." She dipped the piece of bread in some butter, but she didn't eat it. "Obviously he wasn't."

"He seemed smitten to me," Evelyn said. "He hasn't called at all?"

"He left me alone for a few days, but he's called twice."

"And what else?"

She made small circles with her beer bug. "I've received a few text messages." *Several, in fact. Every day.*

"And?" her mother prompted.

"That's it. End of story."

"So what are you going to do about it?"

"Same thing I always do. Pick up the pieces and continue with my life."

The truth was, since she left, she'd been lonely and miserable.

Damien Lowell haunted her days and stalked her nights.

She thought about him when she had to pour her own coffee in the morning. And when she masturbated, she fantasized about the way he'd wielded the crop on her body. He even intruded on her bath time when she remembered the way he'd slicked his hands with soap and run them over her body.

"You're not going to respond to him?"

"No." For the first few days she'd considered it, but had ultimately decided not to. Being in contact with him would only prolong the amount of time she needed to heal.

There was nothing to be said.

Never again would she compromise on who she was.

It was easier to tell herself that they had shared a fun couple of weeks.

She just wished she could convince herself not to miss his touch, and most of all, their easy, magical intimacy.

"You're not at all curious about what he might have to say?"

Her mother and Milton were both staring at her expectantly. "No."

Evelyn patted Catrina's hand. "I want you to be happy. You're one of the strongest people I know." She softened her voice. "It's okay to take your own advice. Protect yourself." She shrugged. "But as I said last time we talked, and you've told your clients, you're allowed to fall in love again."

I wish it were that simple.

No matter how hard she tried, she couldn't be the woman—submissive—that Damien wanted or needed.

Nor had he even indicated that he'd like anything more than a sexy two-week training session.

As she'd told her mother, the best thing she could do was to move on with her life.

She sighed.

If only convincing her heart to accept her brain's decision were possible.

"You're scared of being hurt."

Realizing her mother was speaking again, Catrina forced herself back to the present moment.

"I don't blame you for not wanting to take a risk. But there's a lot of joy to be had out there, just past the edge of your comfort zone." Evelyn looked at her future husband. "No matter what path we choose, there are no guarantees. And there's always the potential for a broken heart."

"Unless he did something dastardly?" Milton asked.

Dastardly? "No." She couldn't help but smile at the idea and the old-fashioned word. "Nothing like that."

"He's not a liar or a cheat? Because if he is, I'll want a word with him myself."

As she shook her head, she marveled at her future stepfather, never imagining he'd be so protective.

Maybe her mother hadn't done so badly, after all.

"Are you trying to avoid failure, my Cat?" Evelyn asked softly.

Catrina sat there, shocked into silence.

Am I?

"Don't you want to be absolutely certain that you're not just trying to protect yourself?" Evelyn asked. "At least talk to your young man." Encouragingly, Evelyn patted Catrina's hand one last time. "The way he tied his hair back…that was hot."

"Mother!

"Evelyn!"

Evelyn giggled and sipped her beer. "I'm about to be married, not buried, my darling Miltey. I notice these things." Then she batted her eyes at him. "Not that there will ever be any other man on the planet for me."

Until today, the last time her mother had scandalized her this much, Catrina had been in middle school. She shook her head to clear the image. "About your wedding... Tell me all the details. Did you decide on" — she so did not want to hear about the honeymoon — "what flowers you'll decorate the chapel with?"

Milton signaled to the server that he'd like another beer and patiently sat back to listen while her mother bubbled over with excitement. His obvious fondness and tolerance of Evelyn's enthusiasm endeared him to Catrina. Maybe Damien had been right about that, too.

After dinner, she drove home, and her phone dinged, signaling another incoming text message. With Damien's tone.

Resolved, she ignored it.

But still, she hadn't blocked his number.

And that told her something.

Over the next two weeks, Damien continued to text, and she continued to ignore him.

Since her discussion with her mom, Catrina's sleep had been choppy, and she was going through her days feeling dazed and out of sorts.

Finally, she'd realized that if she hoped to move on, she had to resume her regular life...even if she would never return to the Den.

For the first time since she'd agreed to submit to Damien, one of her boys was coming over this evening, and she needed to prepare the house and herself.

Even though her heart wasn't in it.

Catrina had believed that Topping was a way to keep her heart safe.

Now she realized she'd intentionally protected herself by disconnecting from her emotions and what she truly craved — intimacy.

With a deep breath, she shook off the uncomfortable thoughts.

She needed to focus on her upcoming session. After all, an orgasm was an orgasm...even if it wasn't from the man — the Dom — she truly wanted.

With Damien's coaching in mind, she'd sent Shaun several emails, building his tension. Yesterday, they'd chatted on the phone, and she'd explored what he liked in greater depth than they ever had before. Before they'd hung up, he informed her how grateful he was.

Two hours before he was scheduled to arrive, she entered her bathroom and pulled out the makeup bag that she used when she wanted to be dramatic.

After not wearing cosmetics or false eyelashes for so long, this seemed unnatural. Getting the dramatic effects right required all of her skill and concentration.

Then she walked into her bedroom to survey the corner of her closet where she kept her BDSM clothing.

She'd grown accustomed to Damien selecting her attire and she agonized over choosing the right outfit.

Instead of a skirt that would leave her ass exposed, she opted for tight leather pants and heeled boots.

Generally, she wore a corset when acting as a Domme.

Tonight, though, she selected a black, button up blouse from the streetwear side of her rack.

Then she surveyed herself in the mirror.

She no longer recognized herself as a Domme. *Was I ever truly one?* This afternoon, she felt as if she was preparing for a role, nothing more.

Still, Shaun would be arriving soon. And she had expectations to meet.

Ten minutes later, the doorbell rang.

He was early, and that was unusual. At least she was ready for him.

When she opened the door, a wall of red roses and dozens of balloons filled her vision.

Slowly, they moved to one side.

Damien.

Larger than life, shadows beneath his eyes, face leaner and gaunter than it had been the last time she saw him, he stood there.

Her legs went out from underneath her.

"Jesus, Catrina. You look beautiful."

He perused her, taking in her attire.

"I'd like to talk to you."

Breathless, unable to respond, she pressed a palm to the doorjamb for support.

"I left you a few voicemails, and numerous text messages telling you I'd stay away if you truly never wanted to see me again." His voice was broken, hoarse. "You never responded, so I'm here."

"I..."

"Invite me in?" he asked softly.

Her heart fluttering, she frantically shook her head.

No way was she prepared to face him.. And she had company arriving momentarily.

"Or I can stand here and say what I need to say."

She glanced down the street. A couple walking a dog slowed their approach, watching what was going on. "Your timing is terrible."

At that moment, a car pulled up to the curb, and Shaun exited.

Slowly, he walked up the sidewalk, and now the couple with the dog watched with active interest.

Not that she blamed them.

Damien held dozens of roses and balloons, and Shaun was wearing skin-tight pants. His blond good looks provided a sharp contrast to Damien's seductive dark hair and blue eyes.

Swinging his gaze from Damien, back to her, Shaun asked, "Am I interrupting something?"

She shook her head but looked at Damien. "As I said, your timing is terrible."

Undeterred, he addressed Shaun. "There's a VIP event at the Den tomorrow night. Not open to the public."

"Err—"

"I'll put you on the list. And I'll make sure you get priority booking for a session with Gregorio. On me."

She gasped.

"Seriously?" Shaun said with a shrug. "All right. Fucking all right."

"Now, go."

Shaun blinked. "Yeah. Sure." He turned to jog down the couple of stairs leading to the sidewalk, then he stopped and looked back. "See ya later, Milady."

With a tight nod, she waved.

"That was unacceptable behavior." She folded her arms over her chest.

"Was it?" he asked, completely unfazed.

So Domlike.

"I've missed you."

His words disarmed her.

When he spoke again, he raised his voice. "I love you, Catrina."

The couple cheered.

The floor spun beneath her, and she couldn't breathe.

"And I was a total idiot."

"*You…?*"

This couldn't be happening.

"You called me Master, and I didn't honor what that meant to you. To me. Catrina, I want to spend the rest of my life with you."

Oh, God.

Surely this was a dream. An impossible one.

Tears burned her eyes.

The passersby now clapped for them, and a man who was about to get into his car stopped to see what was happening.

"Will you invite me in?" he asked again. "Or shall we continue to provide your neighbors with a show?"

If she were smart, she'd shut the door and lock it.

But at what cost?

Deep inside, in a place she'd barricaded years ago, hope stirred, terrifying her.

She wrapped her arms around herself.

"Out here it is. Catrina..." He placed the massive flower arrangements on the porch behind him, and then he lowered himself to knee.

No.

Her mouth fell open.

"Milady... Catrina... I'll do whatever it takes to make you happy. Will you marry me?"

This couldn't be happening...*couldn't.*

"Say yes!" her neighbor shouted.

The dog danced around, barking.

"Damien... I wasn't expecting..."

His smile became a grimace. "That wasn't the response I was hoping for." Still, he dug into his pocket and pulled out a small box.

With his thumb he flipped open the lid.

In the sun, a massive diamond winked up at her.

"I'd love to put this on your finger as a symbol of my never-ending commitment to you."

No matter what the neighbors urged, she couldn't accept.

Taking a deep breath, Catrina attempted to herself.

Love?

Her mind was so filled with fog that she couldn't process what was happening.

With a deep sigh, he flipped the ring box closed and slid it back into his pocket. "Will you at least hear me out?"

When she didn't answer, he tried again. "Ten minutes?"

Because her renegade heart wouldn't let her refuse, she nodded. "Not a moment longer."

Damien stood, then bent to scoop up the flowers.

He glanced over his shoulder. "Fingers crossed," he shouted to the couple with the excited pup.

"Good luck, man!" The man gave him a thumbs-up.

Finally, as she stepped aside, her neighbor climbed behind the wheel of the vehicle, and the young couple continued on. "This is just so we have privacy," she warned him, eyes narrowed as he entered the foyer.

"Understood."

Though she heard his voice, she couldn't see him through the enormous display of roses and bobbing balloons.

"Where do you want them?"

She wasn't sure she had a surface big enough to hold them. "Kitchen island, maybe?"

He laid the flowers flat, and they took up the entire surface.

"Did you buy out an entire store?"

"Two of them." He shrugged.

Between the bouquets, the balloons, and the ring, he'd gone to an awful lot of effort.

"Look, Catrina." He lifted a hand, but then dropped it again. "I meant every word I said."

The world around her reeled.

Once upon a time, she'd dreamed that a gorgeous, adventurous man would sweep her off her feet.

Reality had taught her such a thing didn't exist.

"Say something," he urged. "Anything."

"Damien…"

He waited.

"I, uhm, I appreciate—"

"Not that," he interrupted. "Not an out and out rejection."

"What else did you want?" *An acceptance is out of the question.*

"A discussion, maybe. Unless…"

This time, she remained silent.

"Tell me you don't care for me. Tell me you never want to look at my face again. That my words mean nothing. That what we shared meant nothing."

She looked down.

Immediately, she realized her mistake.

"Then…?" he prompted.

When she looked back, he lifted a hand, as if to touch her.

Shaking her head, she stepped back.

Needing space, distance, she hurried into the living room and perched on the edge of a chair.

Without an invitation, he followed her.

His legs spread wide, he dominated her space, devastating in his black shirt, black trousers with the outline of the engagement ring meant for her in his pocket.

A thin strip of leather cinched his hair at his nape.

Her memories of him were so vibrant, but they were nothing compared to the reality of his powerfully honed body and outdoorsy scent.

Slowly, he took a seat on the couch. "You *do* care."

"So?" A sob caught in her throat. "It doesn't matter."

"Doesn't matter?" he echoed, shock and demand vibrating in his voice. "What the hell do you mean by that?"

"Look…" Her word, fraught with meaning, hung between them. "I think you're in love with a woman who doesn't exist."

"Oh?" He cocked his head to one side.

She was breaking her own heart all over again.

If she were smarter, she wouldn't have allowed him in the house.

Walking away from him had almost destroyed her…so much so that she was still picking up the pieces over a month later.

Trying to project a calm at odds with the turbulence inside her, she brought her chin up.

"Catrina…" His voice was raw, like her own. "My life is empty without you. I want to share my days and nights with you. I want you to share your dreams and fears with me. We're good together." He raked his hair back from his forehead. "I told you once that I didn't believe in love. I didn't. Until you. What I feel for you, I've never experienced before. I want you. I need you."

He stood to pace, but he stopped across from her, honoring her request not to be crowded.

"I respect who you are."

And who is that? A woman who's terrified to risk being hurt.

"BDSM isn't only what our relationship has been about. Not even close."

But it had provided a beautiful foundation…the way he'd taken over in the bedroom, choosing her clothing, taking such exquisite care of her.

She ached from missing it.

"We're compatible, good together. We enjoy our evenings together, working near each other, going out to eat, talking while I cook, grocery shopping, sitting on the balcony, showering together, sleeping in the same bed, you snuggled in my arms..."

The way you made hot chocolate for me.

She held her breath.

Yes. She missed all those things, desperately.

"When I asked you to marry me, I didn't do it with the expectation that you'll be on your knees for me anytime I want. Or ever."

Could he truly mean this? "How do we work this out?"

"Catrina, you never have to submit to me. We can have the same kind of sex that millions of people around the world share."

Studying him intently, she asked, "But..."

"*You* are enough for me."

Catrina pinched herself to be sure this wasn't a dream that she'd wake up from.

In that moment, her thoughts became clear.

She'd loved everything they'd shared.

"I won't be sceneing with anyone else. But if it matters to you to have occasional scenes with your boys, I understand."

That he had made that offer nearly made her swoon.

"I wouldn't necessarily like it," he added. "But if it's something you need..."

She shook her head. "I don't."

"You...?"

Being a Domme had protected her emotions, but subbing for Damien and being with him had filled the awful hole she'd had in her heart. With him, she'd been safe, and he had never made her feel less than a total equal.

Handing over control had liberated her in ways she hadn't imagined possible, and she'd enjoyed sex in ways she never had before.

Damien's caring attention had transformed her life.

"I love you," he said again, voice hoarse, reaching a place deep inside her that she'd thought was hardened forever. "I want to spend my life making you happy." Very deliberately, he stood and extended a hand to her. "Please tell me you'll have me."

Tension thumping in the air, her heart racing, he waited.

A hundred emotions collided inside her soul.

Closing the distance scared her. But the idea of a future without him was bleak and dark. Did she dare risk what he was offering?

Trembling, she rose and took a single, symbolic step toward him.

And he was there, meeting her, capturing her, holding her, kissing her.

"I will protect, honor, cherish you, Catrina."

"And give me dozens of orgasms?"

"That seems like a good place to begin." He smiled.

"Begin?"

"Tell me you love me, Catrina. As long as we're together, as long as we talk, sort through our fears, we can sort the rest out."

"I..." She shook, but he soothed her. "Yes. I love you, Damien."

"Every day, I will treasure you."

She lifted onto her tiptoes to brush a kiss against his lips.

"Be mine?" he asked.

"Yes, Damien. Yes..."

Once more, he pulled out the ring box and lowered himself to one knee. "Catrina, light of my life, will you make me the happiest man in the world and marry me?"

Her breath caught in her throat. "Yes…"

He pulled out her ring, with its beautiful, enormous oval-cut diamond.

In the overhead light, her gemstone winked, with the promise of their commitment.

Gently, he slid it into place.

Then he stood and fisted her hair, pulling back her head.

His kiss consumed her.

"Forever, Catrina."

She nodded. "Forever."

"I have to have you."

"I thought you'd never ask." She knelt, because she wanted to and because it felt right, and reached for his belt buckle.

With a growl, he swept her from the floor and carried her, laughing and crying, to the bedroom.

"Let's get started on our future…"

Epilogue

"I wish I had met you sooner," Milton said as he faced his bride, holding her hands at the front of the small, mountain chapel. "So I could love you longer."

Because she was standing so close to her mother, Catrina noticed Evelyn's eyes well with tears.

Then, because the sentiment was so sweet and a lump had lodged in her throat, Catrina glanced over her shoulder at Damien, sitting in the front row pew, wearing a suit, his hair cinched back, dark and devastating.

He met her gaze and mouthed the words, "I love you."

Her heart skipping, she refocused on the beautiful, small ceremony.

The setting, and the day, with its clear-blue sky couldn't be more perfect.

A window at the front showed nearby peaks. As Milton slipped a plain gold band on her mother's finger, a deer paused, glanced inside, then continued on. Catrina's heart melted even more.

Finally, the beautiful vows exchanged, the minister pronounced Milton and Evelyn husband and wife. "You may kiss the bride."

"Finally!" Milton exclaimed before sweeping his new bride into an embrace.

With a happy laugh, Evelyn reached back. "Hand me my bouquet, my Cat."

Stepping forward, she did so.

Then Evelyn used the gorgeous display to shield herself and Milton from their closest family and friends while Milton gave her a scandalous kiss. The cheers and wild applause proved everyone knew what was happening.

Shaking her head, Catrina laughed.

Their love was beautifully contagious.

After the minister presented them as Mr. and Mrs. Danvers, Evelyn took Milton's hand and all but skipped back down the aisle.

Catrina and the rest of the bridal party followed, making their way to the foyer to form a receiving line, and she enjoyed seeing old friends of her mother's and meeting the people who were important to Milton.

Close to the end, her fiancé stopped in front of her.

Smelling deliciously of the outdoors, and eyes midnight blue with intent, he raised her hand to his lips.

Surprising her, he kissed her right below her ring.

"I'm ready to set a date, Milady. Are you?"

She swallowed.

This had been an almost daily discussion between them.

Because she wanted to adjust to their new life together—moving into his Denver-area house, working on the renovations to her home so she could sell it, finding a local office where she could meet with clients—she'd been reluctant to start making wedding plans.

But now, her defenses were down.

Truly, there was no reason for her and Damien to wait much longer.

"Next month," he persisted.

"Can we talk about it in a little while?" she asked.

"I'll hold you to it." His voice was half growl, half purr, and awareness ricocheted through her. Damien wielded his voice like a sensual weapon, one she couldn't resist.

Again, he kissed her hand, in the exact same spot.

A few moments later, almost everyone else having stepped outside, Catrina hugged her mom before greeting her new stepfather. "Thank you for making my mother so happy." With a small wince, she added, "And for putting up with me."

"Aw, Catrina..." He glanced at Evelyn who was now chatting with her sister, Peggy. "I never imagined I'd be lucky enough to find love a second time in my life. Life and loss taught me to appreciate every moment."

For the first time, she hugged him.

"My day is well and truly happy now," Milton said.

Outside, early spring sunshine warmed the air.

Damien chatted with a group of people, but the moment she started down the steps, he turned, as if he were fully aware of her presence.

Without being rude to anyone, he held out his hand, inviting her into his circle, and he introduced her to some of Milton's old army buddies. As she shook hands, Damien rested his fingertips at the base of her spine, partly signaling his possession, but also offering his comfort and reassurance.

After more photos were taken, guests piled into vehicles to drive a short way to a local country club on Lookout Mountain for the reception.

Dinner was amazing, and so was the big band orchestra.

She wasn't sure whether the music was her mother's idea or Milton's, but regardless, being crooned to by Frank Sinatra and Glenn Miller sent her heart fluttering.

When the opening notes of a forties ballad played, Damien stood. "May I have this dance, Milady?"

Not in a million years could she resist her dashing lover.

Moments later, she was swaying in his arms, content in ways she'd never imagined possible.

Near them, Evelyn and Milton had eyes only for each other.

"I'm glad I didn't try to interfere," she told Damien. "You were right, what they have is special."

"Just like what we share." He brushed a kiss against her temple.

As the evening wound down, the newlyweds began to bid their guests farewell before heading off on their honeymoon.

"Peggy got me a negligee for tonight," Evelyn whispered as she gave Catrina one last hug.

"Mother!"

Evelyn looked around, making sure no one could overhear before adding, "It's black and has holes for my nipples."

I can't even with you. "Go," Catrina ordered. "For the love of God, just go."

She laughed and blew a kiss before catching up to Milton who was waiting by the doorway.

"What was that about?" Damien asked.

"Please believe me...you don't want to know."

The band struck up another sentimental tune.

"Let's dance," she said. Anything to get that exchange out of her head.

"Of course."

Later that evening, because Catrina didn't have any in-person meetings for several days and because there wasn't an event at the Den, they drove to the mountain home rather than return to Denver.

As they entered the main house, Catrina was surprised to find the lights on in the kitchen.

Gregorio was seated at the island, shirtless, a nasty gash marring his chest. A bottle of whiskey in front of him, cap off, he was attempting to clean the wound one-handed, with limited success.

Gasping, Catrina rushed over to him. "What happened? Are you okay?"

He looked up, a mix of surprise and pain in his eyes. "Just a scratch."

A scratch? Blinking, she glanced at Damien.

Not commenting on the wound, he simply said, "Let me do that."

"I've got it."

"Not arguing that," Damien replied.

Neither of you think this is unusual?

Damien disappeared.

And she got a full look at the tattoo on his biceps that she'd noticed previously.

A fierce-looking eagle was framed by words in a foreign language. Latin, she guessed.

Before she could question him, Damien returned with a first aid kit and a bottle of peroxide. "Probably needs stitches."

"Unless you're gonna sew it yourself, Boss, just use the butterfly bandages."

"Damien's right. You need a doctor."

"No doctor." Gregorio's tone was flat, inviting no argument.

With the efficiency of someone who'd done this many times before, Damien got to work.

"What can I do to help?" she asked.

"Pour me some of that whiskey," Gregorio said. "Gonna need it."

She looked at the label, one she recognized from a terrible night in college. "Seriously?" No way would she ever touch that again as long as she lived.

"Or I drink straight from the bottle." He sucked in a breath as Damien cleaned the wound.

Galvanized, she grabbed a glass for him and measured the rotgut into a glass.

"Didn't expect to see you back so soon," Damien said, not looking up.

Gregorio shrugged, then winced against the pain. "Went better than I thought."

"Better?" Catrina frowned. How could it have been much worse? "What were you doing?"

After exchanging a glance with Damien, Gregorio replied quietly, "Trying to make amends." He closed his eyes, shutting out the glimpse of pain and regret that she'd read there. "Atone for past mistakes."

When Damien placed a piece of sterile gauze and taped it into place, an awkward silence descended over the room.

"Jesus." Gregorio tipped back the cheap whiskey then refilled his glass.

There were layers to Gregorio that she knew nothing about.

And Damien, too, it seemed.

Catrina bit her lip, wanting to know more, but Damien caught her gaze and shook his head.

With that, he filled Gregorio's glass again before walking to the sink to wash his hands.

Trusting her fiancé, she forced a fake smile. "I'm glad you're okay. And please be careful. Damien needs you. The Den needs you."

"Not going anywhere." He looked at both of them. "Someone's got to keep this place running while you two are off playing newlyweds."

"Speaking of..." Damien swept his gaze over her. "We should practice our honeymoon."

"Aaand that's my cue to leave." With a grunt, Gregorio eased off the stool, and Damien helped him back into the tattered shirt.

Before leaving, he capped the whiskey and snatched up the bottle.

Then he was gone, leaving Damien and Catrina alone in the kitchen.

"Is he going to be okay?" Catrina asked as Damien locked up. "I'm worried about him."

"He's tough. A survivor. He's been through a lot." A moment later, he added, "More than he lets on."

"And you can't tell me about it?"

"I don't know the whole story." He placed the unused items back in the first aid kit and zipped it shut.

For a moment, he stared out the window looking in the direction of Gregorio's cottage, then he shook his head.

Eyes narrowed with intent, he turned back to her and took two purposeful strides in her direction. "Now...about that honeymoon."

Like he had that night at her home, Damien slung her over his shoulder, making her shriek with surprised laughter.

When she squirmed, he slapped her ass hard.

"Damien! Sir!"

Within seconds of placing her on the bed, he'd stripped off her clothes. "After having you in my arms, seeing you in that maid of honor dress—"

"It was dreadful." Floor-length, the wrong shade of blue for her, and far too modest.

"Gave me fantasies. Maybe I'll ask you to dress up as a naughty schoolgirl at some point."

She shook her head. "You're impossible." And she loved having a man who couldn't get enough of her.

Which was perfect because she couldn't get enough of him, either.

With his eyes narrowed purposefully, he sat next to her and pinned her arms by her sides. "I meant it earlier—I want a date from you, Milady. Why wait?"

Life with him couldn't get any better.

Submission was a beautiful extension of the love and adventure they shared.

He was single-mindedly focused on her pleasure, lavishing his attentions on her...which suited her because she adored being the lucky recipient.

At times, he edged her, and many nights he tied her up. Impact play thrilled her, made her orgasms a hundred times more powerful.

As he'd insisted early on, their relationship was as unique as they were, and he said she was queen to his king, partners.

When they attended events at the Den, they went as Dom and sub, equals.

While Damien coached new Doms on their scenes, he no longer offered demonstrations. Though she and Damien were cohosting a workshop next week about the D/s dynamic and how it could enhance even the most wonderful relationship.

Which meant that most demos were now hosted by Ryder Wolfe, a cocky, edgy, and maybe a little bit dangerous newcomer who liked to push boundaries and take risks.

Because of that, Gregorio kept a close eye on him.

Even though Damien had offered to let her scene with her boys, she no longer felt the need. And in fact, Shaun had recently moved in with a Domme who adored him. He, too, had found the relationship he'd been seeking.

How well Catrina knew the power of the right connection.

For one Dom, and one Dom only, she was willing to submit.

"What do you say, Catrina? Make an honest man out of me. Set a date for our wedding."

She smiled. For a man who once said he didn't believe in love, he'd turned out to be quite a romantic.

"I'm waiting."

When he looked at her like that, holding her gaze, seeing into her soul, she was lost in him. "How about a year from the date you proposed?"

"I was hoping you'd say next week. But I'll let you win this one." He grinned slowly, and he leaned toward her to capture her mouth in a kiss that consumed her.

"You're getting what you want, too, mister."

"Which is why this relationship works. And of course, have your lawyer send me a prenup."

She melted into a puddle of joy.

"I don't want there to be any doubt that I'm in this for the long haul, or that I want you to protect your independence."

He thought of everything.

"What's mine is yours, no matter what. We'll make decisions together. Ones that are the best for us."

Overcome by his thoughtfulness, she struggled away from his grip and sat up to wrap her arms around his neck. "Oh, Damien. I love you so much." So complex, so caring. "I want…"

"Tell me."

"Take me…"

"I want to eat your pussy until you come in my mouth screaming my name."

"Yes."

"Stay there." He left her for a moment and returned with one of his T-shirts. "The dungeon, Milady?"

His tone… Unrelenting. His eyes… Determined.

"Yes…" Desire and a touch of apprehension traced through her.

Even though she should be accustomed to his level of sensuality, he still had the power to send shivers of anticipation through her.

Once she'd slipped into the garment, he had her walk to the dungeon, staying a few steps ahead of him so he could look at her ass.

Taking her breath away, he ordered her into the room with the spindle.

Where it all began.

In seconds, he had her naked.

Then, with a few, quick, efficient motions, she was secured in place, open to him.

"My Catrina…"

She met his gaze. "Master."

"Jesus." He sucked in a breath. "You humble me, Catrina. I don't know what I did to deserve you. But I'm thankful every day. I cherish you and your submission."

Gently, reverently, he parted her pussy lips and lowered his head, bringing her to the precipice of an orgasm, only to step back to fetch a flogger.

With gentle back and forth motions, he caressed her with the leather strands, igniting a trail of frenzied desire.

His motions sure, his gaze on her, he flogged her, covering her breasts, belly, legs, between her thighs, and then, torturously, her heated pussy. *"Damien!"* She squirmed, trying to escape, while simultaneously never wanting his sweet anguish to stop.

On and on he went, covering her body with suede kisses until she thrashed her head back and forth, whimpering, needing relief.

And then her future husband was on knees, parting her labia, sucking, licking, devouring her, finger-fucking her holes, driving her out of her mind. "I can't…"

"I assure you, Milady, you can."

He edged her, drawing out her response until all thought ceased. "Now." He plunged her into a spinning, swirling abyss of pleasure, and he took her there again and again.

Finally, when she came to, managing to open her eyes, they were in a chair, and she was wrapped in the comfort and power of his arms.

As always, he'd taken care of her with no regard for himself.

"That was…" She pressed a palm to his chest and lifted her head as much as she could, considering she had no energy left. "Thank you."

"The pleasure is mine, Catrina."

He snuggled her back into place.

Beneath her, his cock was hard, and insistent. "I think we should do something about that," she mused several minutes later.

"When you have some energy."

She reached up to stroke his chin. "I've recovered."

"Have you, indeed?" He lifted an eyebrow, trailed his fingertips across her pelvis, then he moved lower to find out for himself.

"Promise."

With a possessive growl, he took her back upstairs to their bedroom and claimed her completely, then eased her against him, holding her tightly.

"You did that on purpose," she said.

"Hmm?"

"The spindle."

"Yeah."

Back then, she'd been uncertain, scared to open her heart. Now... "I can't imagine life without you."

She'd confronted her fears and painful past. And now day by day, touch by touch, word by word, they'd built something real and lasting.

"You're mine forever."

"Forever," she affirmed.

Safe in his caring, powerful arms, Catrina was finally where she belonged.

Want to see more from this author? Here's a taster for you to enjoy!

Mastered: With This Ring
Sierra Cartwright

Excerpt

Two years ago

Always the bridesmaid…

This was the fourth wedding where Sasha had been forced into a horrific, frothy, itchy gown that looked terrible on her and she would have never chosen to wear.

If she was ever the bride, she wouldn't make such awful choices.

She shoved the thought aside. The way her dating life looked, Sasha would never receive a proposal.

Leah, today's bride, insisted there was a reason Sasha found every man lacking. She was measuring them against an impossible standard, one that had been set more than a decade ago.

Sasha had shaken her head as she'd informed Leah she was wrong. But deep down, in a place she didn't want to acknowledge, Sasha recognized she was lying to herself.

Around her, the ballroom of the upscale boutique hotel in downtown Denver buzzed with conversation and laughter.

A band played in the corner. Obviously, the quartet with their smooth melodies had been chosen by Leah's grandmother, who was paying for the whole shindig. Sasha hadn't recognized a single tune yet. The music was too refined for her tastes. She craved something with a beat, something she could lose herself in, maybe even a line dance.

Nursing a glass of champagne, she stood at a tall, round table off to one side.

Her whole life, she'd been a misfit. She wouldn't be here tonight if she hadn't been paired with Leah on a college project, when they'd become fast friends.

With a sigh, Sasha took a sip, and the bubbles tickled her nose. The stuff was okay, no doubt uber expensive, but she had little appreciation for life's finer things.

On the dance floor, the bride and groom swayed together, oblivious to everyone. They looked so happy, so in love. What would that be like?

Part of her envied them — a little.

But not enough to settle or give up the life she'd chosen.

"Sasha. Would you…would you like to dance?"

She glanced up at Tristan, the groomsman she'd been matched with for the festivities.

He sidled up to her, his shoulder brushing against hers. His expensive cologne was just as cloying as it had been earlier.

Tristan seemed harmless enough, even if all he talked about were his trips and cars. They had less than nothing in common, and in other circumstances she doubted he'd do anything other than look down his patrician nose at her.

Still, what harm was there in spending three minutes in the arms of a man good looking enough to pose for the cover of a Hampton's fashion magazine?

"Sash?"

Maybe it was the sudden melancholy, a longing for something she might never have or the urge to hurry time along, but she gave him a fake smile. "Sure." She slid her glass back onto the table.

The itchy fabric chafed her inner arms. With a sigh, she attempted to adjust the bodice of the gown.

"Let's go."

Instead of waiting for her, he headed to the dance floor. She trailed, seemingly an afterthought.

A pity dance for the wallflower?

Had Leah or her groom put him up to this?

With a movement that wasn't as smooth as she expected, he turned to her then pulled her into his arms, a little too close for her comfort. His breath smelled of something much stronger than champagne. Whiskey, maybe, or bourbon. No wonder he'd taken a bath in his cologne. Something had to overpower the scent of alcohol.

How much of this song was left, anyway?

Without asking her anything about herself or making polite conversation, he extolled the virtues of his latest purchase, a car reported to cruise along at over two hundred miles an hour.

"Isn't the top speed in this country eighty or eighty-five?"

"My car can be shipped to other places in the world. Or tested on racetracks."

Schooled by the trust fund baby. "I see."

Resisting the urge to roll her eyes, she tuned out as he launched into his next soliloquy.

"What do you say...?"

Realizing she'd completely tuned him out, she shook her head. "Sorry?"

Impatiently, he expelled a breath. "I said we should head somewhere quieter."

Before she could respond, the tiny hairs on her nape stood up, warning of danger.

Someone was watching her.

Surreptitiously, she looked around, scanning the crowd, but she noticed nothing amiss. And yet, the feeling persisted. It was like an itch between her shoulder blades, a prickle of awareness she couldn't shake.

"Are you paying attention?" He pulled her closer, his hand sliding lower on her spine.

She stiffened and eased back a little, not quite ready to bring her heel down on his instep, but getting closer.

From nowhere, a hulking presence appeared and forcefully tapped Tristan's shoulder.

"Get your fucking hands off her."

Both she and Tristan froze.

Sasha would know his voice anywhere. The deep, rich baritone danced through her dreams, echoed through her fantasies.

Gregorio.

God save her.

No.

"Who the hell do you think you are?" Tristan demanded.

Protector. Lethal warrior. Her fiercest defender. And biggest nemesis. The man she'd been certain she'd never see again.

Rather than answering, Gregorio leaned toward Tristan, getting in his face. When he spoke, his tone was controlled and steely, filled with threat. "Do you need me to repeat my question, pretty boy?"

Tristan's eyes widened, but ego—and maybe whiskey—propelled him toward recklessness. "Look, dude, I'll have you know—"

"Tristan," she urged, finally able to shake off her paralysis in order to act. "Don't."

He opened his mouth again, but then he looked at Gregorio, who stood several inches taller and was much broader.

His massive biceps strained against the sleeves of his suitcoat.

No polite, civilized veneer could possibly hide the power coiled in his frame, the barely restrained violence.

A diamond earring winked from one ear.

In a past life, he could have been a pirate.

Gregorio was thrilling and terrifying all at once.

Even though Tristan was lean, in a yoga or runner-type of way, they all knew Gregorio could take him apart in a single move.

What *he* didn't know was that Gregorio would do just that, no matter the setting.

"You're trying my patience, pretty boy. I'll give you the count of three to get lost."

Immediately, Tristan released Sasha and stepped back.

He adjusted his tie as he cleared his throat. "Uh, yeah." He looked her up and down. "Bitch like you isn't worth the effort anyway."

Her mouth dropped from shock as he pivoted and strode away.

Before she could recover, another song started. Gregorio swept her into his strong arms and moved them closer to the band, away from prying eyes.

"Interrupting my dance…" She could handle herself, and a man like Tristan wouldn't have posed much of a challenge. "That was uncalled for."

"Was it?"

He sounded appallingly unconcerned.

For most of her teenage years, he'd repeatedly stuck his nose in her business. He'd been her constant shadow, always watching, always intervening. It had been equal parts comforting and infuriating.

He swept a searing, appreciative gaze over her.

Then before she could protest, he nudged her in closer, leaving her no choice but to inhale his spicy, outdoorsy scent. It was familiar and foreign all at once, bringing back a rush of memories—late night conversations, shared laughter.

"I mean it, Gregorio." She tried to pull back, but he tightened his grip. "You had no right to do that."

"Hmm." He flicked a casual glance toward Tristan, who was making a beeline to the bar. "Pretty boy insulted you. He should drop to his knees and thank his lucky stars I didn't tear him apart limb from limb."

She shuddered. Not from fear, but from a sudden, visceral awareness of his strength, his power. It was like being caught in the gaze of a predator— exhilarating and paralyzing all at once.

"Furthermore, *you* should be thanking me."

"Thanking you?" He thought he could show back up in her life and tell her what to do? "You need to get over yourself."

"He'd have been fun until he fucked you, then abandoned you. He'd have sweet-talked you into not using a condom, then refused to take responsibility."

She gasped.

"You're in investigations, supposedly." He lifted a shoulder in a casual shrug. "Look up the men you're considering inviting inside your home." He paused. "And your body."

"*Jesus.*"

"Tell me he didn't try to take you upstairs."

Flushing, she looked away.

"He'd be good for a minute, maybe two."

She opened her mouth to speak but no words emerged.

"If he could get it up after consuming all that alcohol."

Sasha longed to argue, to tell him he was wrong, but the words stuck in her throat.

"You seem remarkably well informed." She narrowed her gaze. "Or are you merely jealous?"

He chuckled, immediately dismissing her taunt— his sound one of pure male superiority.

"What I do and with whom I do it is not your concern." She paused, then breathlessly rushed on. "And it never was, actually."

"Still telling yourself lies, Petal?"

Petal?

The nickname hit her hard, a flashback, a timeless moment. It was so much more suited to the teen she'd been than the fully capable adult woman she was now, and yet she liked it more than ever.

"You've always needed a protector."

Fuck off. "Just because—"

"Obviously, you still do."

That she didn't have an instant comeback was likely because she was reeling in shock from seeing him again. Leah had talked endlessly about the people who'd be in attendance, and Gregorio's name hadn't been mentioned.

The irony of running into him at a wedding didn't escape her, considering the last time they'd seen each other, she'd been seated in the front row of the divorce proceeding between him and her older sister—a place she wished she'd never gone.

It had been the worst day of her life, watching two of the people she loved most in the world tear each other apart. She'd clenched her hands, body frozen, as the lawyers laid out the sordid details of their failed marriage—the lies, the betrayals, the slow, painful unraveling of a love she'd once thought was forever.

"I was hoping for a memorable experience tonight." Probably wouldn't have happened with Tristan, but Gregorio didn't need to know that.

"Memorable? Maybe I can help you out."

You?

Almost missing a step, she blinked and searched his face for some hint of mockery, but found only an intense sincerity that made her breath catch.

In an instant, he released her, only to immediately clamp a hand around her wrist and all but drag her from the packed ballroom and down the hall into a janitor's closet.

Never pausing, he kicked aside a bucket, sending the mop clattering to the floor, the noise so loud it echoed in her ears and covered the sound of a lock being ratcheted home.

In a single move, he slammed her up against a wall and raised her hands above her head to pin them in place.

"Gregorio..."

He leaned in closer.

Suddenly, the only sounds were her frantic breaths and thundering heart.

She was a competent bodyguard and security agent. People counted on her to protect their lives. But this close to Gregorio, she was helpless, ensnared by his masculine prowess. "What the hell are you suggesting?" *And why aren't I running away screaming?*

"You want something memorable, Petal? I'll make damn sure this is an evening you won't soon forget."

Slowly, he traced his thumb down the column of her throat, bringing it to rest on the frantic pulse that thundered there. His touch was electric, shooting wildfire through her veins.

"Open your mouth."

Desperate to save herself, she shook her head.

"I won't force you." He quirked an eyebrow. "I won't need to."

What cocksure arrogance.

"You want this," he stated. "You want *me*."

Once more, she frantically shook her head. But even as she denied it, she knew it was true. She'd always wanted him, always craved his touch, his attention, his approval. It was a secret she'd carried for so long it had become a part of her, as essential as breathing.

He pressed lightly on her throat. "Your actions say one thing but your body says another. It's speaking to mine, isn't it?"

She should deny what he said.

"Right now, this moment, you're feeling compelled to spread your legs as wide possible, right after you pull up your dress and show me your secrets."

"No."

As if she'd said nothing, he went on in his hypnotic way. "Once you do that, you'll want me to slide my fingers inside your panties and give you an orgasm that would make you scream if we weren't in public."

He leaned impossibly closer and she stared at him, unable to look away. His eyes were dark, almost black in the dim light of the closet, and filled with a hunger that matched her own.

Protests sprang to mind, and each died before emerging. Instead, she was captivated by his air of confidence, worn as easily as the suit hugging his powerful frame.

"But since anyone walking by could hear you, I'd have to silence your cries with my mouth."

Sasha didn't want this. *Shouldn't.* Yet her body betrayed her. Her clit throbbed with need, and an ache built deep inside her.

"Tell me to let you go, Petal. Or use your pretty little mouth to ask me to kiss you and bring you off."

His crudeness made her gasp.

"Or I can walk away right now and leave you wondering, turned on and frustrated."

Embarrassed, she worried her lower lip. But beneath the embarrassment was a thrill, a dark excitement at the thought of surrendering to him, of letting him take control.

Something she'd spent years longing for.

"I'm betting you'd stay behind for a while to masturbate to the fantasy of what you could have had but didn't have the courage to ask for."

Damn you.

"You and I would both know what you were doing, wouldn't we?"

He was impossible.

"Since I'm a gentleman…"

What an absolute lie.

"I'll offer you the same courtesy I gave pretty boy. You've got three seconds to respond." He waited. "Three."

She vowed to remain silent.

"Two."

To keep herself from whimpering with need, she pressed her lips together.

"One."

True to his word, he released her wrists.

Helplessly, she left her arms in place. "Gregorio."

He turned toward the door.

Need consumed her. *"Gregorio!"*

Hand on the lock, he stopped.

"Kiss me?"

He turned to face her. "Now you'll have to use your manners."

Sasha squeezed her eyes shut. *Do you have to make me beg?*

"The words, Petal."

With a gulp, she nodded. "Please. Please kiss me."

"Nice start."

Still, the determined bastard didn't move.

"Now, repeat after me — please use your hand to bring me off."

For years, she'd had a case of hero worship for this forbidden man — since he'd saved her entire family. If it weren't for him, she would never have gone into the personal security field, wouldn't have had the courage to take the risks that made life worth living.

This moment thundered with danger.

If she gave in and asked for what she needed, would her sister see it as a betrayal?

Yet she lacked the conviction to send him away.

"What will it be, Petal?"

She was powerless to resist the sway he held over her. Softly, she said, "Please use your hand to bring me off."

"Very nice."

His approving purr thrilled her, made the awful words worthwhile.

"Now lift your hem and bunch the dress around your waist."

No man had ever been this outrageous with her, yet there wasn't a single part of her that considered denying him. Her hands shook as she reached for the hem, her heart pounding so loudly he had to hear it.

With a deep swallow, she lowered her arms to gather the ridiculous amount of pale pink chiffon and tucked it into place.

"Very nice." He swept his hot gaze over her, taking in her legs, her tummy, then settling at the apex of her thighs. The heat of his stare was like a physical caress on her skin.

Trying not to betray her nerves, she took a breath.

"The thong's unexpected. In a nice way."

Sasha much preferred panties or boy shorts that offered full coverage, but Leah had been very vocal, insisting her wedding pictures would not be ruined by panty lines.

"Now take it off."

Heat flooding her face, she worked the material down her legs. Her hands trembled as she turned over the scrap of silk, the intimacy of the gesture making her feel exposed and vulnerable in a way she'd never experienced before.

"Good girl."

His approval made the room spin.

"Smell it."

The man offered no respite. Before she was finished being scandalized by one request, he made another. *"What?"*

"I want you to smell yourself."

Wishing the floor would open up beneath her, she followed his command.

"Now tell me about the scent."

In the distance the party raged, music reverberating off the walls. An occasional conversation or giggle from the hallway affirmed how absurd being in here with Gregorio was.

"I'm waiting."

The musky, heady aroma made her body flame with embarrassment and desire. After momentarily squeezing her eyes shut, she replied. "It's, ah..." She cleared her throat. "My arousal."

"Mmm." He nodded. "Is the material damp?"

You already know the answer.

Silently, he approached her, something that should have been impossible with a man as large as he was. But Gregorio had always been able to move with silent grace, a stealth that belied his size and strength.

And she'd seen him accomplish the impossible before.

"Now hold it to my nose."

Ready to die from his demands, she followed his scandalous direction.

"Intoxicating, Petal." He then plucked her thong from her and dropped it into his pocket. "I could mainline your scent and feed on it for days."

Who the hell are you?

She'd known he was lethal, but she'd never seen this side of him before. His raw, primal sexuality weakened her knees and made her heart gallop.

"Now, put one hand on the wall next to you and use the other to spread your labia, holding yourself open to me."

This time, she didn't protest. She couldn't, not when her body ached for his touch, taste, possession.

Right now, they both recognized the sway he held over her. She would do anything he wanted.

Once she'd complied, she remembered what he'd said earlier. Without being prompted, she spread her legs wide, made more difficult by her heels and the way her body wavered.

"You really are a good girl. *My* good girl."

She was indecently exposed to the man who'd once been her brother-in-law, and she'd never wanted anything as much as she wanted him in this moment, never needed anything as much as she needed his approval, his praise, his possession.

"Now open your mouth."

He claimed her lips, making it impossible to breathe. He plundered, taking before she offered, as if he had every right to do so.

Exactly the way it should be.

Burying the unwelcome thought in the darkest recesses of her mind, she closed her eyes and surrendered.

A moment later, he changed the tempo to make love to her with his tongue.

When her knees buckled, he was there for her, holding her wrist tight and keeping her steady. Then he slid a finger between her slick folds.

She gasped into his mouth at the sensation of his rough, calloused finger against her most sensitive flesh.

He pulled back long enough to gently nip at her earlobe and whisper, "You have such a beautiful little pussy."

Instantly, he took her mouth again and toyed with her clit, igniting pleasure in the tiny bundle of nerves.

Her body went rigid as he stroked and circled and teased, driving her higher and higher.

Suddenly, an orgasm overtook her, more powerful than anything she'd ever experienced.

Bucking her hips, she sought even more as the waves crashed over her. She rode his hand, grinding against him, chasing the pleasure only he could offer.

If it hadn't been for the way his tongue filled her mouth, she would have screamed aloud, as he'd known she would.

On and on he went, slipping a finger inside her, angling his wrist to find her G-spot.

Desperate for him, she lifted onto her tiptoes and rocked her hips, simulating sex. Her body wanted him to enter her, stretching her, filling her, completing her in a way no other man ever had.

Reading her as if they'd been together dozens of times before, he eased a second finger inside her channel, filling her, fucking her.

Her mouth and pussy were full of him, and the world began to spiral.

As if sensing her need, he pumped his fingers faster, harder, driving her toward the edge.

Gregorio pressed the heel of his palm against her clit and rubbed hard.

She was swimming in sensation and pleasure. *In him.*

Disobediently, she pulled her hand from between them and wrapped her arm around his neck, hanging on with desperation, praying the moment would never end.

How many years had she fantasized about this dark, enigmatic man who was more of a stranger than a brother-in-law? Someone she had probably never truly known, even though she thought she had.

Impossibly, he deepened the intensity by adding a third finger, spreading her wider, forcing her to accept his penetration.

The stretch, the fullness, the sheer presence of him overwhelmed her. But he was also perfect, everything she'd ever wanted.

God.

She was gone, surrendered in bliss.

A shocking, powerful climax rocked her.

Wave after wave of pleasure crashed over her, and she writhed, her pussy clenching him as she drenched his hand.

Only then, when she was shattered, did he release her mouth. "Yeah. My girl."

Still dizzy, she opened her eyes, struggling to bring the world into focus.

Gregorio filled her vision and her senses. In this moment, he was her everything.

Taking his time, he withdrew his fingers, then held them to her mouth.

"Lick them. Taste yourself. Know that I did this to you…brought you this pleasure."

His request was so sensual she almost came again. Her pussy tingled, craving more of him, all of him, in every way possible.

Part of her was shocked that she'd done what he said, but how could she deny him anything when he'd just given her everything?

Once his fingers were clean, he lowered his hand to pull down on her dress, sending the chiffon tumbling back into place.

She blinked.

Are we finished?

He leaned forward to kiss her lips. Tasting her orgasm?

With unbelievable slowness, he traced the plunging neckline of her dress, making her breasts throb with desire. Her nipples tightened, straining against the sheer fabric of her bra, begging for his attention.

For as satisfied as she was, he'd left her wanting and emotionally bereft.

He lowered her arm, and good thing he thought to do so because it seemed to be frozen in place.

Then, in a thoughtful gesture, he rubbed her shoulder, bringing sensation back into it.

"Ready to rejoin the party?"

What the hell had he just done to her? "Wait. I need my underwear back."

"No chance." Gregorio left her to unlock and open the door, then he checked the hallway in both directions.

When it was safe, he beckoned her.

On wobbly legs, her body still vibrating from the physical and emotional aftermath of what they'd shared, her mind reeling with the implications, she walked past him.

Possessively, Gregorio pressed his fingers against the base of her spine, his touch seeming to sear her even through the gown's fabric as he guided her back toward the reception.

His simple touch, the small claim, made her heart squeeze with longing.

"Remember not to make mistakes with pretty boys."

"So I can make bigger ones with dangerous men?"

His quick smile promised sin and salvation.

"Shall we?" He ushered her back into the ballroom.

Then moments later, his touch was gone.

She glanced over her shoulder, but he was nowhere to be seen…vanished into the crowd as if he'd never been there at all.

Stunned, she shook her head.

Gregorio had shown up unexpectedly, turned her life upside down, then disappeared as if the event in the janitor's closet had meant nothing to him.

If it weren't for the fact her panties were missing, the ache between her thighs, the lingering taste of him on her tongue, and the ghost of his touch on her skin, she might have believed she'd made up the entire event.

How am I supposed to go back to my real life now?

About the Author

Born in northern England and raised in the Wild West, Sierra Cartwright pens books that are as untamed as the Rockies she calls home.

She's an award-winning, multi-published writer who wrote her first book at age nine and hasn't stopped since.

Sierra invites you to share the complex journey of love and desire, of surrender and commitment. Her own journey has taught her that trusting takes guts and courage, and her work is a celebration for everyone who is willing to take that risk.

Sierra loves to hear from readers. You can find her contact information, website details and author profile page at https://www.firstforromance.com

Home of Erotic Romance

Sign up for our newsletter and find out about all our romance book releases, eBook sales and promotions, sneak peeks and FREE romance books!